PREY HOUSE

TOROTH-GOL BOOK III

KENNY GOULD

Prey House (Toroth-Gol Book III)

Copyright © 2024 Kenny Gould

COVER ILLUSTRATION BY Tom Edwards

BOOKS BY KENNY GOULD

<u>Toroth-Gol Series</u>

The Castle of 1,000 Doors

Dungeon School

Prey House

The War of Fangs

<u>The School Beneath the City Series</u>

The Potionmaster

<u>Other Work</u>

The Midnight Carnival

Monster Summer Camp

To my cats, Squish and Crumb.
Inspirations for the Smoothie Boys franchise.

THE EMPIRE

The Wastes
Peakskill
Brigadoon
Portside
Cort
Argoston
Oriel
Helios
Spiderhead
Bourdoux
Steel City
Bellablanco
Ironwood
Velda
Mick
The Crescent
Sanmar
Atlantis
Barrier's
Pavilion
Palmer's
Pavilion
The Great Basin
Tabura
Crystal Keep
Aeo
Red Hills
Aramel
Binti
Irbo Jamrain
The Sea of Paradise
Arid Dominion
Hub
Lobster
Isles
Shining Dunes
Fain

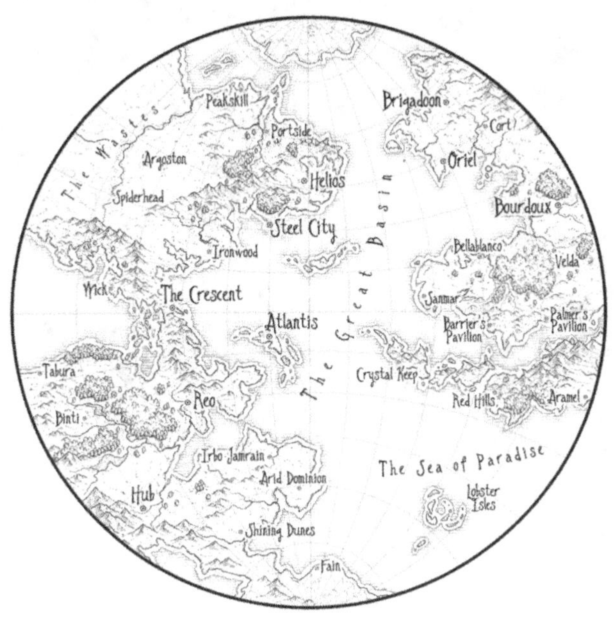

RECAP

Confirming... Live on *Elvis Madden's Hunter Talk* in 3... 2... 1...

For all of those who have sent in your well wishes, thank you! As it turns out, I didn't have a heart attack, but a *stroke*. Isn't that wild? Going through a medical emergency on live TV wasn't exactly in the five-year plan and I'm humbled by your love and support. The vigils outside the studio have been particularly touching.

But I'm getting ahead of myself! My name is Elvis Madden and I'm the host of this eponymous show, where I highlight the wildest, wackiest, and most exciting events to happen in this season of the Hunt! So far, we've had *quite* a doozy, and no one has been more popular than former lightball player Nathaniel 'King Crow' Valentine.

Where has King Crow gone since leaving the Castle of 1,000 Doors? I'm so glad you asked!

After making their way out of the castle, our heroes found themselves on a platform surrounded by four towers. Each tower promised to train the hunters in a different style of combat. Crow's reptilian friend Geeta went into one; the Thuin engineer Brynn picked another; the mysterious mage Rayne chose a third; and Crow and Jocko entered Gray Moor.

At this point in our program, I'll pause to mention that we still have an *incredibly* limited supply of official Spud Spuddington plushies available at our store in the Stadia. We also have plushies of Peristopheles Magnesis IV, King Crow's talking tomato companion! Are you a member of the #SpudSquad or the #PerryPosse? Show your support by picking up a plushie today!

After Crow and Jocko entered Gray Moor, they met Feng, a friendly dungeon native, who helped them choose their room types and prepare for their advising sessions. Feng also told Crow about Sirax Sirco's Personal Armory, a legendary cache of treasure hidden somewhere in the tower.

With housekeeping out of the way, Crow chose his classes. By taking Wisdom, he would learn how to enter a meditative fugue once every week, during which he could gain the answer to a single question. Bulletsmithing promised to help Crow create more weapons like Spud and Perry, but *only* if he could acquire a rare item called a soul core.

After leaving the advising session, Crow learned a valuable lesson about negotiation, fought a rock golem, and made friends with a little-known hunter named Devora. Together, he and Devora battled and defeated a fiery demon named Sor'kodich, and located Sirax Sirco's armory! Inside, Crow found a soul core, which he used to imbue an eggplant with the soul of a necromancer named Xenandor of Kratha, aka Xena.

Was it off the walls? Sure. Bonkers? Yes! But that's the Hunt, people! Just like that, the #SpudSquad—or is it the #PerryPosse?— grew by one!

In previous hunts, the dark forces that run Toroth-Gol have waited several weeks to let the towers get overrun by an army of predators. This year, the predators came early. That was the end of many hunters, but not King Crow! Along with Jocko, Devora, Feng, Spud, Perry, and Xena, Crow escaped into the Valves, a series of old tunnels that ran beneath the tower. There, they faced the mulchers, a strange breed of territorial, toad-like humanoids.

Sad news, viewers: in their initial battle with the mulchers, fan-favorite dungeon native Feng took a fatal blow. It was a sad end to a popular character. Alas!

The mulchers might've killed Crow and his friends, but they once again ran into Sor'kodich. Now inhabiting the body of a long-lost Gray Moor student, the fiery demon gained control of the mulchers and used his newfound power to stop them, but only so he could draw out their deaths.

There were twists! There were turns. Crow and his friends escaped and fled into a forest! But they weren't safe yet: the pirate trio known as Cara, Marland, and Skeev Thorne were also hiding in the woods.

Was I the only one hoping King Crow might consummate his relationship with the beautiful pirate captain?

Really? Just me? Fine.

Over an evening fire, Crow proved himself steadfast in resisting Cara's charm, though he'd barely fallen asleep before Skeev and Marland double-crossed him. During Crow's flight from the murderous pirates, he found himself cornered on the edge of a cliff, Cara's pistol pointed at his heart.

Crack! Was that the sound of Cara's gun? No! It was the sound of Jocko hitting Cara with a club! Though the Thuin didn't move quickly enough to stop Cara from firing.

The bullet hit Crow in the chest. He stumbled backward, right over the edge of the cliff.

Can you believe it? The Empire cut their feed on a *literal* cliffhanger! We couldn't have asked for a better ending to the episode. In my humble opinion, this has been one of *the most exciting* second levels of Toroth-Gol in years. Trust me when I say the excitement is only getting started!

Did Crow survive? Will he be reunited with his friends? What will happen in Prey House? I couldn't begin to…

I'm sorry, *what?* They're in the studio? Right now?

Excuse me, citizens! We appear to be having some, uh, *technical* difficulties. I'll be right back!

PROLOGUE

Elvis Madden, host of *Elvis Madden's Hunter Talk* and one of the most famous celebrities in the Empire, tried to keep the tremor from his hands as soldiers filed into his studio. They were led by Lucca Bert, infamous captain of the Steel City Guard.

"No cause for alarm," Lucca said. While the other guards had rifles, Lucca's only weapon was the holstered knife that hung from a belt around his waist.

That and his reputation, Elvis thought as he eyed Lucca's belt buckle. The buckle featured the Steel City sigil: two silver sledgehammers crisscrossing at their hafts. *I've heard bad stories about him.* And then, in spite of himself: *Why does he look so punchable?*

"Everyone stay seated," Lucca droned. "We're only here for..." Lucca trailed off as his eyes drifted across the writers, programmers, and engineers that made up the crew of Elvis' show. Hundreds of people, all responsible for ensuring the success of the Empire's greatest televised event. His eyes widened slightly as he and Elvis made eye contact, and then his pouting lips curved into a dangerous smile. A *punchable* smile. He pointed an accusing finger at Elvis.

"Him."

Ah. Suddenly, hitting Lucca was the last thing on Elvis' mind;

now he was focused on the soldiers that swarmed through the studio, their boots clomping against the tile floors. He forced himself to stay calm. *Play innocent,* he told himself. *Maybe there's some sort of mistake?*

Weakly, Elvis raised a hand at the approaching soldiers. The cameras had stopped rolling, their shutters programmed to close the moment someone destroyed the sanctity of the filming environment. Behind Elvis, someone dropped a boom mic, which fell to the ground with a clatter. The poor man immediately crouched and covered his head as if worried he'd be shot.

Maybe they will *shoot him,* Elvis thought. He *had* heard stories. But the soldiers didn't so much as glance in his direction.

They were looking at him.

Calm. You've got this, Elvis. You haven't done anything wrong.

Lucca approached at the head of his men and stopped before the desk. He leaned forward, his hands against the wood.

"A pleasure to see you, old friend," he said. "You've been naughty."

Elvis forced himself to meet the captain's eyes. The two had taken their respective positions of power at around the same time. Since then, they'd often seen each other at lightball games and functions around Gomindor. But they weren't actually friends, no more than Elvis was friends with any of the elite in Gomindor.

"A pleasure to see you too, Captain," Elvis said. "To what do I owe the visit?"

Lucca sneered. "Do I need to say it?"

Elvis' heart quickened. "What do you mean? I'm afraid I—ah!"

Elvis gaped at the dagger that now jutted out from his hand. The pommel of the weapon was ovular and smooth, but that wasn't the part that caught his attention. Rather, he was focused on the blade.

A moment before, it had been hanging from Lucca's belt. Now, it stuck out of his hand.

Is that my blood?

Elvis was too shocked to feel the pain. Lucca smirked at him, then turned in a circle, taking in the scared faces of Madden's peers.

"You work for a fraud!" he called, yelling to the farthest corners of the studio. "The great Elvis Madden, supposed citizen of the Empire, is nothing more than a *rotten Thuin sympathizer!*"

There was a collective gasp. It was a stunning accusation, and one Elvis knew Lucca wouldn't have made without proof.

Worst of all, it was true.

Ah, Elvis thought as Lucca turned back toward him. *This isn't good.*

In a single quick motion, Lucca jerked the knife from Elvis' hand. Now, Elvis felt the pain. He grunted and blinked away tears, watching as blood welled from the gash in the back of his hand.

Lucca leaned down to look Elvis in the eye. Their noses were almost touching. "No one is coming to help you, Elvis," he said quietly. Elvis could smell Lucca's breath: mint, with a hint of garlic. "You spent a lifetime building the wrong types of favors. I don't need spluttering. Just cooperation. Now come with me, or bad things will happen."

Lucca nodded to one of his soldiers, who tossed Elvis a handkerchief. No sooner had Elvis grabbed it than the soldier lifted his rifle to his cheek and aimed at the nearest cameraman.

"Oh gods," the man said, lifting his hands. Stuart, if Elvis remembered correctly.

He just had his second child, Elvis thought. *He hasn't stopped showing people pictures!*

There was a *snick* as the guard chambered a round. Poor Stuart's eyes widened as he realized what was about to happen.

"A little demonstration to ensure your cooperation," Lucca said. "Something small, so you know we mean business. On the count of three, Gorda."

"Wait!" someone cried, and it took Elvis a moment to realize the words had come from his own lips. *He* was the one who'd yelled.

By the Dregs, am I going to save him? Elvis thought. *I'm a coward! That doesn't sound like me at all!* But Lucca clearly knew he'd helped Crow. *So what's wrong with admitting it now?*

Elvis looked around. Every eye in the room rested on him.

Watching.

Waiting.

Waiting for *him* to act.

Elvis coughed and pressed the square of fabric to his injured hand. It hurt, though at least it staunched the bleeding.

"I'll cooperate," he said. He reached for his chair's wheel with his injured hand, though merely touching the rubber caused a fresh wave of pain. Elvis hissed in frustration. "I need some help. Can you push me?"

Lucca stared at him. The captain's upturned nose made him look more punchable than ever. *How does a man like that get to the top?* Elvis wondered. But he knew the answer. *He* was on top, wasn't he? In Lucca, he recognized a kindred spirit, a man willing to do whatever was necessary to survive.

Then, Lucca surprised him: he nodded. "Sure," he said casually. "Gorda, don't shoot the cameraman. Go and help Elvis. The poor man recently had a heart attack. Or was it a stroke? I can't remember."

Lucca delivered the last words with venom.

Oh, he definitely knows, Elvis thought, his stomach dropping. *At least I saved Stuart?*

The guard, Gorda, let the rifle drop and swung it onto his back. Stuart, who realized he wasn't going to die, suddenly sagged. It was as if every muscle in his body had given out at once. He collapsed to the ground in a heap and began to sob against the cool tile.

I envy that man, Elvis thought as he watched the broken man. *In a few seconds, Lucca Bert will be gone from his life. But me? I have a feeling we're just getting started.*

Gorda took up a position behind Elvis and pulled on the chair. He did it with more force than necessary. The movement caused Elvis to fall forward, and he only managed to keep from smacking his face on the desk by sticking out his injured hand.

"Agh!" he hissed.

Then, Gorda was wheeling him away.

1

So many things left undone. Feng and Devora dead. The Empire still standing. And...

And... and...

I woke to quiet murmurs, my dreamlike thoughts fading as I smelled antiseptic in the air. I opened my eyes to see that I lay on a bed in an almost blindingly white room.

You survived Level II: Dungeon School. Now, you face Level III: Prey House.

That doesn't explain much. Though I seem to be alive—and on the third level. Did someone bring me through?

I tried to turn, though I couldn't move. My head was held in place by a strap that ran across my forehead. When I glanced down, I saw my wrists and ankles were secured by leather restraints.

"Where am I?" I asked, though no sound came out.

My lips are sewn shut. Why are my lips sewn shut?

I panicked, but the straps held tight. From the corner of my eye, I saw a tray lined with medical gear: gauze, scalpels, forceps.

"Scalpel, please." The sing-song voice came from somewhere

5

behind me. "Slice the scales and peel the skin! Add the bones! Blood goes in!"

Is someone operating on me? Now, I didn't just try to move, but *scream.*

It didn't work. As I already said, my lips were sewn shut.

There was a new voice, closer this time. It came from somewhere just behind my head: "Creepy doctors? I hate to bother you, but the patient doesn't seem to be doing so hot. Guys? Is that a *bone?*"

Spud. That voice belonged to Spud! Hey, Spud! Help me!

For better or worse, telepathy wasn't a skill Spud had mastered. Instead of helping, he continued to offer commentary on what he saw.

"Do organs really glisten like that? They must, because I'm seeing them. Wow! That must be a spleen!"

"You're in good hands, Crow," a new voice said.

Perry. Oh, thank goodness.

"I'm here, and so is Spud," the tomato continued. "And Xena! Say hi, Xena."

"Hi, Xena," Xena said. She was near my head, too. "Man, that joke never gets old. Anyway, hey, Crow. You should calm down before you tear something."

Memories flooded back to me. The last thing I remembered was standing on the edge of a cliff, so close to escaping the second level of Toroth-Gol.

Then, I'd been shot.

Shot by Cara Thorne.

And then I was here. But where was this?

A hospital. With that thought, the smell of the room made sense, as did the medical equipment. I exhaled a sigh of relief. *But why am I awake while they're operating on me?*

"They're fixing up Geeta right now, Crow," Perry said, answering my question. "She's also here. Would you believe it? They're giving her wings!"

"They'll get to you next," Xena said. "Apparently, Geeta's operation was more pressing."

I scanned the room. *Who were "they?"*

The answer hit me like a punch to the stomach.

Back in Gray Moor, when Jocko had taken a powerful blow to the head, I'd rushed him to the Infirmary. Home of the Medics. I'd seen the doctors of their order do incredible things, though their healing came at a cost. If I hadn't managed to scrape together the coin needed to pay for Jocko's treatment, he would've been conscripted into indentured servitude. Who knows what the Medics would've had him doing? After that experience, I'd vowed never to deal with them again.

And yet, here I am.

"Creepy doctors?" This was Spud again. "Can you come check on him?"

"Just stay calm, Crow," Xena said. "You're going to get through this."

Get through what? By the Dregs, where is Jocko?

"Can I read him my poem now?" Spud asked. "Maybe that will help. Crow? Buddy? If you *can* hear me, it's me, Spud!"

"If he can hear you, he knows that," Perry said.

"We need you, Crow!" Spud yelled, continuing as if Perry hadn't spoken. "You're the captain of our crew! The leader of our tribe! The artistically enameled bowl that keeps our fibrous bodies contained upon the table!"

I tried to talk, but no words came out. It was *infuriating*. I heard footsteps, and then one of the Medics leaned over me. Because of his cowl, I couldn't see his face.

Blue Medic (John Cotton)

From a young age, John Cotton displayed a natural talent for healing and a deep empathy for those in pain. At sixteen, he was apprenticed to a skilled medic who taught him the intricacies of the healing arts.

As the years passed, John honed his skills, eventually establishing his own medical practice. But a devastating accident at Ironwood's most notorious foundry changed his life forever. While working

to save the wounded, John discovered the grim truth: the accident had occurred due to the neglect of the factory's owners. Appalled by their greed, John turned over evidence of their crimes to the city's authorities.

Those authorities were related to the factory's owners. Later that day, John was arrested, convicted of treason, and sentenced to Toroth-Gol.

The Medic lifted a thin, black-dyed hand and placed his clammy fingers against my forehead.

"Warm," he said. The voice, soft and low, came from deep within the cowl. "You must be confused, my son. Do not panic. We will take care of you."

The words were soothing, though the effect was ruined when he giggled.

"Tee-hee! Sharpen the blades! Uncap the needles! We'll soon work on King Crow!"

The Medic stepped from my line of sight. Again, I struggled. Again, nothing happened.

Spud noted my distress. "Uh, I know how that sounded, but I guarantee they're really trying to help. They haven't stolen your organs or anything. At least, they haven't since I've been watching!"

"They already reset the thirty-seven bones you broke falling from that cliff," Perry said.

"Thirty-seven!" Spud whistled. "Woo! That's hardcore, Crow. I continue to be impressed!"

I fought. Whatever I'd gone through, *no* healing was worth the cost of the Medics. When Jocko had been hurt, his treatment had almost bankrupted me, and he'd only taken a glancing blow to the forehead.

"I think I'll read my poem now," Spud continued. "Ready? *Crow is here, everyone cheer! Everyone say hooray! Crow is back, so watch your back, and*—oh. Did I just rhyme 'back' with 'back'?"

"He doesn't want to hear the poem, Spud," Perry said. "Crow, can you hear me? I promise, you're going to be fine. We'll get out of here, and find Jocko, and then we'll continue through the dungeon!"

For the second time in a minute, John Cotton appeared over me.

"We have much work to do," he said. "Careful, delicate work. You have become a distraction. Sleep now, my son."

"Okay, I remember how it goes," Spud said. "Crow is back, so watch your—uh, Doc? What are you doing? Why is that needle so *big?*"

I felt a sharp pain in my neck, like I'd just been stung by a hornet. An icy numbness radiated from the wound. It spread through my body, making my limbs feel heavy. I wanted to keep struggling; I needed to figure out the cost of the treatment. I needed to plan for what was coming next.

I couldn't stay awake. Another breath, and then darkness settled over me.

2

I woke. I'd been having a nightmare. I don't remember exactly what it was about, though I was somewhere hot, and things were getting hotter. As soon as I opened my eyes, I sat up and wiped the sweat from my forehead.

I was no longer restrained. My bandolier was slung across my chest, but that was my only piece of gear. I didn't see my gloves. All the other items were missing from my Inventory.

I looked around and saw that I lay on a low metal cot in a room with gray walls and a window along the far wall. There was one other cot in the room, though it was empty and the bed was made, the sheet pulled tight against the mattress. A bare lightbulb hung by a cord from the ceiling, yet most of the room's diffuse light came through the frosted glass of the window.

Spud, Perry, and Xena sat on a table, a game board between them.

Gameboard (Ravens)

Often used to train young Empire nobles in strategy, a typical ravens board consists of sixty-four squares arranged in an eight-

by-eight grid. Each player controls a set of sixteen pieces, making a total of thirty-two pieces on the board at the start of the game.

Pieces are divided into two distinct factions: white pieces, known as guardians, and red pieces, known as sentinels. Games are won when one player captures the other player's pieces.

"Guys?" I said. "Where are we?"

Xena turned first. When she saw I was awake, her eyes widened in surprise. "He's up!" In her excitement, she accidentally upset the board.

"Oh, come *on!*" Spud said as red and white pieces spilled across the table. "I had a chance that game!"

"You really didn't," Perry said. "You lost fifteen moves ago. But hi, Crow! Welcome back!"

I swung my legs over the side of the bed. "What's going on?"

All of my friends replied at once, though it was Spud's loud voice that rose above the din. "We're in Prey House! Domain of the Medics! Why are you heading toward the window?"

I didn't need his questions; I needed to be out of the room, as far away from the Medics as possible. My fingers scraped against the sill, trying and failing to pull the window open.

"That window is locked, Crow," Perry said. "They keep it barred to stop people from doing exactly what you're trying. One of the Medics told me that while you were asleep."

"We're trapped here until they clear you," Xena added. "That's why we're just hanging out."

I couldn't understand how they could be so calm. *These are the Medics we're talking about. The organization that nearly sent Jocko into servitude.*

I checked my Map. We appeared to be on the second floor of a massive building. I rotated the Map as I scanned the floors, trying to find an exit.

As soon as I saw one, I bolted to the door.

"Crow, wait!" Spud shouted. "I'm serious, man. You don't want to do that!"

I threw the door open, nearly slamming face-first into the man who stood behind it.

Or rather, into his chest. He must've been seven feet tall.

Red Medic (Gerald Aberdeen)

Gerald Aberdeen was a scion of the esteemed banking family in the bustling city of Volnarok. Alongside his younger brother, Gray, he inherited the family's legacy of shrewd financial acumen.

Gerald's life took a dramatic turn when he and Gray embarked on a journey to the city of Helios. The purpose of their trip was to negotiate a highly lucrative trading contract, one that had the potential to further expand the Aberdeen family's financial influence across the Empire. Their venture was marred when Empire auditors claimed the Aberdeen brothers had illegally manipulated the trade negotiations to their advantage. The Aberdeen assets were swiftly seized by the Empire and their family's reputation was tarnished.

Gerald and his brother had their hands stained with the symbolic yellow of thieves before they were sentenced to Toroth-Gol.

Gerald was so tall that the top of my head only came up to his nipples. He looked strong, with bare, sculpted pectorals that shone as if they'd just been rubbed with oil. Because I'd just run into him, I could smell his skin, a mixture of baby oil and cloves. A curved sword hung from a tasseled belt at his waist.

The man pushed me. It felt like I'd been kicked by a donkey. I flew several feet, the backs of my knees catching the edge of the cot and forcing me to sit.

"Come on!" I gasped as I rubbed my bruised chest, trying to work air back into my lungs. "I'm a patient here. What was that about?"

The man in the doorway grinned through a mouthful of cracked teeth. When he opened his mouth, I saw he didn't have a tongue. A strange sound escaped his throat: *urk, urk, urk.*

He's laughing at me. And why are so many people in Toroth-Gol missing tongues?

"*Aaaand* that's why we can't escape," Spud said. "I tried to tell you! Gerald is one of several guards they've had stationed outside your room the past few days. None of them has a tongue either, which is pretty awesome, though also quite gruesome!"

I stared at the Red Medic, who leered back at me. He pointed at me, jerked a thumb at the cot, and then drew a finger across his throat. His meaning was obvious: *Stay put.*

"They *really* don't want you to leave here, Crow," Perry said. "Not yet, anyway."

I swallowed, trying to work some moisture into my dry mouth. "And why is that, exactly? What's the deal? Is this level some type of giant medical facility?"

"We don't know all the details," Xena said as I glanced over at her. "Basically, after you fell off the cliff, we thought you were dead. Spud wanted to leave you—"

"Did *not*," Spud said.

"—but before we could figure out what to do, we were attacked by mulchers," Xena continued. "The three of us hid and Jocko was forced to flee. I think he probably meant to come back, but then Brynn found us."

In my mind, I pictured Jocko's friend Brynn, the frizzy-haired engineer. "What was she doing in the Valves?"

"They ran beneath all the schools," Xena replied. "We told her what happened, and we thought about trying to find Jocko, but you were in really bad shape and we needed to get you medical attention. Just our luck that when we came through the door to this level, we ended up right in front of Prey House!"

"That's the name of this facility, as well as the third level of the dungeon," Perry chimed in. "It's a little confusing."

I ran a hand over my head. "But you guys don't know where Jocko is?" My companions all shook back and forth.

My thoughts were interrupted as a Blue Medic pushed past Gerald. Her hands were dyed yellow, which meant she'd been sent to Toroth-Gol as a thief.

Blue Medic (Anne Ya'dar)

Little is known about Anne Ya'dar. She comes to Toroth-Gol from Steel City, though city birth records don't contain a woman by that name. Nor do census records have any reference to an Anne Ya'dar living in Steel City.

The first record of her existence comes from her trial, where she was convicted of thievery and sentenced to Toroth-Gol.

Hmm, I thought as I read the text. *That's odd. Usually descriptions for people are a little more descriptive.*

"Welcome back to the land of the living," my mysterious countrywoman said, her quiet voice drifting out from the shadow of her cowl. She was small, no taller than five feet, and had a clipboard in one hand. "My name is Anne Ya'dar, though you can call me Sister Anne. I need to check your vitals. If you can give me your arm?"

I glanced toward the door. Gerald stood there like a brick wall, his arms folded across his chest and his yellow hands tucked under his armpits. I didn't think I could get past him, though I'd dodged bigger people when I'd played lightball.

On the field, I had a bit more room to work.

Anne lifted a hand to her cowl and drew it away from her face. She was a pretty woman with pale skin and delicate features. Brunette hair hung to her shoulders in tight waves.

"Well, well, hi there!" Spud said from the table. "Spud Spuddington, leader of the Spud Squad. Any chance there's a *Mister* Sister Anne in the picture?"

"You're a pig," Xena said.

"Impossible. I'm a *potato*."

"I wouldn't recommend running," Anne said quietly. She spoke as softly as Perry, and her words were clearly meant for my ears only. "If you ran, the Orange Medics would find you. Then all of us would be sent to the Pit: you for running, and us for failing to stop you. Please. Your healing has already been paid in full. Will you let me get your vitals so I can clear you?"

I froze. "Someone already paid for my treatment? Who? When?"

There was desperation in Anne's eyes. "Please." Her gaze flitted toward the doorway and back, and I could tell she was scared.

The Red Medic. He's watching us.

I didn't want to cause trouble, so I rolled up my sleeve.

"Thank you," Anne said. She lifted my hand in surprisingly delicate fingers and turned it over. Then, she leaned close to me. "Whatever you do, don't join our ranks," she whispered as she slipped something into my hand. "I'll handle the rest."

She'd spoken so quietly it took me a moment to register the words. I wanted to ask her about them, but she hadn't wanted Gerald to hear, and there was no way to continue the conversation without his knowledge. From the corner of my eye, I saw him staring at me, his beady eyes alert for any signs of wrongdoing. Conveniently, Sister Anne had angled her body so Gerald couldn't see what she'd placed in my hand, though I knew what it was by touch.

A single gold coin, the kind used to get an upgrade at a Fountain of Wishes.

Gold Coin (x1)

Throw this gold coin into a Fountain of Wishes to receive one (1) upgrade.

I made the coin disappear into my Inventory. *I don't know why she gave that to me, though I'm not going to turn down a gift.*

Anne pressed two fingers to the inside of my wrist. She was checking my pulse, counting my heartbeats as blood beat in my veins.

After a few moments, she released my arm and wrote something on her clipboard.

"Anne?" I said, speaking as quietly as I could. "Who paid my bill?"

Sister Anne looked up. There was a flash of something sympathetic in her wide eyes, and then it was gone. She glanced toward the door and back, and I saw the sympathy had been replaced by the same fear from earlier.

"All will be explained in time," she replied.

I was about to press her when a gray-robed woman walked into the room. At the sight of her, Sister Anne swallowed hard, drawing in on herself, and her yellow hands started shaking.

Sister Anne hadn't been scared of Gerald, but *this* woman.

The woman was probably in her early sixties, with a helmet of short-cropped white hair. Her bangs were so severe she likely could've used them as a weapon. One hand was dyed red; the other, black.

Gray Medic (Leslie Farrier)

A native of Reo, Leslie owned a bakery that was frequented by Helman Amaranth, liaison to the Helios ambassador in Reo. After several unwanted advances, Leslie poisoned the pastry she gave to Amaranth; unbeknownst to her, Amaranth had bought the pastries for his superior officer.

Leslie was convicted of murder and treason, and sentenced to Toroth-Gol.

Leslie is the founder of the Medics, an organization with branches on every level of the dungeon.

My eyes widened. The *founder* of the Medics? The woman responsible for the treatment in Gray Moor that had almost bankrupted me? And *she* was the one who'd murdered the Reo ambassador to Helios?

I'd heard about that incident. My father had had a trip scheduled to Reo around that time, and though it'd gotten canceled, he'd told me the story. Life had moved on and I hadn't thought of it since.

"Hi!" Spud said before I could say anything. "Spud Spuddington, leader of the Spud Squad. What's your name?"

Leslie ignored Spud. Instead, she faced Sister Anne. "What are you doing here, my daughter? I gave strict orders that this patient was to be my sole responsibility."

Sister Anne looked at her feet. When she spoke, her voice was barely above a whisper. "I'm sorry, Administrator. That wasn't communicated to me. I came to clear this patient for release."

Leslie glared suspiciously at the Blue Medic. "I'll take over from here. You are dismissed, Anne. The worm devours."

"The worm devours." Sister Anne stood, offered me a tight smile, and handed Leslie the clipboard on which she'd been taking notes. She pulled the cowl back over her head and hurried from the room.

Interesting, I thought as Leslie's eyes snapped toward me. In terms of sheer physicality, Leslie wasn't as imposing as Gerald, and yet I was pinned like a moth on a board. The dominant impression was that she wasn't just looking at me, but *through* me, as if she could both see my innermost thoughts and how I truly felt about her organization.

She's perceptive, at the least. Though I doubt you start an organization like the Medics if you can't notice details.

Leslie's severe expression melted into one of apparent warmth. "Nathaniel Valentine!" She reached a hand toward me and I took it, my hand easily enveloping hers. As I did, I saw Gerald tense. "What a fine day! I've been watching you on the screens. I've already had the pleasure of meeting your charming friends, but I'm so very glad to make your acquaintance."

"Uh, nice to meet you," I said. I didn't know why this woman was so pleased to see me, though I wouldn't complain.

Leslie scanned the notes Sister Anne had handed her. "I know you must have questions. Where am I? How did I come to be here? And why has the head of the Medics deigned to visit me personally? I have answers to all of that, and more." She flashed a knowing smirk. "All will be explained in time."

I snagged Perry and set him against his favorite spot on my bandolier—which I was still wearing, though I didn't seem to have any of my other equipment—then set Spud atop one shoulder. Xena jumped to the other.

"That sounds great," I said.

"I'm sure you know a bit of my story from whatever description the dungeon gave you, but let me fill in the gaps," Leslie said. "I *loathe* the Empire. If I could, I'd burn every member and laugh as they screamed. I'd do it happily and never think on it again. Is that not also your goal?"

"It is," I admitted.

"You've lived your life in the Empire, which feeds you a convenient fiction: the dungeon exists to protect a gem known as the Heart of the World. But it's a lie! The Empire is run by a madman. I'm not talking about August Morgan, by the way, but the one you never see: a creature known as Jaguar. He's nothing like the cat, so I honestly don't know where he gets the name. Knowing his taste for ugly theatrics, he's probably wearing the bloody pelt of a skinned beast."

As the head of the Medics, I knew Leslie could order Gerald to tear me limb from limb. She hadn't yet, which meant she wanted something from me. That knowledge made me bold. Not bold enough to try and escape, though I felt confident enough to ask a question: "What does that have to do with me?"

Leslie smiled. "My people have been conducting important research and we're almost done with our most recent project. We've been looking into portal technology, with the goal of escaping the dungeon. Can you imagine what we could do if we brought the dungeon's weapons from here to Steel City or Helios? The Empire would never see us coming."

That would be powerful. But would I ally with the Medics?

"When I saw you were with us, I knew I needed to see you," Leslie continued. "Like I said: I've been watching you on the screens. I admire your performance. I wanted you to understand what we had in common. Because I have an offer for you."

"Oh?"

"Yes. But before we get to that, a question: have you heard of the Purple?"

The change in topic surprised me. "The color?"

"Xena is purple!" Spud shouted unhelpfully.

Leslie shook her head. "It's a noun: the Purple. A potion that makes one lose their memories. Your bloodwork has evidence of Purple poisoning, which is why I ask. Are there swaths of your life you don't remember?"

I tried to hide my shock. There *were* parts of my life from my teenage years that were missing for me, though I didn't want Leslie to know more about me than necessary.

From the way her eyes twinkled, I knew she'd already guessed.

"Well. A mystery for another day, it seems," she said. She shrugged, waving the subject away. "Now! Come. I'd like to show you the facility. *Then* we'll get to my offer."

3

Spud, Perry, Xena, and I trailed Leslie out of the room. Gerald bowed to Leslie as she passed, then grunted at me. To my great relief, he didn't follow.

Based on my experiences with the Medics in Gray Moor, I'd assumed Prey House would be run-down and dilapidated. In that, I was wrong. Prey House was *beautiful.* The floors were made from rich, well-oiled wood, and alcoves in the hallways contained oil paintings and exotic artistic treasures. In one, I saw a clam the size of my head made entirely from crystal, the silk bed in its lower shell adorned with a fist-sized pearl. Another held a clock shaped like the Stadia, the face made from polished opal cut into the shape of the Steel City insignia.

At every turn, Spud commented on the artistry. "Whoa, look at the details in that crown molding!" he'd say, whistling in appreciation as he gazed toward the ceiling. Or, "The fabric on those drapes! Forgive me for gushing, though I'm an absolute sucker for details, and that's high-quality velvet!"

As we turned a corner, Leslie smiled at him. "I'm glad you appreciate the beauty of what we've built here," she said. We passed a couple dressed in yellow robes and she motioned to them. "You see the

20

different-colored garments. Blue Medics handle surgeries. Yellow Medics head our research division. Gray Medics work in administration and Red Medics serve as security."

"And Orange Medics?" I asked, remembering Sister Anne's words: "If you ran, the Orange Medics would find you."

Leslie raised an eyebrow. "How did you hear about the Orange Medics?" she asked. When it was clear I wouldn't respond, she shrugged. "They're our trackers and soldiers," she said. "Like the Red Medics, though they work outside the facility."

The administrator led us down a staircase that descended to a landing before switching back on itself. Now, I saw how foolish I would've been to try and escape. About half the doors we passed were guarded by Red Medics, any one of whom could've sent me back to a hospital bed with ease.

One door we passed looked into a formal dining room. Around a large table, several blue-robed figures sat before a feast. All of them held hands, their heads bowed as if in prayer.

"What's going on in there?" Perry asked.

"That's a dining room for the Blue Medics," Leslie replied. She pushed through a set of doors and I followed her into a truly gargantuan room, easily as big around as the Stadia. We stood on an observation deck that looked down into a hole. Cautiously, I approached the edge, resting my hands on the guard rail that ringed its circumference.

"By the Dregs," I whispered.

Prey House (Red Mine)

A pit dug by hunters in the middle of Prey House. No one knows how far down it goes.

I'd been to enough of my father's mines to know what I was seeing. Far below me, hundreds of tiny figures swung pickaxes at piles of rock. Every once in a while, one of them would stop and grab something from the rubble, which they'd bring to a nearby cart. As I watched, one of the filled carts trundled down a track and disappeared into a tunnel below us.

"Who are these people?" I asked as I stared into the mine. "Prisoners? Do you force these people to work for you?"

Leslie laughed. "Them? No. It's a common misconception that we conscript workers. We have a work program for those who need to pay their debts, but everyone you see here works of their own free will. These are acolytes of the Red Medics."

I watched as one of the men below struggled to heft his pickaxe. "You only have *manual* mining equipment in Toroth-Gol?" I asked.

"That's right. The exercise isn't about production, but the diligent pursuit of a goal in the name of something greater than oneself. We have similar exercises for those who would become, say, Gray Medics, though their work prioritizes mental strength as opposed to physical, as a strong mind is what it takes to excel in their role." She motioned to the scene below us. "By the time an acolyte is done in the mines, he or she has obtained the diligence, patience, and muscle necessary to proceed with the next stage of their training."

"Is that when they have their tongues cut out?" Spud asked. "That's the part I want to hear more about."

"Don't be gross, Spud," Perry said.

Leslie shook her head. "The Red Medics are a silent order, though no one forces them to do anything," she said. "Each acolyte who takes his or her tongue does it as a sign of devotion. Generally, it's part of the final ceremony before an acolyte becomes a full Red Medic. It's cause for celebration, not worry."

I shivered. *Maybe the Red Medics do cut out their own tongues happily and of their own free will, though what type of messed-up organization encourages something like that?*

At the look on my face, Leslie rolled her eyes. "We don't cut out anyone's tongue! Goodness, Crow. You really *do* have a low opinion of us. But come. We're not done with our tour."

From the mine, we pushed through another set of halls, walking through labyrinthine corridors until we came to a library, eight stories of bookshelves connected by a manic array of catwalks, balconies, staircases, and ladders. Gone was the antiseptic smell of a hospital, replaced by the warm scents of cedar and old leather.

Prey House (Library)

In all of Toroth-Gol, few sources of knowledge are more complete than the library of Prey House. A repository for all of the information gathered by Medics across the many levels of the dungeon, the library also contains texts written by the prey forces who originally used this location as a stronghold.

It's estimated that of the thirty million artifacts contained in the library, only ten percent of them have been read and documented.

"Progress is one of the three pillars of our organization," Leslie said as she motioned toward the shelves. "Those are progress, order, and justice. But you can't have progress without knowledge, and that's found here, in the Library. The works here represent hundreds of years of institutional knowledge on everything from history to theory and everything in between."

It was an awe-inspiring sight; I'd never seen so many books. The library in Steel City was equally cavernous, though it held nothing as ephemeral as *paper*. Why bother printing texts when the world's information was only a click away? The minimalist halls of the Steel City Library weren't a place for reading, but a temple to knowledge, a meditation hall in which to consider the life of the mind.

Here, though, was plenty of paper, and the number of yellow-robed Medics who shelved the books was equally inspiring. Hundreds of figures moved around the space, flipping through pages at the tables or scurrying up and down ladders with tomes clutched to their chests.

"So many books," Spud whispered. "Wouldn't they be fun to burn?"

"Writing things by hand *is* surprisingly manual," I said. "Wouldn't a digital system be easier to search?"

Leslie shook her head. "A system like that might reduce clutter, but enchanted paper offers the greatest possible defense against the vagaries of the dungeon. I'm sure you already know that technology tends to go haywire around magic, and in that, at least, the Empire wasn't lying. The lower you go in the dungeon, the more likely tech is to fail. We protect our information by sticking to the old-fashioned."

"And you're not worried about mistakes?" Perry said. "Documents copied and recopied, with inaccuracies compounding?"

"Ugh," Spud said, making a retching sound. "Academia. *Boring!*"

"Hush, Spud," Xena chastised. "I want to hear this!"

"You're talking about the old adage," Leslie said, responding to Perry. "The story about the man who passes a tome to his grandson, who copies it and passes it to his grandson, who copies it and passes it again, each one making a small mistake until the hero of the text becomes the villain. That's a risk, certainly. But we're careful. We subscribe to the doctrine outlined by the scholars of Winter Ridge: if someone makes a mistake while copying a tome, we destroy the entire page and make him start again."

"Impressive," Perry said.

"If you're a *nerd*," Spud said.

I wasn't so taken by Leslie's explanation. "I thought the dungeon has only been around for twenty years. Yet you said these works represent hundreds of years of knowledge. How's that?"

Leslie gave me a sympathetic look. "The Empire only started sending prisoners into Toroth-Gol twenty years ago, which is when Jaguar consolidated his power, but the infrastructure here has been around much longer. There's a world down here, and it has existed for far longer than either of us has been alive."

Leslie took a few steps toward a table where a young woman in yellow robes had her head bent over a scroll. She was probably my age, with shoulder-length blonde hair pulled into a tight ponytail and a thin, equine face. Her hands were dyed the purple of someone sent to Toroth-Gol for practicing magic.

Yellow Medic (Joren Arcos)

Joren Arcos was born in Ilmaya. On her twentieth birthday, she was chosen to represent her people as part of a peacekeeping delegation to Atlantis.

Unbeknownst to Joren, the captain of the ship that carried her and her delegation had a hidden agenda: the vessel's hull was clandestinely filled with precious Ilmayan silver, intended to be smuggled to the Thuins through Atlantis. When a Helios navy vessel intercepted the ship, Joren was taken captive. The young Ilmayan, who'd embarked on the voyage with dreams of peace and diplomacy, found herself amidst a fierce confrontation.

Joren was convicted of witchcraft. Her hands were dyed purple and she was sentenced to Toroth-Gol.

"It's the job of the Yellow Medics to sort the wheat from the chaff and find what might be useful to our organization," Leslie said as she tapped the woman on the shoulder. "We refer to the Yellow Medics as Librarians."

Joren looked up; she'd been so engrossed in her work that she apparently hadn't noticed us talking only several feet away.

"Sorry to bother you, Librarian, but can you tell us what you're working on?" Leslie asked.

"Of course, Administrator." Joren set down a rod, which she'd been using to keep her place as she read. "My current area of research is the work of Grimoria Spaulden, the master builder and recluse who once inhabited the mines of Kentor on the sixth level of the dungeon. I've found that many of her inventions were redundant, though she generated glamours mechanically rather than magically. I had a bit of experience with glamours myself from when I first entered the dungeon, and I hadn't heard of any machine that could generate them, so I cross-referenced this with our current documentation and found that no one else had heard of this, either. I'm now looking into Spaulden's methods. There's a chance this could lead to more effective glamours moving forward."

Leslie beamed. "Excellent work, Librarian. Tell me: do you enjoy your life here? Have you been treated well?"

The Yellow Medic smiled so beatifically I knew her emotions were genuine. "When I first entered the dungeon, I didn't know peace. Now, I have a life." She gestured around the room. "*We* have a life."

Leslie placed a hand on the woman's shoulder. "You're with us now, and we're better for it. Thank you for your service, Librarian."

"And you, Administrator."

"The worm devours," Leslie said, smiling softly.

4

As we stepped away from Joren, I was forced to reconsider my opinion of the Medics. Yes, they'd treated me and my friend poorly on the previous level. But everyone who belonged to their organization appeared content. Together, they'd managed to build lives for themselves in the dungeon.

But something else demanded my attention: "What was that you said just now?" I asked Leslie as we walked deeper into the library. "The worm devours? I also heard you say it to Sister Anne."

"*The worm of justice devours vessels of corruption,*" Leslie said. "It's a line from a text we found here in the library, and it's become a mantra of our organization."

"The full line is a mouthful," Xena said.

Leslie smiled. "That's why we shorten it."

After another hour of walking through Prey House, Leslie led us to a set of double doors. I checked my Map and saw that beyond them was a small room. Beyond that: freedom.

As Leslie had promised, she'd brought me to the exit.

Before we reached the doors, two red-cloaked guards stepped through and held them open for us. We walked in.

Prey House (Back Entry IV)

Prey House has many entrances, each of which is used for a different purpose.

Traditionally, Back Entry IV was used to admit Red Medics returning from Old Town.

One of the lesser-used entrances to Prey House, Back Entry IV opens to a courtyard on the rear side of the facility.

Not for the first time, I found myself missing the manic energy of the descriptions I'd received before Brynn had changed the setting on my eye.

Then again, the grass is always greener.

On the far side of the room, near another pair of double doors, were two parallel glass partitions that looked into some sort of booth. Behind the glass sat a man in gray robes who nodded politely as we approached. He was thin and rat-faced, with a port-wine stain that covered most of his right cheek and spread down his neck.

As I looked at him, I received a description from the dungeon.

Gray Medic (Henry Smith)

Henry was born in Ironwood. Although his family name carried no noble weight, he distinguished himself as a member of the Blacksmith's Guild, becoming a master metallurgist by thirty.

As a blacksmith, Henry specialized in crafting military-grade alloys for the Empire's elite guards. When a shipment of his armor was found in the hands of rebel Thuins in the Wastes, the Empire accused him of treason.

Henry's hands were dyed black and he was sentenced to Toroth-Gol.

"I'll need gear for Nathaniel Valentine," Leslie said to Henry as we reached the partitions.

"We've got everything all ready for him, Administrator," Henry said, lifting a bag from the desk before him. As he did, I noticed his hands were indeed dyed black.

Just like mine.

Henry slid the bag through a gap in the glass. "Mr. Valentine, if you could take a look and make sure nothing is missing?"

I peered into the bag. Inside, I saw my missing equipment. There was something else as well: a pistol made of dark, polished wood and decorated with silver ornamentation. Without looking at the description, I recognized the weapon: Cara Thorne had used it to put a bullet through my heart.

"What's this?" I grunted, holding it up. "This isn't mine."

Henry consulted a paper on the desk in front of him. "It appears the pistol was a condition of your release. When your bill was settled, we also agreed to have you take Cara Thorne's pistol."

"How fun is that," Xena said sarcastically. "A little memento to remember the woman who tried to kill us."

"Yeah," Spud said. "What now, Henry? You gonna give us her body as well?"

Henry gestured behind him. For the first time, I noticed two gurneys covered in white sheets.

Oh. Oh no. I shook my head.

"We're not taking that."

Henry looked at me sympathetically, as if he understood how I felt yet couldn't do anything to help. "In addition to the pistol, you've been given possession of two bodies: that of Ms. Cara Thorne, and that of Mr. Feng Goa. Another condition of your release."

"Whoa!" Spud said. "I'm not usually right!"

I glanced at Leslie, who shrugged. "Just take the weapon and the bodies. We don't care what you do with them."

"We can't let you go *unless* you agree to take them," Henry said. "Those are the rules. We've taken the liberty of preparing the bodies for burial."

I didn't want the pain of being reminded of Feng's death. He, at least, had been a friend. He deserved something from me.

Cara didn't.

For some disturbing reason, Henry swiveled in his chair and pulled the sheet back from the first gurney. Underneath, I saw Cara's face, her tan skin framed by a blanket of shaggy salt-and-pepper hair. When he moved to uncover the second gurney, I held up a hand.

"Don't." I couldn't bear the thought of seeing Feng. "Fine. Sure. I'll take them."

Henry nodded. He looked relieved. "If you'll just reach through here, you can get a hand on them and move them into your Inventory." He motioned to the gap.

I followed his instructions, then made everything disappear into my Inventory except for my gloves, which I slipped onto my hands, and my portable battery pack, which I clipped to my belt.

"So, Crow," Leslie said as I finished reequipping myself. "Are you ready for my offer?"

I knew what it was before she asked. "You want me to join you."

"How astute," she said. "Yes. I'd like you to join us."

I looked up at her. In truth, it didn't seem so bad. The library alone contained millions of pages of original research, much of it about magic and *none* of it censored by the Empire.

What could you find in there? What secrets has Toroth-Gol kept hidden from the Empire?

Additionally, if Leslie was to be believed, the Medics and I shared common goals. We both wanted to escape. We both wanted revenge against the Empire. The kicker was, the Medics had resources.

By yoking my cart to theirs, do I have a better chance of seeing my dreams realized?

The only problem was, I didn't believe Leslie. Something wasn't adding up. Everything I'd seen was a little too perfect, a little too choreographed to represent true freedom.

I was good at detecting lies. It wasn't a magic skill. Just human intuition. I put a lot of stock in it, and it'd never steered me wrong.

Although I hadn't detected any outright lies from Leslie, something about Prey House was rotten. There was Sister Anne's mysterious warning to think about, as well: "Whatever you do, don't join our ranks," she'd said.

Why would she say a thing like that?

"I appreciate the offer," I said. "But I think I'm going to go my own way."

Leslie nodded politely, as if she'd expected that answer. "Understood. Should you want to bury your dead, there's a cemetery on the far side of town. Just follow the path all the way through Old Town and you can't miss it."

"Thank you."

"Of course. So long, Crow." I turned to leave, but as I did, Leslie coughed into her hand. I looked over my shoulder and saw she held up a finger. "Before you go, there's one more thing you should see. It won't take long. It's just down the hall. If you'll follow me?"

"Don't go," Spud whispered.

But I was curious. And arrogant. And naive. Though I didn't know it at the time.

You have your gear back, and she hasn't threatened you so far. Might as well see what she wants to show you.

"Sure," I said. "Let's go."

5

Leslie led me down a hall and around a corner to another set of double doors. These were guarded by Red Medics who looked smarter than the others I'd seen. More cunning. There was intelligence in their dark eyes that I hadn't seen in the eyes of any other Red Medic except Gerald, who stood at our backs.

"The light of the sun will warm the faces of all true soldiers," Leslie said. I thought this might be another mantra, though I realized it was a password, as it was only after she'd spoken that the Medics saluted and lowered their weapons.

"Tight security," Spud said as one of the Medics opened the doors. "I wonder what they're guarding!"

The room beyond the doors was as big as the one that contained the Red Mine. Only here, there was no hole in the floor; in fact, the massive room was completely empty save for dozens of clear glass cells built into a line in the far wall.

Prey House (Cell Viewing Chamber)

Glassinine is a nearly unbreakable substance. Outside of the

Crystal Keep and the Glass Forest, the Cells of Prey House contain more glassinine than any other place on any world.

The glassinine-lined cells of Prey House are only ever opened twice for each prisoner: once when they're placed into the cell, and once when they're released. Prisoners are sent into each cell with all of the food and water they might require for the duration of their incarceration, as well as a composting toilet for solid and liquid waste.

Throughout the history of Prey House, no one has ever escaped its cells.

Disgust crept over me as I realized I was looking at a prison cell. From what I could see, each cell appeared to be about ten feet by ten feet. True to the description, each one contained a box that I assumed held food and water, as well as a smaller box that had to be the toilet. There was no privacy; with their clear glass walls, the cells were not only visible to anyone who walked through the chamber, but also to each other. Standing in a cell on one side of the room, a prisoner could look straight through to the cell at the far end.

"What is this?" Perry asked, speaking aloud the question that was on my lips.

In addition to the toilet and the box for food and water, each cell also contained a single occupant. Some of the prisoners lay on their backs, staring at the ceiling, while others simply sat with their heads to their knees. In one cell, a man stood with his forehead pressed to the wall. Periodically, he'd bang his head against the glass, though no sound escaped.

Leslie sighed. "Much of what you've seen today was built by our organization. These cells were not. I chose to establish my organization here *because* of these cells, which we found while hunting for a suitable site for our headquarters. If you've ever been to Crystal Keep, I'm sure you're familiar with glassinine?"

Crystal Keep was a town outside Toroth-Gol that belonged to the Empire. While my father's mines held iron ore and coal, the pits near Crystal Keep contained glassinine. As the description had said, it was one of the hardest substances in existence. Just a single square foot of glassinine was worth as much as the average lightball player's salary, which made this room more valuable than the combined treasures of Steel City.

"One day soon, we'll find a way to break down these cells and use the glassinine to gird the machines we'll bring to battle against the Empire," Leslie said. "Until then, they serve another purpose."

"What's that?" Spud asked cheerfully, the obvious answer escaping him. Clearly, he hadn't yet realized the purpose of this room.

"The people you see trapped here tried to bring chaos to order," Leslie said. "They defied our rules and ignored our laws. This is part of their punishment."

"These people are prisoners, Spud," Xena explained.

"Oh," Spud said. "That seems unpleasant. What happens to them? They just sit in those glass cages until they rot?"

Leslie offered a grim smile. "These people are on their way to the Pit." She pointed to the cells on the side of the room where we entered. "Just beyond that wall is where we try those accused of breaking order. If someone is found innocent, they're released. If guilty, they're incarcerated. Every so often, the entire line of cells shifts to the left," she moved her finger down the line, "with each cell moving one spot over to accommodate the new one. The cells are on tracks, you see, and a new, empty cell rises from the floor. The cycle repeats."

"Do you ever run out of places to put prisoners?" Xena asked.

"The time it takes to run through a full cycle of imprisonment depends on how many criminals we've incarcerated," Leslie continued. "Several years ago, we had something of a rebellion, and nearly all of our cells were filled. It took us nine weeks to move through all of them, and that was at a rate of one every hour. Today, we're moving prisoners at a rate of one every twelve hours. The rate is adjusted to make sure we always have fresh cells."

"One every twelve hours is a lot of prisoners to get through," Perry replied.

Leslie smiled. "We have a lot of enemies."

I walked closer to the cells, and neither Leslie nor Gerald made any move to stop me. I heard them follow behind. I stopped before a cell, which contained a single woman. She sat with her back to one of the walls, her legs stretched out before her. Her thin cotton shift was smeared with stains, and her brown hair was matted and tangled. If she noticed my presence, she didn't care.

Although I waited for a description, none was forthcoming. The glassinine appeared to block more than just physical attacks. A piece of paper stuck to the cell told me everything I needed to know.

"Jenna Orbin," I read. "Sentenced to the Pit for crimes against the Medics. The worm devours."

I moved to the next cell, which contained the man banging his head against the glassinine. "James de Costa," I said, reading from his paper. "Sentenced to the Pit for crimes against the Medics. The worm devours."

The other papers I saw were written in the same format: the person's name, followed by those same words: *sentenced to the Pit for crimes against the Medics. The worm devours.*

"This is cruel and unusual." The horror of the punishment settled over me. Maybe Jenna Orbin had drowned a puppy, or the man banging his head against the glass had bathed in the blood of a dozen children. Still, there was an element of cruelty to the imprisonment that struck me as discordant, no matter the crime. "Why do this?"

Leslie didn't defend herself. "As I built the Medics from the ground up, I was forced to ask myself philosophical questions about the best way to structure a functioning society. One of those is as old as civilization itself: is it better to be loved or feared?"

"Johann's Discourse," Perry murmured. "I've read the treatise."

"So have I," Xena said.

"I definitely have *not*," Spud added.

Leslie continued. "The answer, I think, is that it's best to be loved *and* feared. Love should be the first course of action. But when gratitude dissolves, a firm hand is the only correcting course. If you want to study fear as a tool of order, there's no better textbook than the Empire."

"You learned from the people you hate?" I asked. "You call that justice?"

Leslie shrugged. "There's something to be learned from everyone. Even our enemies."

Before I could reply, Perry said, "You know the Discourse was written as a satire, right? Johann had been tortured by the Empire for his writings. He'd been brought to Steel City and forced to watch as his family was tossed off the edge of Gomindor. He wrote and dedicated the Discourse to the kindness of August Morgan in *jest*."

Leslie stared at him, her expression hard. "Whether it was written as satire or not is a matter of scholarly debate. Still, Johann's intentions are irrelevant if the path he outlines leads to a greater good. I've seen the wisdom of this path with my own eyes. When you reach Old Town, Crow, look around and tell me the chaos you witness is superior to order. People starving. Living in hovels. Then, think of what you've seen here. The Medics are *order*. A collection of disparate egos marching in lockstep toward the same goal. Everyone is housed, clothed, and fed. You think we maintain order through love alone?"

I felt sick. "Why show me this? I was about to walk out of here. I wasn't in love with the Medics, but I wasn't disgusted by you, either." I turned to look at the poor man beating his forehead against the glassinine, my heart breaking at the sight of him. "This is the work of monsters."

"That may well be," Leslie said. "But tell that to those who have a life within our various wings. A life that was enabled by this so-called cruelty."

She turned and continued walking down the line of cells, gesturing for me to follow. I cast a final glance at Jenna Orbin before joining her.

One foot after the other. Like my father always said. You'll be out of this soon enough, Crow. Just keep walking.

"To answer your earlier question, I brought you here so you know what's at stake if you defy us," Leslie said. "If you keep to your business and don't bother the Medics, we'll have no quarrel with you. Otherwise, you'll end up like *him*."

She pointed to a cell near the far wall.

There, sitting behind the glass, was my father.

6

Though it'd only been a few weeks since I'd last seen Sal Valentine, he'd gone through a substantial change. *This* Sal Valentine was far thinner than the one I'd known, and one of the arms that poked through his Empire-issue jumpsuit was pink and hairless, as if the first layer of skin had been burned away.

My breath caught in my throat as I glanced at the paper on his cell. It didn't say Sal Valentine; it said, "John Petersen."

I wanted to scream. John Petersen was one of the names my father used when he was undercover and didn't want to be discovered. He'd managed to fool the sensors, though I had no doubt this was Sal Valentine.

My father looked up, and I saw the fire that burned behind his eyes. My chest swelled with pride, as it told me he hadn't been broken. Then, the truth hit me, and I felt myself growing despondent.

He's on the wrong side of the glass. How'd the smartest man in the world get himself captured?

My father and I made eye contact, and for the briefest moment, I saw his eyes widen. He gave an almost-imperceptible shake of his head.

What does that mean? Is he telling me not to try and free him? Or am I seeing things?

"I've seen it, then," I growled. "Can I go?"

Leslie smiled. "Right this way." She turned and headed for the nearby doors. I cast one last look at my father, trying to capture every detail of his face in my mind, before I followed.

My father was in the seventh cell. If the cells are moving at a rate of one every twelve hours, my father has roughly four days until... what?

Leslie pushed through the doors and I walked after her, finding myself in a large courtyard. Above me, I saw the darkening sky. After the antiseptic scent of Prey House, the air in the courtyard smelled crisp, though there was a hint of something sour, like rotten meat. A track suspended on struts exited a gate in the wall behind me, running to the center of the courtyard before ending over a yawning black hole.

Prey House (The Pit)

A punishment for those who defy the Medics.

Why did I expect that to be useful? A horn blared, so loud I had to clap my hands to my ears.

"What was *that?*" Tentatively, I removed my hands, though I kept them close to my ears in case of another blast.

"Oh, my poor ears," Xena moaned. I felt for the eggplant, as I knew she had sensitive hearing.

"I wasn't disturbed because I was humming in my own head," Spud said.

I glanced toward Leslie and saw a cruel light enter the Administrator's eyes. "Watch."

Before I could ask what, specifically, she wanted me to see, a cell came out of a gate in the wall, settling onto the tracks and moving along them until it hovered directly over the Pit. Inside, a man sat on the floor, his knees pulled to his chest. Although I couldn't hear him, I saw that he was sobbing. He was of a similar age to Leslie, and when he saw me looking at him, his lips moved. *Help me.* A red light atop his cell started whirling, its glow cast on the gray cobblestones of the courtyard.

"Um, Crow?" Perry said. "Maybe we should go? Because I really don't think we're going to like this."

But I couldn't look away. Even if I'd wanted to run, Gerald had taken up a guard position by the door.

You should've run when you had the chance. Now, it's too late.

Instead of making a break toward the door, I walked closer to the Pit's edge. The Pit was a perfect circle, and though I couldn't see very far into its depths, the lanterns that hung from posts around the hole revealed that I was looking into a gaping maw. The Pit's sides were covered in a glistening membrane that was such a dark shade of red it was almost black. At even intervals along the wall were white spines as long as my forearm. Periodically, the membrane undulated as if beetles moved beneath it, and the spines bobbed up and down.

"You might want to step back," Leslie said. "The show is about to start."

The sour smell I'd previously detected was emanating from the Pit, so I was happy to step away from the edge. Still, I had a feeling I knew what she meant by "show."

Perry had been right: it wasn't something I wanted to see.

"I've had enough," I said. "We understand each other, Leslie. I'm leaving."

I tried to turn, but found I couldn't move. It was as if I was sandwiched between two invisible walls. One held my chest, and one pressed against my back. The wall before me seemed to end just above Perry, so he wasn't squished, but that was the only consolation.

"Crow?" Xena said, a note of concern in her voice as she noticed something amiss. "What's going on? What's happening?"

Again, I tried to move, though I was still frozen. Leslie, a few feet away from me, grunted with exertion as she raised an arm, and I found myself lifted a foot into the air.

"Whoa!" Perry said. "Leslie, are you doing this? Put him down!"

"Stay calm," I told my friends, forcing the words through lips pressed together by whatever magic Leslie was using to hold me. The last thing I wanted was for one of them to get hurt while trying to free me. "She just… wants us… to watch."

I didn't relish the thought of watching the man in the cell falling to his death, though if that's what it took to keep my friends safe, I'd do it.

She'll let us go eventually. Then we can figure out how to free my father. One foot after the other.

Leslie grinned at my useless struggles. "That's right," she said as she manipulated the invisible barriers that held me so I rotated to face the Pit. "I *need* you to watch, because you have to understand what happens to those who break our rules."

The red light above the cell continued to turn, casting the courtyard in an eerie glow. The old man in the cell was mumbling something, though whether it was a prayer or a plea for help, I wasn't sure.

I could've closed my eyes, but I didn't. I forced myself to watch, to etch this memory into my mind, to bear witness to the sorry soul who, stripped of dignity, would be forced to meet his end. I knew this wasn't justice, but torture. Anger rose hot like bile in my chest.

I'll save my father, escape the dungeon, and bring ruin to the Empire. But before I do, I'm going to destroy the Medics.

The Medics *were* the Empire, rebuilt in Toroth-Gol. A collection of people with resources and power who didn't care how many people suffered as long as they got their way.

Leslie came to stand before me and placed her hand on the surface of the invisible barrier before my face. I saw each line on her red-dyed palm, right down to the whorls on her fingertips. Hovering between the invisible planes, I towered over her.

But I was powerless.

"We reserve the Pit for those who defy us," Leslie said. "To them, we offer no mercy."

Another horn split the air. The bottom fell out of the cell, opening along some unseen hinge. I heard the man yell and saw the panic in his red-rimmed eyes. He screamed. He fell. Then the sound cut off, and I could only assume he'd met his end.

The worm devours. Finally, the mantra of the Medics made sense. I shivered, not at all happy that my sense of wrongness about the organization had been validated.

This is the fate that awaits my father. I stopped myself from going further. Right now, it'd only send me into a panic, and that wasn't useful. I needed to focus on my own survival; once that was assured, I'd be in a better position to help Sal.

The red light atop the cell stopped turning and the floor returned to its original position. The cell, now empty, was dragged back along the tracks until it disappeared back through the gate in the wall. Ostensibly, it'd be filled with another sorry prisoner and sent along a journey to the Pit.

With the show complete, Leslie released the invisible walls that held me, and I dropped to the ground. I tried to catch myself, but I was off-balance. I stumbled, landing in a heap at her feet. Spud and Xena managed to stay on my shoulders.

"The Medics won't hurt you, but neither will we go out of our way to help you," Leslie said as she gazed down at me. "Because you turned down my offer, you'll have no special privileges beyond what we provide to any hunter in the dungeon." She pointed to the Pit. "Never forget what you saw here, Crow. I hope the memory is burned so deeply into your psyche that not even the Purple can wipe it from your mind. No one escapes our justice. Know this, and you just might survive the level."

7

I don't remember returning to Back Entry IV, though I do remember my anger. It was a hissing, seething thing, like oil dropped into a hot pan.

Without much fanfare, I found myself on one side of an empty plaza just outside of the building. I was alone save for my friends; Perry was on my bandolier while Spud and Xena sat atop my shoulders. A cold wind blew across the plaza, making me pull my jumpsuit more tightly around myself.

"Hey Crow?" Perry said quietly. "That was your father in that cell, wasn't it? I felt you tense when you saw him, and I thought he looked like Gatekeeper Valentine from the last level."

I nodded. Until today, my friends had never seen my real father, but Perry and Spud had seen a simulated version of him in Gray Moor.

Spud whistled. "Jenna Orbin was your father? I could've *sworn* that was a woman!"

"Not her," Xena said. "The cell marked John Petersen. That was him, wasn't it? I thought he looked like you."

"That was him," I replied dully. "I'm adopted, but people always comment on how much we look alike. Sal Valentine uses the name John Petersen when he doesn't want anyone to know who he is."

"Oh," Spud said. "That makes *way* more sense."

"The disguise must not have fooled the Medics, because Leslie was pretty smug when she pointed him out to you," Perry said. "I don't like her, Crow! That was really cruel."

The wheels in my head started turning. "It was cruel. But here's what I don't understand: my father is meticulous. He's a strategic *genius*. Is he in there because he wants to be? Or is he being held against his will?"

For several seconds, there was only the sound of the wind.

"I'm voting for the former," Xena finally said. "If your father is as smart as you say, we're all dancing to his tune."

I couldn't tell if she was saying it because she believed it or because she was trying to cheer me up. "But I don't *know*," I said. "I hate feeling like I don't know what's going on."

"We're not without resources, Crow," Perry said. "I know things look bleak, but don't give up just yet. You have your Wisdom power, don't you? If I'm not mistaken, it should be ready to go."

I nodded. "It is, though I was hoping to keep that in reserve."

"Maybe we should head to that city?" Xena said. "Old Town? Brynn was the one who brought us here, so I'm sure she's down there. And if we find Brynn, maybe we find Jocko. And what was your other friend's name? The lizard woman?"

"Geeta," I said.

"That's right," Xena continued. "They let her out before you, and she sounded awesome. I bet she's down there right now, just waiting for us to come hang out with her."

Now, I was sure my friends were trying to make me feel better. It was working. Maybe we'd locate our allies or maybe we wouldn't, but there wasn't any reason to give up hope just yet.

"Thanks, guys," I said. "Let's see what we can find in Old Town."

With my spirits marginally improved, I walked across the plaza. It was perhaps two hundred yards long, flanked on either side by high stone walls. The air was colder than it'd been only moments before. I glanced over my shoulder and saw the towering, monstrous edifice of Prey House behind me.

It was impressive, built from brick and crenelated stone. Its thousand windows were lit from the inside, projecting a warm, yellow glow. There were thin chimneys and towers at odd intervals, their roofs angling toward triangular points and capped by lightning rods. Somewhere behind those walls was the Red Mine, the Library, and the Pit, into which the Medics cast their enemies.

"It looks *haunted*," Xena said, putting words to my thoughts.

I turned back to the plaza. In the distance, just beyond the gate that opened to an expansive view of a valley, I saw a fountain. In its center, a pedestal supported a stone statue that had been carved into a shape I recognized well: Sirax Sirco, founder of Gray Moor, returned my gaze. Water dripped down his back like a cape to fill the basin at his feet.

Prey House (Fountain of Wishes)

You'll find one Fountain of Wishes on each level of Toroth-Gol. Drink the water of the Fountain of Wishes to heal your pains. Throw a gold coin into the Fountain of Wishes to claim an upgrade.

"Oh, happy day!" Spud said, his voice giddy with excitement. "Look at this, Crow! See? Things aren't so bad. And just our luck that we have a gold coin!"

I reached into my Inventory and removed the coin Sister Anne had given me. *This has to be more than luck. Perhaps someone is on our side after all.*

"Toss it in!" Spud yelled. "Go, Crow, go! It's time to make me godly!"

There was no reason *not* to get an upgrade, so I tossed the coin into the fountain's dark waters.

You've been granted one upgrade by the Fountain of Wishes. Choose wisely.

That was followed by three choices.

Hellfire (Spud Beauregard Spuddington)

Corrosive Beam (Peristopheles Magnesis IV)

Nightmare Fuel (Xenandor of Kratha)

"Hellfire, hellfire, hellfire!" Spud chanted, bouncing up and down on my shoulder. "Oh, wow! I'm more excited than I was the first time Xena asked me on a date."

Xena snorted. "In your dreams."

"Funny," Spud replied. "That's *exactly* where it happened."

I ignored them as I pulled up the description for Hellfire.

Hellfire (Spud Beauregard Spuddington)

With this upgrade, Spud will be able to channel the flames of Potato Hell to exhibit an awe-inspiring display of pyromantic prowess.

Spud's body will now trail an iridescent oil. This oil, akin to liquid fire, adheres to the surfaces it contacts and quickly ignites, generating an infernal conflagration. Ranging from deep amber to fiery crimson, the oil is notably viscous and capable of sticking effortlessly to various materials and surfaces.

The trail of burning oil persists for a limited duration, with its

lifespan directly influenced by how forcefully Spud was initially fired.

"Pyromantic prowess," Spud whispered. "It's beautiful. No need to wait, Crow, take it."

It certainly wasn't a *bad* upgrade, though it seemed highly technical, and I wasn't sure about the potential for friendly fire.

"I'm reading the others first," I said. "Then we'll make a decision. Let's see what we get with Corrosive Beam."

I opened the description for Perry's power.

Corrosive Beam (Peristopheles Magnesis IV)

With this upgrade, Perry gains the ability to project a searing ray of corrosive acid from his mouth. Once released, the acidic residue of the beam lingers, continuing to erode surfaces and materials after the initial strike.

Perry can control the intensity at will, allowing for precision in dealing with a wide range of obstacles and adversaries.

Upon acquiring this magical ability, Perry will emanate a subtle, iridescent aura, indicating the heightened magical potency now coursing within his plump form.

"Ha," Spud said. "Plump form."

I rubbed the bristles on Perry's head. "Not bad, eh buddy? Think of how many mulchers you could blast with that!"

Perry laughed nervously. "It *is* pretty good, though I don't know if it's as good as Hellfire."

"It's *way* better than Hellfire," Xena said. "Awesome upgrade, Perry!"

"Let's see what you've got, Xena," I said, before Spud could argue.

Nightmare Fuel (Xenandor of Kratha)

On the shores of the Kingdom of Death, the souls of those who have left the physical realm wait to cross the veil. Once they do, it becomes impossible to bring them back. This threshold, first theorized by necromantic researcher Xenandor of Kratha, is known as Xenandor's Veil.

With this upgrade, Xenandor of Kratha gains the ability to surpass the eponymous veil. Nightmare Fuel will augment the power behind her resurrections, enabling her to anchor in the Kingdom of Death more fully.

I read the text again. And then once more.

"Xena, what does this mean, exactly?" I asked.

From my shoulder, the eggplant was silent. Then: "It means I was right." When she spoke again, she yelled so loudly that I jerked to one side. "I was right!"

"Ow!" I said, pressing a hand to my ear. "Right about what?"

Xena bounced up and down excitedly. "This is what my entire dissertation was about. Three hundred and twenty pages, not including the bibliography. I submitted it to Kanebrook when I was trying to get a post-grad residency. They rejected me. Told me there wasn't enough supporting evidence."

"Supporting evidence for *what?*" Perry asked. He was as confused as I was. "What's all that stuff about souls and the veil?"

"Necromancy isn't an exact science," Xena said. "The best way I can describe it is like Crow's Wisdom power. It's like, a state of mind. When I go into a state where I can bring someone back from the dead, I enter a whole other world. *I* think it's a real place, but that's currently a hotly contested issue in the field. Necromancers who believe in this world call it the Kingdom of Death."

I waited for her to say more. For the first time since our heart-to-heart in Gray Moor, Xena was telling us something about her past and her powers, and I thought it was important to let her talk. Clearly, so did Perry, because he was silent as well. Even Spud was quiet, though I couldn't tell if that was because he was interested in what Xena was saying or distracted by a nearby flock of birds.

"For me, this world looks like a beach, and the souls of the recently deceased line the shore," Xena continued. "These are the souls I can bring back. But wait too long and the souls leave. There's something at the edge of the water, like a curtain made of fog. In my dissertation, I called it the veil. Xenandor's Veil. Once the souls go past it, they can't come back. Well, sometimes someone who isn't too far gone can hear you and fight their way back, but the times I've physically tried to walk into it, I've been kicked right back into my body. I've talked to other necromancers who have experienced the same thing. So that's where this new power comes in. If Nightmare Fuel allows me to better anchor my subtle body in the Kingdom of Death, I should be able to venture deeper beyond the veil."

I heard Perry breathe in sharply. "Which means…"

"*Dragons*," Spud whispered.

"What?" Xena said. "No. It means I might be able to bring back people who have already crossed the veil. Like Feng! But it wouldn't be a done deal. This is uncharted territory. To my knowledge, no necromancer has ever gone more than ten steps into the veil. Not even Seraphina Grimwood herself."

"That *can't* be a real name," Spud said. "Seraphina Grimwood?"

I considered the upgrades. If I was going to bring my fight to the Medics, I needed as much firepower as I could get. That meant the logical choice was Hellfire or Corrosive Beam. Unless Xena could bring back Feng, in which case Nightmare Fuel was the best option. Feng had saved my life twice, and I felt like I owed him.

Even if Nightmare Fuel isn't guaranteed to bring back Feng, I have to try. If Nightmare Fuel turned out to be a lemon, so be it. It was a small price for the chance to repay a debt.

"I'm going to go with Nightmare Fuel," I said, explaining my reasoning to my friends.

"I figured you'd say that," Spud said, sighing as if he bore a grievous weight. "I support it. It's always the right move to help those who have gone out of their way to help you. I suppose I can wait a *little* longer to reach my ultimate form. For the record, though, you know who else died for you twice?"

"We're all in agreement, then?"

"Do it!" Perry said. "Nightmare Fuel!"

The eggplant nodded solemnly. "I'll do everything I can to bring him back."

"I agree, too, as I've told you," Spud grumbled.

Mentally, I selected Nightmare Fuel. The text winked out from my vision, and Xena gasped.

"Oh," she said. "I feel the power! Crow, get Feng's body out of your Inventory and lay him on the ground."

I followed her instructions and she rolled across the stone to take a spot near Feng's head.

"Now whatever happens, don't disturb me," she said. She glanced at Spud, who still sat on my shoulder. "That means you. No quips. No snide comments. No exclamations. This is going to be hard enough as it is without interjections on mini-golf."

Spud groaned. "I make *one* joke about a made-up sport in Potato Hell." Xena didn't flinch. "*Fine.* I'll stay quiet. You don't have to worry about me."

Xena narrowed her eyes at Spud, then turned back to Feng. She let her eyelids close. "Here we go. Uncharted territory. Crow, cross your fingers for me."

As I sat on the edge of the fountain, purple smoke drifted out from Xena's body. I wanted to bring Spud into my hand and light his flames, but I knew how much he'd moan if I did, and Xena had requested no distractions. I brought Perry into one hand and Spud into the other, taking comfort from their round forms.

"I'm not big on physical contact," Spud whispered, his voice barely audible above the wind, "but this is actually nice."

As we waited, time seemed to stop. I remember holding my breath, though in hindsight, that wouldn't have been possible, because at least ten minutes passed.

What will I say to Feng, if Xena manages to resurrect him? Maybe I won't say anything for a while. Then, I'll thank him. Tell him I've got his back. And I've got to get that soda recipe from him. That stuff was delicious!

Finally, the purple smoke stopped rolling off Xena's body, and the eggplant opened her eyes. My adrenaline started pumping when I saw the look of wonder on her face. I jumped to my feet, placing Spud back on my shoulder and Perry on my bandolier.

"What happened?" I asked. "What was it like?"

"It was incredible," she gasped. "I've never seen anything like it. There's a city beyond the veil, Crow. I only got to see it for a second, but it's real as anything you see before you. The *true* Kingdom of Death!"

She went quiet, and my stomach dropped. I looked down at Feng, who hadn't moved. Xena shook her head.

"I'm sorry, guys," she said. "I tried. He wasn't on the shore, and I got past the veil, but the city is *massive*. Give me weeks to explore, and I still don't know if I could find him. Or bring him back."

"I understand," I said. Xena had told us this was a possibility, but to have had just a glimpse of hope, and then to have it dashed…

"You tried your best," Perry said, trying to sound encouraging. "That's what counts."

I scarcely heard him. Although I was sure I'd chosen the right power from the Fountain of Wishes, I couldn't help but feel a pang of regret. The fact that Feng's body still lay on the cold ground before me didn't help. I reached forward to touch his leg, which sent his body back into my Inventory. I knew I should say something comforting to Xena, but I couldn't muster the energy.

"It's going to be dark soon," I said instead. "I'd like to find somewhere to sleep before the sun sets. It's cold enough already."

"Wait," Xena said. "There's one tiny thing. Hardly worth mentioning, really. When I was on the shore, I saw Cara. You know, the pirate who tried to kill you? She was just standing there by herself, staring over the water. Souls do that sometimes, before they cross the veil. I didn't say anything to her, and I don't think she saw me, but if you wanted me to try, I think I could bring her back."

8

There were a million reasons *not* to resurrect Cara Thorne. Most of them were blindingly obvious.

One: she was a pirate.

Two: she was a liar.

Three: because she'd shot me in the heart, I'd fallen off the side of a cliff, broken thirty-seven bones, and found myself in the care of the Blue Medics.

At the same time, I was alone, in unfamiliar territory, and considering the best way to break my father out of Prey House. Given my situation, I'd be smart to take every additional gun I could get.

"You can control the people you resurrect, right?" I asked Xena.

The eggplant shook herself back and forth. "Not exactly," she said. "For something as simple as a mulcher, the answer is yes. Animals, monsters, and other entities without developed prefrontal cortices are highly suggestive, which is functionally akin to control. That was why I could convince the mulchers I raised to fight their brothers, while Feng maintained autonomy."

"So if you resurrected Cara, she wouldn't be beholden to your suggestions?" I said.

Xena looked thoughtful. "If I understand your question, you're worried about what will happen if I bring her back and she isn't, uh, grateful? Is that it?"

"That's right."

"I see the concern," Xena said. "Once I bring her back, my magic will be the only thing anchoring her soul to the physical realm. If she threatens you and I end the connection, her soul will be returned to the subtle realm. The effect would be instantaneous."

I ran a hand over my head. *So Xena can let her die again if she threatens me. That's comforting. But what do I do? It would be so easy to bury her and be done with it. I don't owe her anything.*

But a part of me felt that I *did* owe her something: an explanation, perhaps, or maybe an apology. I hadn't been the one to swing the club that had killed her, but I could've warned her. Tried to find a more diplomatic resolution to our conflict. In spite of everything, I hadn't wanted to see her dead. She and her brothers weren't my enemies; that distinction belonged to the Empire.

"I say we go for it," I said. "We'll bring her back and we can tell her the circumstances. Maybe we can convince her to help us."

Perry, ever the voice of reason, chimed in from my hand. "You sure about that, Crow? She hasn't exactly proven, uh, trustworthy."

Of course I'm not sure.

"Let's do it," I said, sticking Perry to my bandolier. "Xena, if she looks like she's going to cross us, cut the connection."

"On it."

With a thought, I summoned Cara's body, which was lighter than Feng's. I bent, my knees cracking, and laid her on the smooth stone where my friend's body had lain only moments before.

"What now?" I stepped back from the body.

"Now you wait," Xena said as she closed her eyes. "And once again, don't disturb me. I'm going to talk to her. See if I can convince her to come back. If she's amenable, try to bring her back without accidentally bringing something else. Stand a little ways back, Crow. You might want to aim Spud at Cara's head. If I come back and say, 'Clear,' the resurrection worked. If I shout 'Fire,' it's not Cara that came back, but something else. I don't think that'll happen, though if it does, don't hesitate."

"Wait," I said. "What?"

"Here we go. Get ready!"

I stepped back, switched on my battery pack, and set Spud to hover over my hand. Purple smoke leaked from Xena's body and drifted toward Cara. When it got close, it was drawn down into her skin.

"What if Xena resurrects a dragon?" Spud whispered. "Or resurrects Cara *as* a dragon? How cool would *that* be?"

"No distractions, Spud," I replied. "This is tense."

At that moment, Xena took a long, shuddering breath. The smoke flowing from her body cut off, and the streams that had connected her to Cara dissipated.

I feared the worst, and my fingers twitched as Xena's eyes snapped open.

"Clear!"

I exhaled a sigh of relief, then deactivated the magnetism in my gloves and let Spud fall into my palm. "You handled that quickly."

"She wanted to come back, so it didn't take much convincing," Xena replied. "Give her a moment. Sometimes the dead can be a bit disoriented when they're brought back to life."

I set Spud on my shoulder and fell to my knees beside Cara's prone body. "Cara?" I whispered. Her eyes fluttered open.

She looked exactly as she had in life, save for her left eye. Her right eye was like mine, a piece of machinery built by the Empire. But her left, which had once been the dark brown of waterlogged bark, was now the same violet color of the smoke that drifted from Xena whenever she wielded her necromantic powers.

Cara pushed herself to sitting. Her one real eye looked glassed-over and she was moving her lips, yet no words came out. I could tell that she was disoriented, so I got one arm behind her and helped her up.

"Easy now," I said. "Take it slow."

That violet eye took in the square and the fountain. "My brothers. Where am I?" Then, her gaze fell on me.

She *slapped* me.

It was a good hit, and the *crack* echoed across the quiet square.

"Ow!" I brought a hand to my cheek. "What was *that* about?"

Cara scrambled to her feet and backed away from me. "We were so close to the end of the level!" Her tone was just like I remembered, husky and sensual despite her anger. "We were going to get through. Then you let me die, Crow. You let me *die!*"

I couldn't believe it. I almost told Xena to end her right there, though I managed to hold my tongue.

"That's not how I remember it!" I pointed at her. "*You* had me at gunpoint. By the Dregs, Cara, you shot me in the chest! Do you know how many bones I broke when I hit the ground? I'd *still* be under the care of the Medics if someone hadn't paid for my release!"

Cara shook her head. "No, no, no. We were *negotiating*, Crow. You and I were talking." Her face took on a confused, faraway look. "Oh. I did shoot you, didn't I?"

"Uh, yeah," I said. "You did."

Cara looked uncomfortable. "Well, it wasn't intentional. I swear. The gun *should've* stayed unfired, but then your idiot friend cracked my skull." Her eyes lit with fire again. "Yes! *That's* what happened. We were standing at the edge of the cliff, and we were very calmly negotiating. Jocko got me from behind. I saw him when my soul left my body! Before I went to that beach. Oh my gosh. I'm *so* mad at you."

My head spun. Cara was mad at *me?* "So you didn't mean to shoot me?"

"No! We had that special moment by the fire! Of course I didn't mean to shoot you. But a funny thing happens to me when you let someone bash me in the head: I lose all control of my hands!"

As I stared at the fuming pirate, I felt a twinge of recognition, like we'd been in this situation before. In my mind's eye, I saw Cara not in her sailor's clothes, but a sheer red dress. We stood on a balcony that overlooked a city. It was night. She was so close to me that I could smell the perfume on her neck. I held the fragile stem of a glass and

Cara clutched the sweating neck of a brown bottle. She leaned toward me, wrapping an arm around my neck.

"What?" Cara said, raising an eyebrow at me. "Why are you looking at me like that?"

Her words shattered the memory. I blinked. Once again, I found myself next to the fountain outside Prey House. I tried to call back pieces of that nighttime scene with Cara, though nothing came to me except the peculiar feeling that, beneath her gruff exterior, Cara was important to me.

"It's nothing," I said, shaking my head. What was I supposed to tell her? That I had a feeling we'd met at some other point in life, somewhere outside Toroth-Gol, and maybe even loved each other? Was *that* what I'd felt?

I felt a flush creep up my neck. "You hate the Empire as much as I do," I continued, "and you clearly have a knack for surviving. I want your word that if I arm you, you won't harm us."

She started to say something, but I cut her off. "One more thing." I pointed toward Prey House. "I woke up in that facility not so long ago. It's run by the Medics from the last level. In addition to agreeing you won't hurt us, I want your help rescuing my father from inside that place. There are only four of us, so we need all the help we can get. Do we have a deal?"

I thought she might say no, but she only flashed a grin. Perhaps that should've been my sign not to trust her.

But I want to trust her, I thought, right as she said, "Of course, Crow. Deal it is."

Spud cleared his throat. "I don't mean to be a naysayer, Crow, but as your advisor on all things personal and professional, I advise you *not* to give Cara back her pistol."

Cara's eyes darted to Spud, then back to me. "You have nothing to worry about. I already told you, I didn't mean to shoot you the first time. I can help you, Crow. Promise."

I summoned Cara's pistol from my Inventory.

"You sure about this?" Spud said.

"Spud and I never agree on anything, but this is a bad idea," Perry said.

My father had always told me trust was a two-way street. "Give a little and get a little," he'd said. If I had a choice, I would've picked a more trustworthy partner than a pirate, though I didn't.

I handed Cara the pistol.

As Cara took hold of the weapon, her demeanor changed. She appeared to melt, like a mother who angrily discovers a messy kitchen, only to soften once she realizes it was because her beloved children had tried to bake her cookies. With a flick of her wrist, she popped out the cylinder and brought the chamber to her eye.

"Loaded," she said. "You even oiled it for me. You *are* a gentleman."

I wasn't the one who'd oiled the weapon, but I certainly wasn't going to tell her that. Cara snapped the cylinder closed, nodded, and shoved the gun through the waistband of her pants. Then, she swept into a low bow.

"Thank you for bringing me back," she said. "And for the weapon. So long for now! I'm off to find my brothers."

So much for trust.

"Wait!" I said. "Cara, we brought you back because we need your help. You can't just leave! You promised!"

Cara smirked. "Meh. I'll avoid killing you and call us even."

She turned. Before I could say anything else, Xena spoke up. "That's not going to work."

Cara ignored her.

"Well, she's not going to like *this*," Xena murmured.

Cara was maybe thirty feet away when she gasped, her hands flying to her neck as if she was being strangled. At the same time, she jerked back toward us. When she got her bearings, she whirled on Xena.

"What was that?" she asked. "What did you just do?"

"For better or worse, you need to be near me," Xena said. "See, the equation is—"

"Never mind the equation," Cara snapped. "I don't have a head for numbers. *What just happened?*"

Xena was quiet. I took the opportunity to take a few steps closer to Cara, because I had a feeling we were about to see some violence, and I'd do better against Cara at close range.

"When you died, your soul was severed from your physical body," Xena said. "I brought it back, though we need to stay in close proximity. You saw what happened when you got beyond a certain range."

"I'm on a leash." Cara's forehead creased. In one swift motion, she pulled out her pistol and pointed it at me. "Okay, new plan. I know I said I wouldn't shoot you. But I'm a pirate, Crow. You can't trust me. I've got the biggest gun, and it's pointed at you, so now *I'm* calling the shots."

9

I stared down the barrel of Cara's gun. *I don't believe this.* But was it really all that surprising? Barring the aforementioned moment by the fire, Cara had lied to or threatened me during each of our inter-actions.

You chose to ignore that based on a feeling. Now you're going to pay for it.

"Probably not the best time to say I told you so," Spud said.

"Here's what's going to happen," Cara continued. "You're going to give me the eggplant, and then I'm going to…"

Cara trailed off as three figures in orange robes broke the treeline behind her and started toward us up the path.

Who are these? I wondered, though from their robes, I had a feeling I knew. The figures were androgynous, their heads shaved and their apparel covering any distinguishing body features. Each rode a wolf as big as a horse; two of the wolves had shaggy gray fur and the wolf in the lead was jet black.

As Cara glanced toward them, I knocked Perry from my bandolier. The small tomato dropped to the ground without a sound and rolled away. By the time Cara looked back at me, he was well hidden behind a rock, and I could only hope she didn't notice his absence.

For the time being, at least, she seemed oblivious. "These friends of yours?" she said, still not taking her gun from me. I shook my head; I didn't know who these newcomers were.

Alpha Warg (Zannius)

Zannius was born to a pack in the frigid tundra far to the north of Prey House. From his earliest days, it was clear he was destined for greatness, displaying an intelligence that set him apart from others in his pack. His young life was marked by savage conflicts with other would-be leaders, though his brute force and cunning led him to become the pack's alpha.

Under Zannius' rule, the pack flourished, becoming a formidable hunting force. But Zannius' leadership was put to the test when a severe blizzard swept through his lands, destroying the pack's primary food sources and leaving them vulnerable to starvation. In that moment of dire necessity, a traveling contingent of Orange Medics extended an offer of assistance, providing sustenance to Zannius and his pack.

After the storm had passed, Zannius and his pack traveled south to Prey House, offering a year of service to the Orange Medics in exchange for the food they were provided.

The good ol' Orange Medics. Leslie mentioned them.
I glanced at the orange-robed, green-handed Medic who rode atop Zannius.

Orange Medic (Skor Dratvir)

When Skor Dratvir was a teenager, his younger sister came down with summer pox. In an effort to save her, he killed one of the sacred white deer that lived in the fields around his village, as its heart was rumored to be a key ingredient in a remedy that would

stop the pox. The moment Skor's transgression was discovered, he was banished from the city.

Alone for the first time in his life, Skor traveled from Volnarok to Neilos and caught a ship to Akka in the Nightlands. There, he joined a crew headed to Wick, and then traveled the rugged mountain path to the Empire-controlled city of the Crescent. At the city's central market, he got into a drunken brawl with a group of Empire Guards.

Skor's hands were dyed the green of one who has assaulted a citizen of the Empire, and he was sentenced to Toroth-Gol.

As I finished reading, Zannius' nostrils flared and he gnashed his fangs, each the size of my index finger. A low growl escaped his throat and his black lips pulled back from his teeth in a snarl.

"Uh, hi!" Spud said from my shoulder. "It seems like you're the Orange Medics. We've heard about you. Don't mind us. We're just having a little domestic disagreement. But we've got it under control! Carry on, fine Medics, carry on."

Zannius stopped, and the other two wolves stopped behind him. Their breath steamed in the chill air. With a jump, I knew, Zannius could have me in his jaws, and I doubted Cara's weapon had enough firepower to stop him. Who knew if she'd even fire on my behalf?

I glanced at Xena, who raised an eyebrow at me. Her question was clear: *should I release her soul?* I gave a small shake of my head. A minute ago, that might've worked, though if Xena severed the connection now, I didn't know how I'd explain to the Medics why a woman who'd been holding me at gunpoint had dropped dead at their feet.

"I'm not your enemy, Cara," I said. "I've never lied to you. Besides, if they take me, you're coming, too. Xena is connected to me like you're connected to her, and she's the only thing keeping your soul anchored to your body."

Xena *wasn't* connected to me. I knew that from back in the Valves, when she'd been with Sor'kodich while I'd been in his cells. But Cara didn't know that. She looked into my eyes, searching for the lie, and I schooled my face to stillness.

Please buy it. The last thing I wanted was to end up back in Prey House, especially so soon after escaping.

"Can we help you?" Skor Dratvir asked. His voice was tinged with the accent of those who came from beyond the western edge of the Empire's borders.

I held my breath. Although Skor had spoken to both of us, he was looking at Cara, even though she was the one who held me at gunpoint. At a word from her, I knew, the Orange Medics wouldn't hesitate to take me into captivity. I'd already seen what happened to those who broke their order.

"Ah, no," Cara said. "As the potato said, we're just having a small disagreement. Everything is under control. Thank you, though."

I exhaled. Skor glanced over to me, then nodded. He seemed content to let us handle our business. Zannius started moving again, growling as he passed me, and the other wolves followed him. They slunk toward Prey House, then rounded a corner and disappeared.

"Where was I?" Cara asked. "Oh, that's right. You were just about to give me the eggplant. But since you're connected to her, that means you're coming with us, too."

"Not so fast," Spud said from my shoulder. "Lower your gun, Cara. My best buddy Perry is ready to spread his acid across your legs. If you think a club was painful, just wait for that."

Cara looked at him quizzically, then followed his gaze to her feet. The tomato sat on the icy ground, staring up at her with a worried frown on his round face.

"Sorry, Cara," Perry said. "I hate to do this, but I really want to help Crow save his dad. Maybe we can help you find your brothers when we're done?"

Cara groaned. She knew she'd been beaten, and she let her arm drop. "Well played. Though I promise you I won't make the mistake of trusting you again."

"That makes two of us," I replied.

Cara moved to put the gun into her waistband, but I shook my head.

"Forgive me if I ask for that back," I said. "Put it on the ground. Now, or I'll have Perry do his thing."

Anger flashed in her eyes. For the briefest moment, I remembered another scene, and I saw that anger repeated as she raised a pistol toward the shadows in the corner of some long-forgotten room. Then, just like the last memory, it was gone.

What is happening? I thought, though I had more immediate concerns. Cara still held her weapon, and she'd made no move to drop it.

"*Now*," I repeated. "If Perry won't sway you, I'll have Xena return you to the Kingdom of Death."

I didn't want to do it, though if Cara couldn't cooperate, it was my only choice. Cara seemed to recognize it.

"You'd kill me so soon after bringing me back?" she asked. She looked hurt.

"Don't put me into a corner, Cara. If you want to play nice, you know I'm a man of my word. Help me and I'll help you. But you've been alive for ten minutes and you've already tried to cross me multiple times, so forgive me if I can't trust you with that weapon right now. Set it down."

Finally, Cara complied. I snagged the gun and made it disappear into my Inventory. I set Xena on the shoulder opposite Spud and then grabbed Perry, who I set against my bandolier.

"All right, Crow," Cara said. "You've got me. I'm not happy about it, and I won't hesitate to take the upper hand. When you're a pirate, mercy is weakness. You make one mistake and you're done." She snapped her fingers. "Don't close your eyes, Crow. Don't let your guard down for a second. You do that and I'll have a blade to your throat in less time than it takes you to blink."

"Thanks for that," I said. "Let's head into town."

10

The path that led from the gates of Prey House was lined with pine trees. It wound down the side of a mountain into a small village, crisscrossed by cobblestone streets and filled with houses that I could see even from a distance.

That must be Old Town. I looked down at the village.

Prey House (Old Town)

Before Prey House was built, those who lived in this area inhabited Old Town.

Today, the crumbling buildings and poor conditions serve as a reminder of a better time, and a warning to those who would cross the Medics.

A babbling river ran alongside the town, fed by a waterfall that flowed in a pencil-thin stream down a distant cliff face. Although the air was cold, the grass and trees were green. It was beautiful, the kind of image I used to imagine during my worst nights in the Dregs. At least, it was beautiful from up here. Leslie had told me I wouldn't like what I saw up close, and the description had pretty much said the same.

"The prettiest villages always hold the ugliest secrets," Perry said thoughtfully. "Or perhaps it's the juxtaposition of the natural beauty before us with knowledge that the town itself isn't going to be nice."

"I have no idea what you just said," Spud said. "Come on, Crow, let's keep moving. It's freezing!"

True enough. I glanced at Cara, who shrugged.

"It *is* pretty cold up here," she said.

We continued down the path. I didn't have a plan, exactly, other than to reach the town and see if I could find my friends. *I bet Brynn is down there. Perhaps Jocko. Maybe even Geeta!*

"So, Cara, what's the Kingdom of Death like?" Spud asked. "Are there ghosts? Dragons? Ghosts of dragons?"

"I'd prefer not to talk about it," the pirate replied.

"Excuse me for trying to make conversation," Spud grumbled, though he shut up.

I tried to call back the strange memories I'd had of Cara, though they weren't forthcoming. In fact, the more I tried to remember them, the more they eluded me, until they didn't seem like memories at all. Eventually, all that was left was the dominant impression that I'd known Cara before the dungeon, and the recurring sense that the pirate was important to me.

But you don't know her. Not really.

Ten minutes later, when we reached Old Town, I was still trying to sort out my feelings. By then, I had more pressing things to worry about.

"This town doesn't look so bad," Spud said. "Look at that cottage! If you ignore the hole in the wall, it's cute as a button. And those hedges! Actually, have those been trimmed into the shape of—"

"Yup," Perry said.

"Oh," Spud said quietly. "Oh! Maybe those aren't so nice."

At one point, I was sure the town had been beautiful, though it'd seen better days. The walls of the buildings were crumbling and the roofs sagged. The cobblestone streets were missing pavers so I had to keep my eyes down to avoid falling into the gaps. I glanced over my shoulder and saw Prey House on the ridge above us, well-built and impressive. Each of its many windows was illuminated by a single candle.

A warm bed would be nice right about now.

Although it wasn't particularly late, the streets were largely empty, save for a few people that moved past us without making eye contact, their heads bowed and cloaks pulled tight against the wind.

"Where are we going?" Cara asked.

"I'm not sure," I replied. "We're looking for Jocko. Or Brynn. Geeta. Any of my friends, really."

We turned a corner and I saw what was unmistakably a bar. There was a smiling cherub carved into the wooden sign that hung from a chain above the door.

It seemed like the perfect place to begin a search for my lost friends. And there was something else as well: "This is a replica of a bar near my old house," I said. "The Empire's Guard. I never thought I'd see it again!"

"The Empire's *Lard*, you mean," Spud said. "Ha. That's pretty good."

I was about to chide him for making a stupid joke when I looked more closely at the sign. It *did* say "lard." Now that I looked more closely, I saw other subtle differences between my favorite bar and this one: the cherub on the sign above the door wasn't exactly the same as the one on the Empire Guard. That one gazed down at incoming drinkers, a sweet smile on its dimpled face. This one also flashed a smile, though its trousers were down around its ankles, giving everyone who walked beneath it a view of what lay beneath.

Old Town (Empire's Lard)

One of the oldest bars in Steel City is the Empire's Guard, renowned as the institution that created the Soldier's Fortune cocktail.

The Empire's Lard was built as a replica of that bar.

"Should we go inside and warm up?" Cara asked. "I could use a drink. Or five."

I couldn't tell if the bar was open or not. With the sleeve of my jumpsuit, I cleared the foggy window and peered inside. I still couldn't see much.

Something slammed into the other side of the window, making me stumble backward and fall down hard on a pile of rubble. From inside the bar, I heard raucous laughter. Someone yelled, their voice muffled by the glass: "Come on in! We'll show you a good time!"

"I'm pretty sure it's open," Perry said.

"I think you're the butt of someone's joke!" Spud said. "But better the butt of a joke than the butt of… nope, don't know where I was going with that. But you can't let them impugn your honor, Crow. Let's go back, exchange Xena for that Hellfire upgrade, and fry the lot of 'em!"

I stood and dusted off my jumpsuit. "Maybe we'll skip the Empire's Lard," I said. "I don't think we'll find friends in there."

Cara groaned. "Fine," she said. "But this means you owe me five drinks."

I remained quiet as we continued down the street, looking for an inn or a bar where I thought we'd have a chance of getting a lead on my friends. Only, I must've gotten turned around, because a few minutes later, I found myself back at the Empire's Lard.

This time, as we walked past the door, three men stumbled out. I could smell the alcohol coming off them like body odor. They hadn't consumed anything good, because good alcohol didn't smell like that. In the dim light, I could see that all three had their hands dyed red.

Murderers. Just our luck.

Cara also noticed their hands. "Uh, Crow?" she said from behind me. "Maybe I could have my gun?"

At the sound of her voice, the man in the lead glanced over at us, an ugly grin spreading across his face. The man was as tall as me, with fur-lined boots and a wolf's pelt hanging over his neck. Leather bracers covered his muscular arms and an axe haft peeked over his left shoulder. The other shoulder was covered in a leather pauldron.

Rabid Barbarian (Wolf Durgar)

Wolf was born in the frozen heart of the frigid city of Neilos. His given name has long been forgotten, replaced by the moniker he earned due to the wolf's pelt he wears over his shoulders.

Wolf's downfall came with a daring heist that saw him and his gang infiltrate the opulent mansion of Lord Thalgrim, a powerful and corrupt nobleman. During that event, Wolf was betrayed by one of his men, and Lord Thalgrim was waiting for him with a band of mercenaries. Rather than surrender, Wolf ordered his men to fight. The ensuing battle saw Lord Thalgrim killed and Wolf and his men captured.

Wolf was convicted of murder and sentenced to Toroth-Gol.

Wolf flashed a mouth full of yellowing teeth. "Well, well, well. What do we have here?"

A smirk curled on the lips of the man to Wolf's right; he wore fur-lined boots and carried a small hammer. He was clean-shaven, with a single long braid hanging over one shoulder. According to the text that appeared in my vision, his name was, somewhat implausibly, Dromac Flail.

Hammer Fiend (Dromac Flail)

Etched into the annals of Neilos' most dangerous criminals, Dromac Flail learned the art of survival in the city's unforgiving streets.

At fourteen, he first crossed paths with Wolf, who recognized his potential for mischief, mayhem, and loyalty. As the years passed, Dromac became Wolf's right-hand man. Together, they formed a gang of like-minded miscreants, though their partnership reached its zenith during the infamous heist at Lord Thalgrim's mansion.

Following the botched infiltration, Dromac was captured, convicted of murder, and sentenced to Toroth-Gol.

"I could be mistaken, but these look like the fools who responded so rudely when you tried to introduce yourself earlier," Dromac commented, his tone laced with mockery.

"Now would be a really good time for that gun, Crow," Cara said.

"Should we give them the Old Town welcome?" the third man said. He was the drunkest of the group, his words slurred, and he ended his sentence with a hiccup.

Shadowblade (Silas Viperkin)

Silas was the youngest member of Wolf and Dromac Flail's notorious gang. An orphan who swept the floors at a local pub, Silas stumbled upon one of their heists by chance. Amused by the boy's audacity, Wolf and Dromac allowed him to join them. Silas became the gang's unofficial mascot, bringing a sense of youthful zeal to their otherwise grim endeavors.

Despite his lack of experience, Silas proved surprisingly resourceful. His small stature allowed him to slip through tight spaces and avoid detection, and his boundless energy made him a useful scout.

When the alarm sounded at Lord Thalgrim's mansion, Silas swung his dagger with all the bravado of a seasoned swordsman.

The youngest member of the gang was convicted of murder and sentenced to Toroth-Gol.

"Just need a tree and some rope," Dromac said.

"A tree?" Spud whispered from my shoulder. "Why would they need a tree?"

Mentally, I'd just committed to arming Cara when Wolf stepped forward and raised his hands. "Let's not be hasty," he said, and I knew he'd be on me before I could get the pistol out of my Inventory. "I'm sure we can come to an arrangement so no one gets hurt."

I sighed. *Leave it to me to cross paths with three inebriated bullies in an unfamiliar town.* My mind raced. *Maybe I can talk my way out of the situation?*

"Hello, gentlemen," I said, trying to inject some cheer into my voice. "I'd like to discuss this out of the cold. Drinks are on me, of course."

Apparently, it was the wrong thing to say. "He called us *gentlemen,*" Dromac said, squinting at me through red-rimmed eyes. "Is he making fun of us?"

Wolf jabbed a thick finger into my chest. It was as large and thick as a summer sausage, which is what his breath smelled like.

"We don't want your company," he said. "We want your coin. Give it here, now, or we'll see you hanging from the rafters." He glanced over my shoulder. "You and the lady, both, though it'd be a shame to see her swing. Hello, lovely."

I didn't like the way he spoke, or the way he looked at Cara, though it was too late to arm her. If I tried to run, the man's threat would undoubtedly come to fruition. I could surrender my coin, a gesture which would leave me penniless, but might give me and Cara a better chance of survival.

Or, I could take my chances and fight.

"We'll never give you our coin!" Spud shouted before I could clamp a hand to his mouth. "Knaves! Brigands! You might as well attack us now!"

"You sure about that?" Wolf asked.

"No!" I said. "Spud, shut up!"

"Yes!" Spud yelled. "Do your worst!"

Wolf's eyes widened in surprise, then he grinned. "We'll be happy to oblige. Boys? Get him!"

Dromac and Silas moved forward, their movements reminiscent of predators closing in on their prey.

"Wait just a minute," I said. "We can fix this!" When the bullies continued advancing, I realized the talking was over. "Run, Cara! Get yourself out of here at least!" I activated my battery pack, and the low hum of its energy began buzzing in the cold air.

"Where am I gonna go?" Cara said from behind me, her voice close to my ear. "I can't move farther than thirty feet away from you."

That was a good point. Spud moaned with delight as I pulled him into my hand and activated his flames. "*Ugh,*" he said. "Let justice —*arghhh!*—be done!"

The alley was narrow at least, limiting Wolf's ability to maneuver. *They'll have to take me on one at a time,* I thought, raising my palm toward the oncoming bullies.

At least, that was the plan.

"Behind you!" Cara called. Before I could turn, something hard crashed against the back of my head. I staggered, my vision blurred, and I barely managed to glimpse the figure behind me: Dromac. He now stood between me and Cara, hammer in hand.

How did he get behind me? I wondered before realizing the answer: he must've had a teleportation skill like Jocko.

"I look forward to pulling the treasures from your dead body," Dromac said, twirling his hammer. He caught the weapon, lifted it above his head, and stepped forward to deliver a killing blow.

"Back off!" Perry hissed, his usually thoughtful tone replaced by a deadly seriousness. He retched, spewing a stream of acid that splashed across the cobblestones. Although it didn't reach Dromac, it did burn a few holes in the man's boots. Dromac jumped backward, staring incredulously at his feet.

"Are you kidding me?" he shouted. "A talking tomato that spits acid? That was good leather you just ruined! Now I'm *really* going to hurt you."

A peal of laughter echoed through the alley, coming from Silas. "A talking tomato that spits acid!" he said. He doubled over and clutched the wall for support. "That's the funniest thing I've ever seen!"

"Shut up, Silas," Wolf growled.

I lurched toward Dromac, for all the good it did me. We were outnumbered and outmatched. After my head injury, I was barely conscious.

Think, I told myself, trying to clear my thoughts. *There has to be a way out of this.*

"Hey!" I heard the shout from behind me and spun, glancing toward Wolf and Silas in time to see a towering figure appear at the entrance of the alley. Such was my confused state of mind that I couldn't read the text that appeared in my vision when I saw him. "Leave them alone, or you'll have to deal with me!"

When Dromac and Wolf saw the figure, their bravado dissipated. "It's *him!*" Wolf shouted, sharing a look of terror with Dromac. They turned tail and bolted past me, leaving their young, drunken comrade behind.

"Guys?" Silas said. "Guys, come back! Don't leave me!"

As the towering figure strode toward us, his fist shot out, connecting with Silas' jaw. The blow was so powerful the boy was lifted off his feet before he landed, unconscious or perhaps even dead, in a nearby heap of trash.

I'm so cold, I thought, my mind still reeling from the hammer blow.

Then I succumbed to the enticing lure of unconsciousness.

11

I woke up groaning, my back seizing from what seemed like hours spent on an unfamiliar surface. Slowly, I sat up, trying to work some relief into my muscles. I'd fallen asleep on my right arm and it prickled with pins and needles.

"Why do I keep waking up in strange places?" I grumbled aloud. I wasn't fully awake yet. "And why do I keep waking up injured? For that matter, where am I?"

I blinked the sleep from my eyes and realized there was a man standing across the room from me. Strangely, I recognized him.

To my knowledge, there was only one giant in the dungeon who wore spandex shorts.

"Mega?" I said. "What are *you* doing here?"

The big man who I'd last seen headed into the Valves lifted a whistling teakettle from the stove before turning toward me. He looked much as he had the last time I'd seen him, right down to the too-tight spandex shorts. He held the kettle by the unprotected handle, which must've been scalding.

A broad grin split the man's chiseled face. "King Crow!" he rumbled. "Glad you're awake. I knew our paths would cross again." He brought the kettle to the table in the center of the room, where he poured water into a chipped ceramic cup. "It's only been about an hour since I found you. The others are downstairs. They're safe, and in much better condition than you. I thought we could talk a moment before we joined them." He sat at the table. "How do you feel?"

I raised a hand to my throbbing head. "Like I just took a goaltender's bat to the back of the skull."

Mega nodded. "That's to be expected. You didn't break anything, and I don't think you're concussed, so you should be good as new with a good night's sleep. Can I offer you some tea?"

The big man set the kettle on the table. I heard it sizzle against the wood, and that was when I noticed the surface was covered with dozens of round burn marks.

"Uh, sure," I said as he motioned to the seat across from him. I stood and walked to the table. As I did, I looked around the spartan room and realized it really didn't contain much. There was a cot, a table with two chairs, a sink, the stove, the teakettle, and two chipped cups. There was also a cupboard against one wall, the face lined with glass so I could see inside, but it only contained a single glass plate.

"Where are we, exactly?" I asked as I sat.

Mega smiled as he poured liquid into a second cup. "You're in a house in Old Town. Home to all those who rejected the Medics. Like those men you met in the alley. How did you like them?"

I raised an eyebrow. *Is this a trick question?* "I didn't like them at all. They're thieves and murderers and clearly weren't afraid to fight over something trivial."

He nodded as if he already knew this. "Some would say those are the *exact* skills one might need when facing a stronger enemy. That beggars can't be choosers. That the enemy of my enemy is my friend. You know these aphorisms?"

"Sure," I said. "But what do they have to do with anything?"

For a few seconds, Mega turned his teacup, which looked tiny in his massive hand. Steam rose above the rim. Finally, he spoke: "Have you heard of the Right People?"

"I have." The Right People were an organized crime group that operated throughout the Empire. Supposedly, they smuggled weapons to the Thuins.

I still didn't see where he was going.

"When I lived in the Crescent, I was a member of the Right People," Mega continued. "The Empire painted us as terrorists, but of course they would. Internally, we had our own code: we never hurt women or children, and we never smuggled weapons for the Empire. We treated everyone like our brothers and sisters. We watched out for each other, and for others as well. The organization worked because we were unified around shared ideals, and we never let the ends justify the means."

"So?"

He sighed, and I could tell I'd disappointed him. "Let me spell it out for you. If I learned anything from the Right People, it's that division is the killer. We can't afford it. If we're to have any hope of escaping the dungeon, we need to work together."

"Who is 'we'?"

"Everyone who'd oppose the Medics," Mega replied. He jerked a thumb toward the window. It was still dark out, though I could see Prey House glowing atop the distant hill. "They want us fragmented. They want us fighting each other for every crumb so we're not united against the true threat: *them*. See? The hunters who didn't join the Medics need to band together."

"Easier said than done."

Mega shrugged. "People respect power. You have potential, though you need to get more aggressive. You have to get it through your head that when survival is your only option, the only solution is to fight like your life depends on it."

I scoffed. I didn't need some giant in spandex shorts telling me how to behave. "If you just want to insult me, I don't know why I'm here," I said. "I'd just as soon collect my friends and leave."

Mega held up his hands in a placating gesture. "Now hold on a minute, Crow. There's another reason I wanted to speak with you. The last time I saw you, a platform beneath Gray Moor was spiriting me and my friends to the Valves. We found our way through, just like you. And when we arrived in Old Town, we found ourselves in a similar situation to the one you just faced: hopelessly outnumbered and overpowered by both Medics and other hunters who would've taken advantage of us. To be honest, we probably would've died if we hadn't met your father."

My stomach lurched, and I found myself paying attention. "What do you know about my father?"

Mega sipped his tea. "I saw him in the street not long after we arrived. He was going by the name John Petersen, but I recognized him right away. The Right People make a point of looking past pseudonyms."

"You met him?"

"Met him? This is his place!" Mega gestured to the room around him. "He's the one who took us in. He's also the one who's been preaching unity. But then he disappeared. I suspect the Medics caught him."

I looked around the ill-appointed room. *This was my father's place? He was working with Mega?*

I glanced back to the giant, who stared at me impassively. "I saw my father earlier today. Inside Prey House. The Medics have him in a series of time-locked cells. Every twelve hours, the cells shift, and the cell at the end drops its prisoner into a pit. If the pattern holds, my father only has a few more days before he's dropped. I came down to Old Town to see if I could find a way to help him."

Mega tapped his chin. There's a common misconception that all big guys are louts, but I've known a great many sensitive, thoughtful minds that inhabited larger bodies.

"I've only been here for a few days, though your father got here weeks ago," Mega said. "He must've cleared the second level of the dungeon in record time. The last time I spoke with him, he was trying to join the forces he'd gathered with those of the Ghosts, a local organization that has been waging a secret war against the Medics. Your father told me the Ghosts were run by an assassin named Tigereye, but I heard he was killed recently, and that presents an opportunity."

My tea had finally cooled enough to drink, so I took a long sip. "How so?"

"A few days ago, I sent a message to the new leader of the Ghosts. Told her I had some powerful weapons for sale, because who can resist a message like that? They bit like a fish on a line. In two days, I've been invited to have a chat. My hope is that I can convince them to join us. With our combined forces, we'd have the numbers to make a play for Prey House. We could take over the facility and rescue your father."

I nodded. "And if the Ghosts don't want to play nice?"

Mega slammed a fist on the table, causing me to jump. "Then we kill them. What else would we do?"

I had to think there was a way to get through the level without killing everyone who disagreed with me, but I didn't say that to Mega. Instead, I said, "It doesn't sound easy."

Mega stood, pushing his chair back from the table. "*Nothing* is easy. But you've got to start somewhere. One foot after the other, right?"

I recognized my father's words. Until then, I'd harbored a niggling doubt about the veracity of Mega's claims. I thought that maybe this was a setup, or that he was lying for some other nefarious purpose. But the moment Mega said those words, I knew he was telling the truth. My father *had* been inside this house.

"Yeah," I said. "Right."

Mega brought his cup to the sink before turning back to face me. "So we wait for the meeting," he said. "There's an inn near here where you and your crew can lay low. But before you head there, I have something to show you."

The last time someone had said similar words, I'd seen my father in a glassinine cell. For some reason, I didn't think Mega would show me anything half as grim.

"All right," I said. "What have you got?"

Mega walked to the stove. It only had four burners, I noticed, but five knobs.

Mega turned the fifth knob, then walked to the cupboard and

pushed on one side. The piece of furniture slid to one side as if on tracks, revealing a hidden staircase that descended into darkness.

I raised an eyebrow at him.

"Like I said, this used to be your father's place," he said, lifting a lantern from a hook beside the cupboard. "Fighting the Medics is tough business. A few secrets make the job easier."

"A secret staircase behind the cupboard," I said. "Not bad. Where does it go?"

Mega brightened. "Don't you want to see?"

I followed him into the darkness; we didn't have far to descend. I'd expected to enter a series of labyrinthine passages, though the stairs deposited us into a small cellar. The room held several cots and shelves filled with provisions: pickled vegetables, jarred peaches, and more.

It also held my friends.

"Hey there, Crow!" Spud said cheerfully. He sat at a table in the center of the room with Robyn, Esmé, and Jinx, the three women I'd originally spoken with the first time I'd met Mega. Cara also sat with them, as did Perry and Xena. The group watched Spud face off against Robyn in a game of ravens.

"Uh, hi," I said. "Hi, Esmé. Robyn. Jinx. Good to see the three of you. Jinx, is that a new haircut?"

The mute girl smiled shyly at me, running a hand through a vicious hack job that, combined with her metal teeth, made her look feral. I remembered the description I'd gotten of the girl in Gray Moor; she was something called a Metal Masticator, which I imagined involved tearing things with her teeth.

"Did it myself," Esmé said. "Looks good, right?"

"Yes," I lied. "Quite fierce."

Mega set his lantern on a table beside the stairs. Behind us, the cupboard slid shut.

"Welcome to headquarters," Mega said, motioning around the room. "This is where we've been planning our escape. Continuing your father's research, actually."

He pointed to the far wall. It was covered in pages of notes, each one connected to the wall with tacks, and I recognized my father's looping cursive.

"Research?" I said, approaching the far wall. I picked a page at random and started to read.

Red Medic (Gerald Aberdeen)

Thirty-eight years old. Six feet, ten inches. Three hundred and fifteen pounds. Sentenced to Toroth-Gol for theft.

In the entrance to the dungeon, Gerald took a mimic ability that allowed him to copy the likeness of any other hunter he saw. In the Castle of 1,000 Doors, he went through a door marked 'Plains of Doom,' where he used a Fountain of Wishes to upgrade his mimic ability so that he could shift into monsters as well as hunters.

Gerald successfully exited the Plains of Doom to Dungeon School. He attended Gray Moor and took Hand-to-Hand Combat, Physical Toughness, and Mental Protection. After that, Gerald successfully exited to Prey House, where he joined the Red Medics.

My eyes widened as I picked another page.

Gray Medic (Leslie Farrier)

Five feet, one inch. Sixty-three years old. One hundred and twenty-three pounds. Sentenced to Toroth-Gol for treason and murder.

In the entrance to the dungeon, Leslie took a barrier generation ability that allowed her to create and wield a single, impenetrable, invisible, six-foot-wide barrier within ten feet of her person. In the Castle of 1,000 Doors, she went through a door marked 'Snake River Delta,' where she used a Fountain of Wishes to upgrade her ability to be able to wield two barriers at the same time.

Leslie successfully exited to Dungeon School. She attended Winter Ridge and took Pathifery. Another upgrade from a Fountain of Wishes allowed her to extend the range of her barriers to a hundred feet.

Leslie successfully exited to Prey House, where she founded the Medics.

My father had notes on *everyone* who worked in Prey House. Hundreds of pages, each with more information than he could've gotten from the dungeon's descriptions alone.

"How did he do this?" I asked incredulously. "This should've taken years!"

Mega shrugged. "I'm not sure. Your father said he had someone on the inside, though he never told me who it was."

Count on Sal Valentine to accomplish the impossible. I read Leslie's notes again.

"Does anyone know what 'Pathifery' means?" I asked.

"It's similar to my Charm ability," Cara said. "It allows the user to play on the emotions of the people in their presence. They can inspire, calm, that sort of thing."

"Interesting," I murmured. "I wonder if she uses that to convince people to join the Medics. She can use her power to play on their emotions."

"In hindsight, I guess it *is* a little weird that so many people voluntarily chose to cut out their tongues," Spud said. "This makes way more sense."

"Her power must not be complete, though," I continued. "Otherwise she'd be able to convince everyone to do exactly what she wanted. But she didn't do that to us."

"Unless we're dancing to her tune right now," Xena said.

It was a sobering thought. Yet I didn't think that was the case. "Maybe it only works on the weak-willed?"

"Unlikely," Spud said. "It didn't work on you, did it?"

"We suspect she needs permission to get inside people's minds,"

Esmé said. "We imagine most people don't know it's happening. Maybe she pretends she's helping them, so they open their minds to her and then *bam*! She's in. Or perhaps she's able to get leverage on those she can't convince to join willingly."

I thought of my father in his cell. "That makes sense," I said, turning back to the wall of notes. After a column of pages detailing the constituency of the Orange Medics, I found notes on Prey House itself. There were blueprints and floor plans. Notes on which areas were guarded, which weren't, and which were guarded sometimes and not others. From what I could see, there were no secret passages or tunnels that led into the facility, but once inside, we'd know exactly how to navigate the halls.

My eyes continued to roam. About halfway down another column, my eyes found an ink drawing of Prey House, each room rendered in exacting detail. I located the Red Mine; from there, it was easy to find the Pit. In the drawing, the Pit dropped through the earth, and a room at its base was filled with equipment, each piece labeled in my father's looping hand. There were capacitors, resistors, transistors, and batteries.

"Is this some type of generator?" I asked.

Mega nodded. "The Medics built that room to—"

"Don't spoil the fun!" Perry interjected. "I want to see his face when he gets it. Crow, what do you think that is?"

I looked back at the drawing. Wires ran from each piece of equipment, all of them leading to a coil of rope at the center of the room, directly beneath the entrance to the Pit.

Not a coil of rope. I leaned forward. *A tail.* I followed the tail and saw how it stretched up into the Pit, where it became a body. Now that I was looking more closely, I could see that the body was attached to the sides of the Pit with spikes. Near the top of the Pit, the body became a head, the lips pulled back around the outer edges.

"They have some type of creature hooked up to batteries," I said. "But why? What type of animal produces electricity?"

The answer hit me.

"The worm devours," I said. "Or, the *wyrm* devours. That's not just any creature: they have a subterranean wyrm queen stretched out inside the Pit! Like the one the dwarves in the Electric Fortress used to power the Castle of 1,000 Doors!"

"Bingo!" Perry said. "Nice work, Crow!"

"If what your father believed is true, the Medics have harnessed a similar technique to try and open a portal out of the dungeon," Mega said. "To make it work, they need a bigger setup. More scale."

He pressed a thick finger to another sheet of paper tacked further down the wall, and I glanced over to see a map of the area drawn from above. There was Prey House and Old Town. Far beyond the outer gate that ringed Old Town was a cemetery, and then a forest. Beyond that was a smattering of buildings; my father had labeled the area "Decrepit Ruins."

"This is where the Medics are conducting their research on portals," Mega said as he tapped the page. "If we want to steal their tech, we'll go here."

Excitement shot through me. *Is it possible? Can we actually defeat the Medics, rescue my father, and escape the dungeon?*

"Tell me how I can help," I said.

12

I found the inn where Mega had recommended that we find lodging until he had a chance to meet with the Ghosts.

"Here we go," I said aloud. Xena and Spud sat on my shoulders and Perry was on my bandolier. Cara followed just behind me.

Inside the door, I saw what looked like a gift shop. There were numerous cabinets that held sundry goods, each one of them marked with a price tag. There was a wooden spoon, a bouquet of dried flowers, and a small pile of bones. They didn't appear to be magical or enchanted. Why someone would need any of it, I had no idea.

Sitting behind a desk was one of the ugliest people I'd ever seen. *She looks like a head of boiled cabbage.* I corrected myself: *she could be a really nice person!*

Paperback Writer (Gertrude Grunt)

Driven by ambition and a desire for wealth and influence, Gertrude was determined to climb the ladder of success. Although one might not believe it to look at her now, the young Gertrude was comely, and she hatched a plan to secure her place among

Reo's most influential circles. She targeted the heir of a powerful and wealthy family, intending to seduce and manipulate him into marrying her.

Gertrude's calculated seduction worked, and she soon found herself engaged to the young heir. Anxious to collect her fiancé's inheritance, she began to secretly poison him.

Gertrude's scheme was not as covert as she believed. Suspicion grew within the family, and they launched an investigation into the sudden decline in the heir's health.

When the truth came to light, Gertrude's hands were dyed with the red of a murderer and she was sentenced to Toroth-Gol.

Maybe not.

"Ah, good evening," I said as I strode toward her. The cover of the book in her hands featured a muscular reptilian standing over a woman in a shift so thin it'd barely cover Perry. It was called, *Tamed by Lizard Men*. I saw a larger stack of romance novels sitting on the desk before her. "Do you have any rooms available?"

Gertrude didn't look up. "Welcome to Medic's Rest," she said in a bored voice. "Rooms are a hundred marks per night, and that includes breakfast, which is served from six to eight. Showers are in the bathrooms at the end of each hall. Don't use all the hot water. Dinner is fifteen marks per person and gets served at seven. It's after seven, so you get no dinner. Drinks are extra."

Her voice would've sucked the energy from a puppy.

"Okay," I said. "Do you have two adjacent rooms by chance?"

"No."

"A single room with two beds?"

"No."

"What do you have?"

"I have a single room, which is a king. We don't have cots." Now she looked up, her bulbous eyes taking me in before darting to Cara, who stood behind me. As they did, she wrinkled her nose as if to say, "Him?"

I wonder what fits her tastes. And then, before I could stop myself, *Probably a man who also looks like boiled cabbage!*

I counted out the money and put the coins on the counter. The room wasn't particularly expensive, though I was loath to give away any coins, especially to someone like Gertrude.

"We'll be here two nights," I said. "If we need to stay longer, do we just let you know?"

Without looking up, the woman scooped up the money. "If you know you'll want the room longer, you should put down a deposit. Otherwise, the best we can do is try to accommodate you." She pulled a key out from beneath the desk and set it on the counter. "Your room is on the second floor. Number eight. Second door on the left."

I took the key and started toward our room, glad to be away from the dour Gertrude. Cara followed close behind. We entered a long hallway, the walls covered in divots and stains except for where they were hung with framed portraits of ugly men and women. I took the stairs, which creaked so loudly I thought I might plummet through at any moment. One step was missing entirely. The landing contained a single window, but it was so covered in filth and grime the drapes might as well have been drawn across it.

My tenement was preferable to this, I thought, thinking of my time in the Dregs as I found the door to our assigned room. When I turned the key, it swung open on rusty hinges.

The room beyond was little more than a closet. It smelled of mothballs and held a single, cobweb-covered bed and dresser. A table had been crammed into the alcove before the window; the table held a board for playing ravens, the cracked red and white pieces already lined up on their respective sides. The room was musty and damp, like someone had sprayed it down with water several days ago and it still hadn't dried out.

Old Town (Medic's Rest Room #8)

A shabby room on the second floor of an inn called Medic's Rest.

"This is unpleasant," Perry said, his words echoing my thoughts.

"Well, it's definitely not a king room," Spud replied. "But I doubt we'll get anywhere by arguing with Gertrude."

"I've slept in worse places," Cara said as she strode past me and flopped onto the bed. "Sleep tight everyone. Crow, you'll be a gentleman and take the floor, won't you?"

Sighing, I stepped into the room and closed the door behind me. As I did, Spud jumped from my shoulder and landed on the edge of the bed.

"You don't mind if I share, do you, Cara?" he asked. "I've got a bad back, and I hardly take up any room at all!"

"It's really just Crow I'm worried about," Cara said. "Produce isn't a problem."

"Oh, great!" Xena said, jumping from my other shoulder and landing next to Spud. "That's good, because the bed looks way more comfortable than the floor." She looked at me awkwardly. "Sorry, Crow. The floor looks super comfortable!"

"I'll stay with you, Crow," Perry said from my bandolier.

I shook my head as I dropped him onto the bed. "Only one of us needs to be uncomfortable. Might as well be me."

"You're a martyr, Crow," Spud said. "I'll never forget this."

I woke when the sun's first light streamed through the grimy window. I stretched, then pushed myself to a seated position to find Spud, Xena, and Cara staring at me from the edge of the bed.

"Whoa!" I said, unable to contain my shock. "Were all of you just watching me sleep?"

"I promise it's not as weird as it looks," Xena said. "We just got up ourselves and were debating whether or not to wake you."

Perry, who'd been lying nearby and snoring loudly, woke suddenly.

"Linguine!" he shouted, coming out of some strange dream. He looked around the room. "What's going on? Are we having a team meeting?"

"Not exactly," I said. Remembering what Gertrude had said about the bathrooms, I got to my feet. "I'm going to take a shower. Can I leave all of you alone?"

"Of course," Xena replied. "If Cara tries to steal me and run away, I'll end the connection. And that would be a bummer since we all appear to be friends again!"

I grabbed a towel from beside the door and left the room, moving down the hallway toward the bathrooms. There were separate facilities for men and women, accessible via doorways at the end of the hall. When I crossed the threshold to the men's bathroom, I almost jumped in shock at the sight that greeted me. On one side of the room were stalls, each containing a toilet and a shower. On the other, three sinks lined the wall, and sitting on the counter between the sinks were...

Dolls.

"By the Dregs," I muttered. Although the dolls didn't appear to be alive or magical, their beady gazes seemed to follow me. There were eight of them, all dressed in frilly dresses with lace accents. One of them, a cherubic little angel with thin eyebrows, rosy cheeks, and a sun hat, had her cherry-red lips parted slightly so I could see her wooden teeth, each smaller than my pinky nail.

I cast the creepy dolls another glance before stepping into one of the stalls and locking the door behind me. There was a gap at the bottom of the door, just big enough for a porcelain doll to crawl beneath if it came alive and decided to eat me. The lock provided some small measure of comfort.

I folded my jumpsuit and underwear into squares that I set on the toilet's lid, then hung my towel from a hook in the wall. A few minutes later, I stepped into the shower and pulled the curtain behind me. The water heated, and only once I was beneath its soothing rain did I finally start to relax.

Freeing your father from Prey House seems impossible, but you have help now, I thought as I took soap from the dispenser on the wall. It was light purple and smelled of lilac. *Mega has a good plan. It could work.*

I shook my head.

You're distracting yourself. Trying not to think of Cara.

It was true. I knew there was a reason I couldn't stop thinking about her, even if I didn't know exactly what it was.

Maybe you knew her once. There are large parts of your life you can't remember. Perhaps you knew her then?

I wasn't sure. Unsettled, I finished my shower, dressed, and walked back to my room. Cara sat at the table by the window, my three friends across from her. A ravens board sat between them.

"You're just in time to witness my victory," Cara said, completing a triple jump. "Winning always makes me hungry. Anyone want breakfast?"

The first meal of the day took place in a large dining room off the inn's entry, which contained multiple doily-covered tables.

"This doesn't look half bad," Xena said. "Gertrude might not have been the most pleasant, but it sure seems like she can cook!"

The first tray on the buffet contained eggs, the yolks as richly orange as the robes of the Medics. There were hash browns, seasoned mushrooms, baked beans in a red sauce, sausages, bacon, and ham. The tray at the end contained cinnamon toast, a specialty from the Crescent. Two little bowls shaped like seashells sat before it, one filled halfway to the top with maple sap and the other containing powdered sugar.

"You better not get the hash browns or you'll never hear the end of it," Perry whispered.

I loaded up my plate and made my way over to Cara, who had taken a seat at a table on one side of the room. There was a glass of orange juice before her, and more food than one person could possibly expect to eat. I put my friends on the table and sat across from her.

Act normal. Don't say anything awkward.

"So," I said. "Did you, uh, sleep well? After you fell asleep?"

Spud rolled his eyes. "Dear god, send me to Potato Hell."

Cara didn't look up as she answered. "I did, thank you," she said. "Quite a buffet they've got here. Based on our welcome, I expected fried mealworms."

"Right," I said. "Say, do you think that—?"

My words were interrupted as a hand came down on my shoulder, and the barrel of what was unmistakably a pistol pressed against the base of my skull.

13

High highs and low lows. That's life. One moment you're up; the next, down. You're laughing one minute and crying the next. The peaks come with valleys, so I suppose I should've expected a boot to the chest the moment I felt like cheering.

"Hello, Crow," a voice said from behind me. "Hands where I can see 'em."

"Oh *wow*," Spud said. "Skeev Thorne is behind you, Crow. Marland, too! How did none of us notice that?"

I let my fork clatter to my plate. "Mr. Thorne," I said to Cara's brother, without turning around. "I'm sure we can resolve this without violence."

The barrel of the pistol dug deeper into the back of my head, hard enough to be painful. As I raised my hands, I glanced toward Cara.

Say something! They listen to you. Tell them not to kill me!

The pirate captain only stared at her plate.

"Take off your gloves and put them on the table," Skeev said. "Then get on your feet. You gave us the slip once and it's not happening again."

"Crow?" Xena said quietly. I looked down at her. She had an eyebrow raised, the question obvious, but I shook my head.

If Xena sends Cara back to that beach, her brothers have no reason to keep us alive. But they should know I have her life in my hands.

"I have Cara's soul," I said as I peeled off my gloves. "Anything happens to me and she's dead."

I tossed my gloves on the table and stood, my chair scraping the floor. When I turned, I saw Skeev Thorne standing behind me, a pistol in his hand. His silent brother Marland was nearby, the barrel of a blunderbuss following the track of his eyes as they swept across the room. The way he held his weapon spoke volumes, and I knew he wouldn't hesitate to fire.

Skeev took the gloves from the table and made them disappear into his Inventory before glancing toward his sister, who'd just finished the last sausage on her plate. I'd expected him to look angry, or at least thoughtful, but he offered a grin that chilled me to the bone.

"We've sailed into a standoff, mates. We're playing chicken. You know how our father taught us to end a situation like this on the high seas? The superior captain calls the weaker captain's bluff." He pointed his pistol at me. "You kill her, I kill you. You walk, she survives, you survive, and I show you the solution we've got to this little dilemma. Simple as that. Now grab your produce and follow us."

It was as simple as that. If I wanted to live, I didn't have another choice. I set Perry on my bandolier and then reached for Xena and Spud, slowly loading them up as well. As I did, Skeev looked at the shocked faces around the room.

"Any of you have dealings with this scallywag?" he said, motioning to me. When no one spoke up, a self-satisfied smile crept onto Skeev's face. "Good. So this stays a private matter." Again, he nodded to me. "Come along, Crow. Hope your legs are warm, because you're set to dance with fate herself."

I exited the dining room ahead of the pirates, my eyes drifting toward anything that might provide an escape. *The candelabra near the door? No, I wouldn't be able to grab it before they shot me. The innkeeper, then? Could she call for help?*

One glance at the homely woman told me everything I needed to know about Gertrude's likelihood of helping. The grin on her face said she knew exactly what was happening, and that she wouldn't do a single thing to stop it. I didn't know what I'd done to personally insult her, but when she saw the pirates walking me out of her establishment at gunpoint, she gave a short chuckle and went back to the book she was reading.

Outside, the winter air bit through my jumpsuit. With Cara at our mercy, I didn't think Skeev would shoot me, though I also didn't trust him to be sensible.

We continued across the square. At this early hour, the only ones outside were two Orange Medics, who sat on their wargs near the gazebo at its center. If they were bothered by the nipping cold, they didn't show it. Despite the low light, I could make out their eyes as they saw us, but they made no move to help.

"Here's what I'm thinking," Spud whispered to me from my bandolier. "Crow, you pretend to stumble and drop Perry, who hides behind that carriage stone. Then you get up and keep walking, and when the pirates are beside the stone, Xena cancels Cara. At the same time, Perry jumps out—*whabam!*—and blows chunks all over Skeev. You toss me at Marland. Underhand, if you want, but preferably overhand, so I can really get my speed up. Wham, bam, thank you, ma'am. The #SpudSquad earns three points and those pirates get a goose egg."

Cara rolled her eyes. "We can hear you. That reminds me: give me my pistol. You make a sudden move and my brothers will end you."

I wanted to scream. *Come on, Cara, don't betray us like this!*

My moment of hesitation caused Skeev to cock the hammer of his gun.

"Do what she says," he barked. "Now."

I reached into my Inventory and pulled out Cara's pistol. If I could've gotten a shot off before Skeev blew a hole through my skull, I might've tried, but the angry pirate kept his barrel trained on me and didn't blink until Cara had a firm grip on the stock of her weapon.

"That's better," Skeev said as Cara shoved the gun into her belt. "All right, Crow. Keep walking."

"Can I ask where we're going?" I asked.

Skeev grunted. "I'm not going to tell you my master plan so you can pick it apart while we move. We'll get to where we're going, and *then* you'll get instructions. Until we do, follow your orders and keep that tuber quiet, or I'll do us all a favor and smash him."

"Hey!" Spud said. "That's super mean!"

At least I know Skeev does *have a master plan.*

We passed plenty of alleys on our walk, but there were three guns at my back and no chance I could slip into one without picking up a few pounds of lead. Even if I did manage to escape, I'd be condemning Cara to death.

She had her chance, though. So what if she goes back beyond the veil? At this point, why do you even care what happens to her?

But I *did* care. There was still a mystery to solve.

After fifteen minutes or so, we exited the other side of the town through a gap in a wooden fence. The path, which led up a rise and into the trees, changed from cobblestone to packed dirt. There was a sign at the top of the rise, though I couldn't make out the writing on it. No description was forthcoming. Still, I recognized the stones arranged in orderly lines just beyond the trees.

The cemetery. I remembered the map from Mega's secret cellar. This was where I'd been planning to bury Feng. Cara, too, before we'd managed to bring her back from the dead. Now, it looked like it might be my final resting place, too.

As we entered the cemetery, I saw something swoop through the trees beside the road. I only caught it out of the corner of my eye, but it was big, much bigger than any of the birds I'd previously seen. When I glanced up, all I saw were the pines, their evergreen boughs dancing in the breeze.

"Eyes down," Skeev said, prodding me in the back with his gun. "Don't give me any reasons to start shooting early."

We walked through the cemetery, stepping around gravestones and over the gnarled roots of haunted pines. The headstones were old and weatherworn, many of them too faded or covered with moss to read. After another few minutes, we came to a clearing where there were no trees and only a single headstone at its center. When we reached the stone, Skeev called a halt.

I stopped. Cara's second-in-command leaned against the grave and flicked an invisible speck of dust from his gun. "On the last level of the dungeon, I took a class called Gemsmithing," he said. "I learned how to make soul cores, and I came to understand the theory behind them. The course was taught by someone you wouldn't know, but he was once the student of Justice Maron. That's who taught you Bullet-smithing, eh?"

I looked at him curiously. "How did you know that?" I asked, thinking of the surly dwarven teacher from Gray Moor.

Skeev grinned. "A little bird told me. But I know what I know, so I'm going to make this easy."

He reached into his Inventory and drew out an object.

Master Soul Core (Empty)

Combine with additional Special Materials and a Schematic to create a Special Item.

I gasped. I didn't know much about soul cores, but from what I *did* understand, they each had a different grade, and master soul cores were the rarest of them all. They possessed the ability to store a soul indefinitely, with no loss to the soul's memories once they were extracted. In Gray Moor, the master soul core I'd found in Sirax Sirco's Personal Armory had contained Xena; my Bulletsmithing ability had allowed me to transfer her soul from the core to an eggplant.

Skeev tossed the priceless artifact into the air before catching it. "I believe this is the key to solving Cara's problem," he continued. He raised the orb, which glinted as it caught the morning light. "Your power lets you move souls from cores into other objects. So if we get Cara's soul from her body into the core, you can then move it from the core back to her body. Permanently this time."

My heart quickened. *That might actually work. But how do we get Cara's soul from her body into the core?*

Skeev stared at me. "Aye, I know what you're thinking. You can move souls from a core to a body, but how do you move one from a body to a core? Let me help again. That language you speak when you activate your Bulletsmithing ability is called Old Thuin. It's the language of magic, and it was used by those who built the dungeon. Old Thuin is reversible. Which means a word or phrase spoken backward takes its opposite meaning. Savvy?"

If what Skeev said was true, all I had to do was reverse the words Justice Maron had taught me to activate my Bulletsmithing ability.

I've got to give him credit for being smarter than I thought.

I looked down at Xena. "Is it possible?" Although she couldn't see me, she realized I was talking to her.

"There's an entire realm of scholarship built on this," she replied. "It's called Old Thuin Anadromy. I haven't studied it, though I know the basics. Just like the original spell, the intonation, stress, tempo, and phrasing of the reversed spell need to be exactly correct. If not, it's possible nothing happens. More likely, you'll get a worst-case scenario."

"What's that?" I asked.

"Typically, you summon the type of demon that makes Sor'kodich look like Perry," she said. "So if you're going to do this, you need to do it right."

I glanced back at Skeev. I had a good two inches on him, but height didn't matter here. In my experience, the best way to deal with bullies was to confront them.

"You heard Xena," I said. "Are you willing to take the risk that something goes wrong?"

Skeev smiled at his sister. "Anything for the captain."

I nodded. "I'll do it, but I want assurances. I'll do what I can for Cara, no threats necessary, but then you let us walk. You stop your petty drive for vengeance, or however you justify it. I don't want to keep going through the dungeon while looking over my shoulder. I have bigger fish to fry."

Skeev looked at me thoughtfully, then let the soul core drop back into his Inventory. "Not gonna work, matey. The crew protects its own. We take what we need, and we can't be making bargains to the contrary." He lifted his other hand, which still contained his pistol, and I found myself looking down the barrel. "Ah well. It was worth a try."

"Wait!" Perry yelled. "This can't be it. He's not asking for anything unreasonable! Cara, help Crow out here!"

Before Cara could do anything, a figure dropped out of the trees and landed behind Skeev.

"Drop the gun," the figure said as the blade of a black stiletto appeared at Skeev's throat.

14

High highs and low lows. Isn't that what I said?

Just as it looked like a group of murderous pirates was about to kill me, Geeta swooped in and saved the day.

The shadow. I remembered the figure I'd seen from the corner of my eye as we'd entered the cemetery. *It was Geeta! But something was different about her. She has... wings?*

Now, I remembered Perry saying something about that when I'd awoken during my surgery in Prey House, though I hadn't thought about it since.

"Hands in the air, pirate," Geeta said as the tip of her blade drew a bead of blood from Skeev's neck. She nodded at Cara. "Either of you make a move and I slit his throat."

Skeev released the hammer on his pistol and raised it over his head. "Take it easy," he said. "I was wondering when we'd see you again, slave. Cara said letting you go was a mistake, but I bet her you'd die in agony before exacting your petty revenge. Looks like I owe her a thousand marks. Which, incidentally, is the exact value they put on your lover at market."

He was trying to goad her, to raise her ire so she'd make a mistake.

I'd seen the technique used in lightball games. Heck, I was famous for it. But Geeta didn't take the bait.

"Crow, come over here," she said.

Before I could move, Skeev said, "Not so fast. Anyone know where Marland went? Makes so little noise, people always forget him." With one hand, he kept his gun in the air, but he used the other to cup a hand around his ear. "But you can still hear his music."

At first, I had no idea what he was talking about. A strange sound reached me: the faint, sad notes of a violin. It occurred to me that I'd been hearing music since we'd entered the cemetery. At different times melodious and mournful, it'd always been there, a backdrop to the unfolding drama.

Why is someone playing music?

The music stopped. When it did, it was as if a skin had been peeled away from my eyes. There, standing behind Geeta with a saber pointed at her back, was Marland.

By the Dregs! He's been there this whole time, too. Standing right there, holding that blade, masked by the magic of that instrument on his belt!

"Drop the weapon," Skeev said to Geeta. "Then fall in beside your friend. I want both of you on the shooting end of my gun."

Geeta didn't look worried. "You think I did not come to understand you, with so many days behind your oars?" she said. "You think yourself brilliant, Skeev. A strategic mastermind. You are a boy playing pirate in breeches that do not fit him."

As Marland pressed the tip of his blade into Geeta's back, the reptilian continued. "I brought insurance," she said, and Jocko's friend Brynn materialized behind Marland. She arrived in a fuzz of static, her frizzy hair sticking out in all directions. In one hand, she clutched a wand with two prongs; blue electricity arced between them.

"Hello, friends!" she said.

Before she could say anything else, she winked out of existence.

"Uh, was that supposed to happen?" Spud asked.

"Reporting for duty and ready for action!" Brynn said, reappearing some three feet away. Her free hand fiddled with a device that hung from her belt. "Oh, wow. Darn magic screwing with my—" She disappeared *again*, then immediately reappeared behind Marland, so close she could've stuck out her tongue and licked his ear.

"Come on!" She smacked a hand against the device. "Stable. Phew! As I was saying, I'm here now and I'd thank you pirates not to kill my friends. After all, I went through so much trouble to save them." She pressed a button on the wand in her hand and the stream of electricity that arced between the prongs doubled in size. "Hurt them and I'll shock you into oblivion," she said. "That would *truly* be a tragedy."

Cara rolled her eyes. "This is getting ridiculous," she said. She looked around the clearing. When she next spoke, her voice was loud enough to shake the nearby birds from their perches. "Anyone else want to make themselves known before we spend the day going back and forth like this?" she shouted.

Dozens of black crows went cawing into the distance, and two more figures appeared in the clearing around us, their weapons drawn. I didn't know if they were friend or foe until I saw their hands: they were dyed blue, for piracy.

Big Boom (Roderick Smythe)

Born to a life of comfort in the sun-soaked city of Atlantis, Roderick was once the heir to a prosperous trading family. His philanthropic nature and jovial disposition made him a beloved figure among the city's elite, and his future appeared set on a path of opulence and privilege.

However, Roderick was not content with a life of stuffy dinner parties and pompous social gatherings. From a young age, he'd been captivated by the thrilling tales of the pirates who sailed the Great Basin. While other children played with toys, Roderick devoured books about swashbucklers, hidden treasures, and uncharted islands. He dreamed of a life at sea, far removed from the constraints of his family's fortune.

Roderick's opportunity for escape came when he met Captain

Whitemane Thorne, a grizzled pirate with a notorious reputation who happened to be visiting Atlantis. The two forged an unlikely friendship, and Captain Thorne offered Roderick a chance to join the crew of his ship.

Roderick became the ship's accountant, a role he served until he was captured along with the rest of the crew and sentenced to Toroth-Gol for piracy.

Roderick was a heavyset man with wispy brown hair that clung to the sides of his head like spun sugar. At one point, he must've had a bad case of the pox, and he still bore scars from the infection on his spotted pate. A massive cannon was strapped to one arm, so big it looked like he needed to use his other arm to support it. He was dressed flamboyantly, with a loose-fitting blouse and a sash around his waist.

The second man carried the piece of machinery that must've been responsible for their invisibility. He was about half the size of Roderick, lupine in every way that his counterpart resembled a walrus. He wasn't particularly tall, though he was muscular, with a pronounced jawline and honed physique that spoke of quick, powerful displays of violence. In many ways, he reminded me of Jocko, though there was nothing friendly about this man.

Fell Sapper (Craven Beaumont)

Craven Beaumont was born to destitution in the gritty, Empire-controlled streets of the Crescent. Abandoned as an infant on the doorstep of an overcrowded orphanage, he eventually became a master of theft and deception, navigating the perilous alleys of the city and dodging the Empire Guard as he fell into a life of crime.

It was during a daring heist that Craven first crossed paths with Captain Whitemane Thorne. The young Craven had targeted a merchant ship loaded with valuable cargo, as had Whitemane.

However, rather than imprisoning or punishing Craven, White-mane saw potential in the scrappy street urchin. He recognized Craven's cunning and resourcefulness and offered the young thief a choice: join his crew or face the consequences of his crimes. Craven chose to join the crew, which meant he was on the *Rancid Pearl* when the ship was captured.

Craven was convicted of piracy and sentenced to Toroth-Gol.

"Awaiting your orders, Captain," Roderick said. "And may I say, it's nice to see you again. That violet eye looks excellent on you."

Brynn sighed. "To be honest, I was wondering what happened to the other crew members from the *Rancid Pearl*," she said.

Geeta, who realized we had the worse hand, made no move to stop Skeev as he stepped away from her. As he did, he brought his hand to his neck where her stiletto had left a shallow cut. Then he dabbed his fingers against his tongue, licked his lips, and plastered a grin on his face.

"Captain Thorne," he said, bowing to Cara. "Your crew has assembled and awaits your orders. What should we do with the hostages?"

I stared at Cara, holding my breath, though she still refused to meet my gaze. Finally, she pointed toward one side of the clearing. "Humans and reptilian over there," she said. "Craven, you watch them." She pointed to the other side of the clearing. "Produce over there with Roderick. Skeev and Marland, you're with me. I'd like to call a council."

Without another choice, we followed her instructions, which meant it wasn't long before I was kneeling in the cold dirt. Twenty yards away, I could see Roderick holding Spud, Xena, and Perry at gunpoint. Just beyond them was the pirate council. From my vantage point, I saw the animated gestures of the pirates, though I couldn't hear what they were saying.

But for now, at least, we were still alive. Which meant I wanted some answers.

"What are you doing here?" I hissed at Geeta.

Geeta glanced over at me, fatigue evident in her swirling eyes. However, it was Brynn who answered.

"We came to save you, dummy," she said. "I wasn't gonna drag your butt out of the Valves only to let you get shot up by pirates. You're welcome, by the way. No need to thank me. It was all in a day's work."

"Thank you," I said sheepishly. "But how did you get here? And why are you only showing yourself now? Start at the beginning."

Brynn sighed. "I left Wicked Field and was about to head through the door to Prey House when you fell from the sky," she said. "Almost crushed me, mind. I found your friends, who told me what had happened, and brought you through. I was the one who paid for your care."

I stared at her. "Was there a reason you insisted we take Cara's body?" I asked. "The Medics told me that was a condition of my release."

Brynn shrugged. "I thought you'd want to bury her," she said. "Feng, too." She nodded to the pirates. "I obviously wasn't expecting this."

I wanted to be angry, though I knew Brynn had only been trying to help. "It is what it is," I said. "Was the bill expensive?"

Brynn stretched like a sunning cat and leaned against a headstone. "Sure," she said. "But I had plenty of scratch. Sold little odds and ends to the other engineers in Wicked Field. They told me they'd never seen anything like the stuff I'd built. It was right flattering."

"I'll repay the favor at some point," I said.

"Think nothing of it," Brynn said. "Anyway, I was waiting for you to get better. Sitting outside Prey House right near the door to the Valves. That's when I saw Geeta stumble on through, and she almost looked worse than you."

I glanced at Geeta. "Our final exam at Talon Lake was to get through a maze," she said. "We could work in teams of three, and I had aligned myself with two other reptilians. Humans have rarely been kind to me, and I figured our kind would take care of their own. I was wrong about that. I got us deep into the maze before they turned on me. Stole everything. Let me keep my stiletto, but then they split. I was injured by mulchers, then found myself stalked through the dark by something called a *beli'ezel*. But I made it out alive. Barely, though I survived."

"She looked like a sack of ground beef!" Brynn interjected. "But ol' Brynn doesn't forget a face, so when I saw her, I thought, *That's Geeta, Crow's friend. And Crow is friends with Jocko, and Jocko is like a brother to me, so that basically makes Geeta my sister!* So I checked her into Prey House, too."

"She had them give me *wings*," Geeta said. From the tone of her voice, she wasn't pleased about it.

"That's a bad thing?" I asked.

"In the Emerald Isles, birds are hated," Geeta said. "They steal our fruits and leave their droppings everywhere."

Brynn rolled her eyes. "She's a rare raptor, isn't she, Crow?" she asked. "A pearl of the plumed! I thought the wings would be helpful."

"An angel of death," Spud chimed in from across the clearing. "Honestly, Geeta, the wings look great!"

"Shut him up," Craven growled to Roderick. The paunchy man pointed his hand cannon at Spud, then thought twice about using the massive weapon to shoot a potato three feet in front of him. When Spud didn't say anything else, he shrugged and let the weapon drop.

"We don't have anyone on the team who can fly," Brynn continued. "Could I have gotten you something all flashy and full of fire? Sure. But where would you be on the next level? What happens when that tech stops working? As you get deeper in the dungeon, magic makes tech go haywire. Those wings will never go out of style!"

Geeta narrowed her eyes. "I will not say thank you," she said.

Brynn sighed. "*Anyway*, I waited outside Prey House for them to finish healing you guys," she said. "Geeta came out first, and then we waited for you. By the time we realized the facility had a back door, you'd established yourself at that horrible inn. Made our way there, though we'd apparently just missed you. But someone had seen which direction the pirates had taken you when you crossed the square. Well, there's only one path leading from the north side of the square, and only one place it goes, so we made our way here. We thought ourselves pretty slick for getting the drop on Skeev, with a backup for Marland. We didn't expect them to have the crew." She patted her now-empty belt. "If there wasn't so much darn interference, I might've picked them up. But magic wreaks havoc on tech. Everything was glitching."

I waited for her to continue. When she still hadn't said anything, I shifted uncomfortably.

"Now what?" I asked.

"Hmm?" Brynn raised an eyebrow at me. "Oh, I was hoping Jocko might swoop in and save us. He's good at that." She paused expectantly. "Jocko?"

I looked at the trees surrounding us. When the Grass King failed to appear, Brynn shrugged. "It was worth a shot," she said. "I'm out of ideas. Geeta? Anything happening behind those shining reptilian eyes?"

The reptilian shook her head. It was cruel to be reunited, only to find ourselves at death's door. But what could I do? The only card I had left to play was my Wisdom power.

I glanced across the clearing; the pirates were still arguing about something. Maybe it was all the creative ways they could use to kill us, though I had a feeling there was more at play.

Could Cara actually be a decent person? Could she help us?

I tried to bring back memories of her. I knew that if I could pinpoint how I'd known her, I'd be more effective at reaching her. But no specific memories were forthcoming.

If there's even a chance she takes our side, I won't waste my Wisdom power yet. It's too powerful to use if we're going to get out of this anyway.

After another few minutes, Cara and her brothers came back to the clearing. I held my breath as Cara cleared her throat.

"After much discussion, we've agreed to your terms, Crow," she said. "If you successfully anchor my soul back to my body, you'll have a one-week grace period where my crew and I won't attack you. We give you this, our solemn word, and treat you as fellow pirates in this situation. The reprieve will also apply to your friends," she added, casting a doubtful eye at Brynn.

Yes! I wanted to cheer. I didn't know what Cara had said to her brothers, though she must've spoken on my behalf, because they certainly hadn't wanted to let me live. I looked over at Skeev, who met my gaze with murder in his eyes. I almost laughed. For some reason, his fury made me think of Magnus Croyden, my old lightball rival.

One week. Enough time to save my father, or not.

"Thank you," I said. "Do you want me to do this here? Now?"

Cara nodded. I stood and approached Skeev, who summoned the empty master soul core and reluctantly handed it to me.

"Don't mess this up," he growled. "Your life depends on it."

I turned away and looked at Cara. "Here goes nothing," I said, lifting the core. "Cara, you might want to sit down for this."

15

Just like the last time I'd used my Bulletsmithing power, my view changed between eye blinks. One moment I was in the frosty cemetery; the next, I stood on a beach. About twenty yards away, the turquoise waters of an ocean lapped against the shore. Moored a hundred yards beyond was a ship with the words "Rancid Pearl" emblazoned on its side.

And it was warm. The breeze carried the scent of dried seaweed and salt.

I was alone. The waves sent shells and sand tumbling, but there were no seagulls crying overhead, nor any sandpipers trying to outrun the frothing surf. The timbers and rigging of the pirate ship creaked in the surf, but no pirates ran along its deck.

More importantly, I didn't see Cara. Just the beach, with fine white sand stretching in either direction. Before me was the ocean, and I squinted at the horizon.

In the distance, I spotted a storm.

The last time I'd appeared in a soul space, I'd quickly found its owner. "Cara?" I called. There was no response.

Maybe this isn't her soul space? Is this the beach from the Kingdom of Death?

But I knew that wasn't the case.

That's her precious ship. This has *to be her soul space. But then where's Cara?*

I looked inland, where a line of sea grapes gave way to tall grasses that stretched as far as I could see. I couldn't see Cara there, either. I turned back to the ocean. I couldn't be sure, but during the seconds I'd looked away, the storm appeared to have gotten closer.

For the first time, I wondered what my own soul space would look like.

A lightball field, I imagine. Would the holes in my memory manifest somehow? Maybe as divots in the field?

The clouds above me were puffy and gray, with a tinge of purple around the edges. Once again, I squinted at the horizon. Now, I was sure of it: the clouds had *definitely* gotten closer.

At that moment, I wanted to be anywhere except that beach. "Cara?" I called again, not really expecting an answer. I didn't get one. "Cara, where are you?"

In those few seconds, it became clear the storm was barreling toward the beach at a breakneck pace. Even in the short time I'd stood there, the waves had turned into whitecaps. Now, they slammed the shore, the surf hissing and spitting as it ran back to join the ocean. Just off the shore, the *Rancid Pearl* bucked, the sails snapping and the rigging creaking.

"Okay," I said nervously. "Experiment over. Time to take the loss and try something else."

I tried to cancel the power, but nothing happened. My stomach dropped and I experienced a spike of fear as I realized how deeply I was out of my element.

A wall of rain slammed against the beach. Within seconds, I was soaked. The clouds were only a few hundred yards away. They moved like a living entity, bubbling outward and growing protuberances that looked like limbs. The purple tinge had deepened, the color shifting from slate gray to deep purple. I didn't know what would happen if they reached me, though I knew it wouldn't be good.

"Cara!" I shouted. I don't know why. She clearly wasn't there.

There's something strange that happens when athletes face a tense moment. I suppose the same thing probably happens to soldiers or firefighters or anyone who regularly faces stressful situations. But my experience is as an athlete, so I can only speak to that experience.

In the heat of a major moment, athletes lock in. That is, the world around us slows and everything snaps into perfect clarity. Thoughts come more quickly and we gain the ability to sort them more critically than usual.

In that moment on the beach, I locked in. The storm continued to charge toward the shore. There was only one thing to do, I realized, and though it was unlikely to save me, I didn't have a better option.

I stood my ground.

I don't know what I expected to happen. But within a second, I knew I didn't have a chance. The storm was simply too powerful.

This is it. Still so much left unsolved, though I suppose that's the way it goes.

I looked around for any type of weapon, my eyes falling on a coconut in the sand before me. *Better than nothing.* It was only as I bent to scoop it up that I realized it wasn't a coconut, but Skeev's master soul core.

The storm hit me just as my fingers closed around the core. I blinked, and appeared back in the clearing.

I was no longer surrounded by the warmth of the beach, but the cold of the forest. The sand had been replaced by frost-caked dirt, the sea grapes by uneven rows of headstones. In place of the sand were the pirates and my friends.

"Crow?" Perry said, concern in his voice. "You okay?"

"Did it work?" Skeev growled. I turned to him, then glanced at the core in my hands. It seemed unchanged. My eyes went to Cara, who shrugged, then to Xena, who stared back, fear in her eyes.

"I don't think it worked," I said.

From his belt, Skeev drew his pistol. "You tried your best, Crow." He raised the weapon. "I'll be sorry to take the contents of your Inventory."

I didn't know why the spell hadn't worked. Perhaps I'd said the words incorrectly. Whatever the reason, I only had one option left.

"Wait!" Instinctively, I raised my hands. "There's one more thing I can try. In Gray Moor, my other class was called Wisdom. It lets me receive the answer to one question per week. I was saving it, but I'll use it to help Cara."

It was now or never. Skeev looked suspicious, but he didn't shoot. Cara got to her feet, caught his wrist, and made him lower the gun.

"He's too good-hearted to betray us," she said to her brother. She nodded to me. "Do it."

I closed my eyes and steadied my breath. I'd wanted to use Wisdom to help my father. Since seeing him in Prey House, I'd had plenty of time to think of the question that would help me to save him while allowing for the least amount of variation in its interpretation. For instance, I didn't want to ask how we could break my father out of Prey House and get to the next level, because that wasn't specific enough. Maybe we'd reach the next level, but only be able to bring along my father's corpse, like we'd done with Feng.

But now, I needed to change the question. *Or do I?* I wondered, as it occurred to me that maybe the way I dealt with Cara and the way I could help my father were one and the same. If I figured out a way to phrase my question that got myself, my friends, and my father safely to the next level, alive and in our own bodies, couldn't I add Cara to the same request?

It was worth a shot. I didn't know how the Wisdom power would respond, but it was the only way I saw to handle both situations. I let my breathing slow.

What is the next step I need to take that would put me on a path to rescuing my father in a way that also allows me and Cara to survive this level?

That was good. I offered my truth to the universe: *Even though my father has manipulated me, I want to save him more than anything.*

There was the soft *ding* of a chime as my truth was accepted.

The Wisdom vision started, and I found myself in the cemetery. Rather, I was *above* the cemetery. Below me, I could see *myself*, still surrounded by pirates. Despite the distance, I spotted Spud, Perry, and Xena as well.

A chill wind blew against the body I inhabited as I swooped through the trees, nimbly dodging branches. Then I folded my wings and landed lightly on the ground behind a thick oak.

Swooped? Wait... wings?

I was in *Geeta's* body. That was the only explanation. I—as in me, King Crow, the *real* King Crow—was an athlete, accustomed to moving with grace and agility, yet the lithe movements I felt in this body were wildly, *absurdly* quick. This was new for Geeta, I realized, because I'd fought her back in the Castle of 1,000 Doors. I'd won that fight, though if *this* was the body I'd fought, I wouldn't have stood a chance. I felt proud of my friend for how she'd improved, and more grateful than ever that the quiet reptilian was now on my side.

It seems like the group is hanging back while we send Geeta scouting, I thought, narrating the scene to myself as Geeta picked her way through the trees. She moved like a ghost, quick and quiet, making no more noise than if she were walking on sand. *She's walking, she's walking, she's... stopping?*

The Geeta whose body I inhabited pressed her back against a tree as I caught a scent on the air, a mixture of wet fur and rotten meat. She leaned around the trunk. A hundred yards away, I saw a group of wargs.

I stared at the wolf-like creatures. *What are they doing here?*

We were still a good ways off from where the wargs stood by a low stone wall, fighting over several old bones. It was good they were distracted, because even in Geeta's agile body, I didn't relish the thought of fighting them. Somewhere in the distance, I could hear the hum of machinery, and the *clang* of pickaxes against rock.

Is someone mining? Something else?

Beyond the low wall, I saw the ruins of a city.

Prey House (Decrepit Ruins)

The remains of an ancient city known as Korolo. Once the city fell,

its ruins were too irradiated to inhabit, so post-fall explorers settled in Old Town. The concentrated radiation has now dissipated, though there's little reason to try and find a home amongst the dead city's bones.

This site now serves as a research station for the Medics.

The path was made of yellowed stone, and the buildings had been so worn by the elements that many of them had collapsed, leaving nothing visible but their foundations. Other nearby buildings were in better repair, though none had escaped the ravages of time. Even those that still had roofs were missing chunks from the walls, which meant I could see the empty rooms inside.

As Geeta crept forward, it occurred to me this was already the longest Wisdom vision I'd ever had. It was at least longer than my first and showed no signs of ending.

Good. Because if the vision ends here, I don't see how it helps me.

Geeta slipped past the wargs, still not making so much as a whisper as she tiptoed over frozen ground. Behind us, the wolves kept fighting over their bones, though Geeta ignored them as she moved deeper into the city.

The sounds of mining got louder. When they stopped, Geeta ducked into an alley, putting her back against a tree that sprouted from a nearby building. With a few flaps of her powerful wings, she rose to the roof, landing behind a waist-high wall of weatherworn stone. There, she crouched, looking into the distance at a group of six Orange Medics who'd just stopped work, gathered their things, and were now headed toward the wargs, pickaxes leaning against their shoulders. Their bald pates glistened with sweat and they looked tired, as if they'd spent the last hour or two swinging those heavy tools against stone.

With Geeta's sensitive hearing, I could hear the men as they spoke.

"Did the boys bring their surprise to Old Town?" one of them asked. From the text in my vision that appeared when Geeta looked at him, I saw his name was Matt.

"Nah," another Medic replied. His name was Gunner. "You would've heard it by now." He glanced at the horizon, to where the sun had started to set. "Bet it happens soon, though. The boss won't wait much longer."

I didn't know what they were talking about, but my attention drifted away from them as Geeta glanced from the Medics to the building where they'd been working.

This is what I'm supposed to see. The building towered over its neighbors, and black cables rose from the ground outside and ran through gaps in its walls. Alcoves carved into the first few stories once held statuary, though of what, it was hard to say, as only the pedestals and feet were still visible. The only thing left from the higher stories was a single arch in the middle of the building. The rest of those floors were gone.

Behind us, the Orange Medics reached the stone wall. Whistling, they gathered their wargs and headed into the forest. Only after they were gone did Geeta fly down from her perch and land before the building.

Now we'll see what they were working on, I thought as Geeta circled the building. Through her eyes, I saw that every point of egress on the first floor was covered by yellow lines indicating multiple traps.

No way inside. Not unless we disable those traps. Though I suppose Geeta could fly over them.

No sooner had the thought crossed my mind than Geeta's wings snapped out, and we rose into the air.

The Medics had prepared for this potentiality. Yellow strings blocked the only opening from above, a dark staircase that led down to the first floor. Without another way to enter, Geeta came back to settle in front of the building.

I had a feeling the vision would end, yet it continued. We stood there, smelling the chill air and the hint of woodsmoke from distant fires. It was calm. Peaceful. The nighttime breeze might've bothered another person, but not one with a collar that allowed her to regulate her internal body temperature.

A few moments later, I heard the sounds of footsteps coming from the forest. With Geeta's sensitive hearing, I could tell whoever made the noise was trying to be quiet, though they sounded like an elephant attempting to move stealthily. They were oafish in spite of themselves. Anyone with a decent set of ears would've heard them.

Then *I* walked out of the forest. The real me. King Crow. Spud sat on one shoulder, Xena on another, and Perry was attached to the bandolier that crossed my chest.

I was the one who'd been trying to sneak through the forest like I had ingots tied to my ankles.

The King Crow that had just exited the forest raised a hand in greeting, and Geeta responded in kind. Then Cara came out of the forest behind Crow.

"You were right about those Orange Medics, I'll give you that," Cara said to me. Not *me* me, but the King Crow at the edge of the forest. Skeev and Marland exited the woods behind her, and finally Brynn, Craven, and Roderick.

"Here is the situation," Geeta said, quickly telling them about the trapped building. When she was done, Craven stepped forward.

"I'm a Fell Sapper," he said. "Got the ability to set and disable traps when we came down here. Let me take a look." He stepped to the yellow strings that ran across the front door. "Hmm. If anyone has ever wanted to see an earth elemental, I can trigger this one. Probably best if I disable it."

There was a *pop* of static and the yellow strings disappeared.

Maybe let Skeev go through first. But no: King Crow had to be brave. Through Geeta's eyes, I saw myself pull Spud into my hand and step through the doorway. Geeta followed.

The ruin in which we now stood was about fifty feet square. In its center was a freestanding wooden door. The cables I'd seen entering the building ran to the platform beneath the door.

Experiment #4853

When the Medics first took over Prey House, they discovered many books on magical theory left by the area's previous inhabi-

tants. One badly burned tome contained research on portal generation, though it was too damaged to discern a complete model.

Over time, the Medics have added their own research to the theory outlined in the tome, developing a working model of portal generation that they've tested in the Decrepit Ruins.

This door is the result of test #4853.

"It's like the door we went through to reach Dungeon School," Perry said from my bandolier. "It looks to be powered the same way, too. Only, that one told us we were going to the next level, while this one is labeled as an experiment."

Through Geeta's eyes, I saw King Crow reach for the doorknob. As he did, Skeev shouted, "Not so fast!" From somewhere outside, there was a loud *bang*. The ground rumbled, like an earthquake had started.

From the volume and direction of the noise, it was clear something in Old Town had exploded. Before the body I inhabited could turn around, the vision ended, and I found myself back in the cemetery. I sat with one ankle pressed into my thigh while the other dug into the opposite shin. My left leg had fallen asleep.

Cara stood over me, her bright eyes wide. "Did you get the answer you needed?" she asked.

Not at all. But I couldn't say that. Instead, I nodded.

"Of course," I said. "We just need Geeta to do a little scouting."

16

I watched Geeta take a running start before her wings snapped out and she rose into the sky.

"Follow her," Skeev said to his brother. Marland slipped out of the clearing.

I wasn't trying to cross the pirates. Not intentionally, at least. I'd asked Wisdom to help me save Cara, and I intended to follow through, if only because the same solution would help me and my friends. I wasn't surprised when everything proceeded as I'd seen, right down to the moment I broke the tree line and lifted a hand to Geeta in greeting.

"You were right about the Orange Medics, I'll give you that," Cara said as she exited the tree line behind me. I hadn't told her to say those words, though they were the exact ones I'd heard in my vision. Then the rest of the group joined us and we approached Geeta. As I'd seen in the vision, Craven disabled the traps, and then Geeta and I stepped into the building.

My pulse quickened. I didn't know what was behind the door, though I knew I needed to jump through it as soon as I heard the explosion. I reached for the doorknob.

Here it comes. In a second, Skeev is about to raise his gun and yell...

"Not so fast!"

From the direction of Old Town came a *bang* that rattled dust from the stones above us. But I hardly noticed it as I threw open the door and jumped through. Halfway across the threshold, I realized bringing Xena through a portal might have an adverse effect on Cara, but it was too late to stop.

I was in the midst of a battle.

The smell of sulfur assaulted my nostrils, and the air was thick with the sound of battle cries, the clash of weapons, and...

Electronic music?

The cavern was a storm of light and shadow. I counted maybe fifty hunters, clustered in small groups of four or five. I scanned the faces of those in the closest group, but I didn't recognize them. Then I didn't have time, because I realized what was happening.

The strange hunters were fighting at least a hundred mulchers.

Now the music made sense. All around the cavern, the battle raged, with mulchers braining hunters and hunters shooting mulchers. To my right, I saw several hunters engaged with something that looked like a troll from the storybooks I'd found in Sal's library, a monstrosity that took out two of his adversaries with a single swipe of his club.

Mulcher Shaman (Gorta the Behemoth)

In his youth, Gorta the Behemoth gained renown during an expedition to hunt a dangerous and elusive beast known as the Shadowclaw Panther. As Gorta and his companions delved deeper into the jungle, they were picked off one by one. Gorta, the last of his companions standing, bested the Shadowclaw Panther in single combat and brought its body as tribute to his chieftain, though his chest still bears scars from the beast's savage claws.

He looks dangerous. However, he was nothing compared to the creature at the center of the cave.

Sor'kodich. On the tip of a peninsula that reached into an underwater pond, the demon I'd last seen in the Valves was fighting Jocko.

I was so shocked by seeing Jocko and Sor'kodich that I stopped in my tracks. Cara, who'd come through after Geeta, almost ran into my back.

"What have you gotten us into, Crow?" she yelled.

Skeev came through the door and bumped into Cara. He tried to raise his gun, but Geeta surged toward him, knocking it away and sending it skidding into the fray. Skeev stared at it wide-eyed, then glanced at Geeta, who bared her sharp teeth at the now-weaponless pirate. Skeev pivoted toward the door just in time to run into Roderick, who'd tried to join us in the cave.

After that, I didn't wait around to see what happened. I turned and ran, my eyes tracing a path to Jocko, and Cara had no choice but to follow. Although the pirate captain had her pistol, she didn't dare shoot; as soon as she hit me, she was dead, too.

Still, that didn't stop her from cursing my name. "Stop!" she yelled. "I stood up for you, Crow! You yellow-bellied, truth-bending land weasel! For the love of your own honor, quit running!"

I didn't listen. Instead, my attention remained fixed on the scene at the center of the cave. Jocko's sword danced in his hand and the Grass King himself flickered in and out of view, leaves following each lunge and feint as he tried to stab the demon. For his part, Sor'kodich met Jocko's attacks with his pitchfork, or turned them away with the bracers of his red armor. He didn't seem to have any trouble following my friend as he teleported. Whenever Jocko disappeared, Sor'kodich pivoted, lifting a pitchfork or an arm to parry a swipe.

How is he tracking Jocko? I didn't know. Sor'kodich tried to catch him in one of the bubble shields he'd once used on Perry, but Jocko teleported out of danger. The Grass King appeared behind the demon, yet Sor'kodich didn't turn; he just lifted his pitchfork over his head to meet the blade before whipping his weapon around in a wide sweep. Jocko was forced to teleport again, though he wasn't fast enough. There was a spray of blood, and a flutter of fabric drifted to the ground.

He'll be fine. I knew that wasn't true. We were heavily outnumbered, and Sor'kodich was a monster. The odds definitely weren't in our favor.

Then again, when were they ever?

I entered the thick of the battle. The smell of blood and the guttural cries of the mulchers were nearly overwhelming. Although I didn't have my gloves, I still had options. I threw a fist at a shocked-looking mulcher, connected with his bony temple, and dropped him. I didn't think that was enough to kill the mulcher, so just to be sure, I stomped on his head. *Once. Twice.* They were vicious stomps, each delivered with murderous intent. On the third, I felt something crack and give.

"Way to go, Crow!" Spud said as my foot hit the ground. "Ew. Mulcher brains are gross!"

Over the next few minutes, I killed a lot of mulchers. In fact, I killed so many of them that I must've earned something of a reputation, because as I slogged toward the center of the cavern, the mulchers before me started to howl. I'd never heard them make the noise, though the meaning was obvious. They were the cries of an animal alerting its pack: *danger. There's a predator on the loose!*

I was the predator.

At least, that's what I told myself until I almost ran straight into another mulcher shaman. He was eight feet tall, all corded muscle and mismatched, jagged teeth. His skin was a mottled gray and he had eyes like polished obsidian. He held a club the size of my torso.

One hit and any dream of rescuing my father would be over.

Mulcher Shaman (Zarnak the Seer)

In his early years, Zarnak the Seer displayed an inquisitive nature. While exploring the jungle around his home, Zarnak stumbled upon an ancient and sacred grove. In the heart of the grove stood a massive, centuries-old tree known as the "Eldertree." Zarnak's bond with this tree further augmented his powers, making him

second to only Tharok the Mauler in terms of the magical power he's capable of wielding.

I dodged and the club obliterated the boulder behind me. Blood and mucus flecked my face as Zarnak roared, causing mulchers and hunters engaged in battle around us to look up in alarm.

I ran.

"Wait for me!" Cara called, pounding after me.

Fighting was everywhere. There was a wet, sticky humidity to the air, which stank of blood and damp stone. The rock beneath my feet was slick with water, blood, and who knows what else. Already, sweat covered my skin.

I dodged two mulchers locked in battle with a fire-breathing hunter. Behind me, I heard Zarnak bellow, and the ground shook as he stomped after me. Then a body smashed against the ground before me, seemingly fallen from a great height. Human or mulcher, I didn't know; I vaulted it just the same. I glanced over my shoulder in time to see an admirable display of grace from Cara; she slid beneath another crashing body.

That one had *definitely* been human.

"Turn around, Crow!" Xena called, and I had just enough time to turn before a mulcher hit me. The text that appeared in my vision told me it was Gorta the Behemoth, the shaman I'd seen when I'd first entered the cavern.

He must've finished off the hunters he was fighting and come after me. Great.

As I bounced off Gorta, I caught the leering, satisfied grin on his toad-like face, as well as something I hadn't seen before: a necklace of human teeth that hung from rings pierced into his shoulders. I was still trying to find my balance when Gorta snatched me by the neck, the motion too quick to dodge.

From behind me, I heard a delighted bellow as Zarnak the Seer caught up with us. *Just my luck.* Gorta grinned at me, lifting me several feet above the ground, and I couldn't stop my feet from kicking as a black tongue rolled from his mouth. His breath smelled like rotten meat and wet fur.

"Uh, Crow? You should probably stop fooling around," Spud yelled from my shoulder.

"Reach down!" Perry shouted from my bandolier. "I can't get off the bandolier without your help, but I think you should be able to grab me."

I had both hands on Gorta's fist, trying to prevent him from choking the life out of me, but I let go with one hand and dropped it to my side. Sure enough, I snagged Perry and tossed him forward.

The tomato did the rest. *"Blargh!"* I heard him yell as he vomited.

Gorta howled as Perry's acid connected with his stomach. Reflexively, he threw me against a nearby boulder. My head cracked against the stone and I fell to the ground, Perry skittering out of my grip. I felt myself starting to black out.

"Look alive!" Spud shouted, startling me back to consciousness. "Stay with us, Crow!"

Gorta was flailing, seemingly unable to believe he'd been injured by something as puny as Perry. But Zarnak the Seer, who'd been watching us with a bemused expression, was still hale and hearty. I'd fallen near where he was standing, and he raised his club as he stalked toward me, speaking some low, guttural language I didn't understand.

Thunder cracked. At first, I thought it was the result of a magic spell and whatever strange language Zarnak had been speaking; a split-second later, when Zarnak's head exploded, I realized it hadn't been thunder at all, but Cara's gun.

During the few seconds in which Gorta had been choking the life from me, I'd lost track of Cara, but the pirate captain had used the time to get an angle on Zarnak and dropped him with a single shot. As his headless body fell to the ground, she blew smoke from the barrel and twirled the pistol around her finger before leveling it at Gorta, who, somewhat miraculously, remained alive. He leaned against a rock and moaned, clutching his ruined stomach.

A second shot took the creature out of his misery.

"You can't help me if you're dead, Crow," Cara said.

"True enough," I said, my voice raspy from the choking. If I survived until the next morning, I'd undoubtedly have bruises.

I found Perry, shocked but uninjured, and lifted him to his favorite spot on my bandolier. "Good going, friend," I said. "You saved me."

"Thanks," Perry replied. "Spud and Xena are always helping. I figured it was my turn."

"It was a decent display of power," Spud admitted from my shoulder. "You weren't on fire, so negative points for that, but you *did* save Crow. Oh, look! Jocko is about to get murdered by Sor'kodich!"

I glanced toward the center of the cavern, where the Grass King still battled the demon. He wasn't exactly in danger of getting murdered, though he wasn't doing well.

"Hold on," I said to Spud and Xena.

I ran.

17

Although the remaining hunters were outnumbered, they fought with tenacity. Now that I'd had more time to see them in action, I noted something interesting: they all fought in a similar manner. I don't mean they had the same stance or way of punching, but they battled with stealth and subterfuge rather than brute force.

After my time in Gray Moor, I expected hunters to use guns, swords, or flashy magic spells. These hunters wielded daggers, needles, and illusions. As I ran past one hunter, a blob of acidic mucus splashed against his chest, only for his body to flash, grow fuzzy, and disappear. It was like the body had been a projection. When the same hunter appeared behind the mulcher that had thrown the mucus and drove twin daggers into his back, I realized that was *exactly* what it'd been.

Just past him, a hunter dressed in skin-tight black leather stabbed a mulcher with a thin needle as long as my arm. It didn't look like a killing blow, but the mulcher immediately fell to the ground, white foam bubbling from his fleshy lips.

"Do you think these are graduates from Talon Lake?" Perry asked, referencing one of the towers we hadn't entered on the last level of

122

the dungeon. It didn't seem to be directed at anyone in particular, though Xena replied.

"That's what I suspect," she said. "Look at the way they're fighting. See that hunter in the corner? Her clothes keep changing color to keep her blended in with the cavern wall. That has 'stealthy fighter' written all over it."

I was about to respond when a mulcher leaped at us, his mouth opening wide to reveal rows of serrated teeth. On instinct, I lifted Perry, who once again vomited a stream of acid, this time spraying it directly into the mulcher's face. The creature let out a gurgling cry as he fell, his head dissolving into a puddle of goo.

"Gross!" Spud cheered. "But effective. Do it again, Perry!"

The cavern echoed with the reverberating music that always accompanied the mulchers. In the middle of it all, Jocko's sword collided with Sor'kodich's pitchfork.

Sparks flew.

"I'll be interested in hearing what happened to Jocko after the incident on the cliff," I said to my friends as I ran. "But first, we've got to make sure he survives!"

I was maybe thirty yards away when Sor'kodich finally caught him. The demon knocked Jocko's sword away and landed a punch on him, sending him sprawling. At first, I thought Jocko had only been knocked off balance, but when he didn't get up, I realized he was unconscious.

"That's not good," Xena said from my right shoulder.

"No kidding," Perry replied, his tone filled with anxious anticipation. "Crow, you've got to do something!"

He was right. If I didn't intervene, Sor'kodich was going to kill Jocko. "Sorry, Spud," I said as I pulled the potato into my hand. Although I didn't have my gloves, I still had a decent arm. "You're gonna be the distraction."

"I'm used to it," Spud said. "Throw at will!"

I threw him. Only after he left my hand did he flare his flames.

"*Yearrgh!*" the potato yelled. "Watch out, demon. Here I—*ugh* —come!"

Sor'kodich, who'd lifted his pitchfork to finish the Desert Blade, looked up just in time to see a flaming Spud rocketing toward him. He twisted and raised his pitchfork, barely getting it up in time to block the incoming projectile. With a grunt, Spud hit the haft of the weapon and bounced away.

Then Sor'kodich turned toward me, his eyes narrowed to slits behind his helm. When he realized who I was, he snarled.

"King Crow!" he said. "You're just in time for the main event."

From behind the rock where he'd landed, Spud started rolling toward me. "Great throw, Crow," he said. "Now say this: 'Sorry I'm late. Traffic was a nightmare.' That's, like, a killer line."

"I'm not saying that," I replied.

"It's good!" Spud hissed. "It's from *Smoothie Boys*! It'll keep him focused on us instead of Jocko!"

I shook my head. *Smoothie Boys* was one of the biggest franchises in the Empire. There was *Smoothie Boys, Smoothie Boys II: Even Smoother,* and *Smoothie Boys III: Legend of the Smoothie Beast.* Right before I'd been sent to Toroth-Gol, they'd started putting up ads for the fourth movie, which was called *Smoothie Boys IV: Lost in the Smoothieverse.*

Spud stopped at my feet and I bent to pick him up. "I've got another idea," I said to him. "Gonna play with his ego."

I stopped ten yards away from Sor'kodich. Staring into the eyes of his helm, I said, "I've killed you once. I can do it again."

From my palm, Spud groaned. "Meh. Two out of ten."

Sor'kodich's laughter echoed through the cavern, a chilling sound that raised the hairs on the back of my neck. "You may have caught me off guard once, but you won't get lucky again," he said.

"But I might!" Cara jumped out from behind a rock, her pistol held before her. She squeezed off three shots.

All three ricocheted harmlessly off the demon's armor.

Sor'kodich laughed again as Cara cursed and ducked behind a nearby boulder. The demon shook his head. "You humans are weak," he said.

I threw Spud; once again, the potato exploded into flames. But Sor'kodich was ready. He waved his hand and a shimmering, red-tinged orb appeared in front of him. The summoned sphere worked like a shield and the potato bounced off its surface.

"Bummer," Spud said as he fell to the ground. "I—*yeargh!*—really hoped that would do more."

Now Sor'kodich looked angry. "You want to fight me, Crow?" he said. "Come, then. Let's fight."

He surged toward me and I reacted instinctively, moving an arm across my body. I managed to turn aside the first thrust of his pitchfork, though the act sent a painful shock lancing through the right side of my body. It was only a matter of time before the tines of his weapon pierced my skin.

And then what? Devora's body disappeared the moment he'd stabbed her, and then that light appeared inside the weapon. Did it trap her soul? Or something else? What will happen to me?

I didn't know, but I had a feeling I was about to find out. Sor'kodich was *strong*. Cara had unloaded several shots into his broad chest and hadn't managed to scratch the armor. And Jocko, the Desert Blade himself, had trained in swordsmanship his entire life, yet he'd already been bested by the demon.

If neither of them could hurt Sor'kodich, what chance do I have?

But I couldn't give up. That simply wasn't my style. I dodged and weaved, using all of the speed I'd acquired from years as an athlete to keep Sor'kodich from landing a fatal blow. While Cara continued shooting at the demon, I tossed Perry at Sor'kodich.

Again, the demon summoned one of his orbs to knock Perry away. The tomato grunted as he hit the ground, his squishy body compressing. Then I didn't have time to think about Perry, because Sor'kodich surged toward me. Once again, I stumbled backward, narrowly dodging the tines of his pitchfork.

This isn't working.

In less than half a minute, I was battered, bruised, and bleeding from several different cuts. At least the battle had moved away from the unconscious Jocko; I'd lost sight of his body as I led Sor'kodich on a chase through a collection of nearby boulders. Soon, I found myself with rock at my back and no way to escape.

Cara, where are you? I thought, praying for a miracle. Spud and Perry were gone too, knocked away by Sor'kodich's orbs. Until my friends rolled closer to me, I couldn't grab them.

It was just me and Xena facing down an armored demon.

"There's a rock at your feet that appears to be a good size for throwing," Xena said. "Maybe you could try that?"

What hope was a rock? Not much, though I had to use what I could get. I snatched it up and hurled it at Sor'kodich's helm; again, I prayed for a miracle, but instead I got nothing. The rock clanged against his armor, though it was even less effective than Spud.

"Foolish," Sor'kodich said, not even trying to dodge. "I will enjoy taking your powers, Crow. They will fuel me as I begin my fight to the surface."

"I didn't know you could steal powers," I said. I'd do anything to keep him talking. "Do you do that through your pitchfork?"

Sor'kodich growled. "I steal *souls* through my pitchfork," he replied as he dropped the weapon to the ground. "I steal powers through my hands. Like this."

The demon charged forward. There was nowhere for me to go, and he finally caught me, grabbing my head between both hands. His armored gloves were hot, like they'd been inside an oven. I heard screaming and then realized it was coming from *me.*

Right before Sor'kodich cracked my skull like an egg, he stopped. Instead, he stared into my eyes, his great helm filling my vision.

"I know you," he said.

Of course we know each other. I defeated you in Gray Moor, and then Jocko and I escaped you in the Valves.

As if he could sense what I was thinking, Sor'kodich shook his helmeted head.

"No," he said. "From before. A lifetime ago. The Facility. I didn't recognize you earlier, because—"

His voice cut off as his own pitchfork exploded through his chest, the tines stopping just shy of my jumpsuit. Blood spattered my face and I blinked it away.

"No," Sor'kodich whispered. He dropped me. I didn't know how I'd been saved, but I didn't waste a moment: I grabbed the tines of the pitch-fork and pulled it the rest of the way through his body. As Sor'kodich stumbled backward, I saw Jocko behind him, the Grass King's arm extended. Spud sat on one shoulder and Perry sat on the other.

"Never... take an eye... off an enemy... *pacho*," Jocko said, his voice leaden with exhaustion.

"And never drop your weapon to the ground," Spud added. "That's like, rule number one of fighting."

The faceplate of Sor'kodich's helm retracted and I could see his face. Or maybe it was only the face he'd most recently stolen. Sweat dripped down his forehead and there was uncertainty in his eyes. He said he'd recognized me, but I certainly didn't know him.

It was a mystery to solve at another time. Right now, I needed to put Sor'kodich down for good.

I glanced at the pitchfork in my hands.

Pitchfork (Soulskewer)

The legend of Soulskewer traces its origins to a forge hidden deep in the Valves beneath the dungeon's four schools. There, a shadowy group of necromancers runs Mystic Cavern, a fifth school focused on forbidden arts.

Soulskewer's tines are inscribed with Old Thuin words that allow them to capture souls before they depart for the Kingdom of Death. The haft is made from the same material as soul cores. When an entity is stabbed by Soulskewer, their essence flows through the tines and is held in the translucent haft, where it appears as glowing, colored smoke.

For many years, the pitchfork remained locked in the vaults of Mystic Cavern until it was captured during a daring raid by Sor'kodich, a cunning and malevolent demon. Most recently, the

cursed relic has fallen into the hands of Nathaniel 'King Crow' Valentine.

My eyes widened. *When Sor'kodich stabbed Devora, he didn't kill her, but trapped her soul inside the weapon. Could she still be in there?*

Inside the haft, I could see the red smoke that had leaked from Devora's body when she'd been stabbed. It was faint, but unmistakable.

If that's her, could I bring her back?

In spite of my fatigue, I flipped the pitchfork and lashed out, but Sor'kodich rolled beyond the reach of my thrust. Behind him, I saw the Grass King shake his head. There was a literal *hole* in the demon's chest, and neither Jocko nor I expected him to have any fight left, though he was still alive and kicking.

However, the chest wound must've disoriented the demon, because as he tried to recover, he stumbled over the body of a slain mulcher. With a roar of frustration, he toppled backward, throwing one of his orbs between us.

"This is for Devora," I spat.

I lifted the pitchfork above my head and drove it down with as much force as I could muster.

There was a *crack* as the pitchfork went through Sor'kodich's magic shield. The tines of the weapon continued through his armor, and then through his neck, pinning him to the stone floor. He wriggled like a fish, trying to get free, but I roared and twisted the haft. Both of us were scrambling. Spitting. Blood flecked his lips, and I could taste it on mine. There was no glory. Just two predators matching strength in an arena where only one would survive.

Sor'kodich's face contorted in agony. I'd pierced his neck, so when he tried to speak, his words were wheezy and shallow. Still, he managed to spit out the words: "You... don't remember. That was me you saw, when you were... younger. I was the one who—"

I twisted the pitchfork again, cutting him off. Sor'kodich gasped, and blood spilled from his mouth. Finally, he fell still. Black smoke flowed from Sor'kodich's body, up through the tines of my weapon, and into the translucent haft. It looked similar to what had come out of Devora's body when Sor'kodich had stabbed her, though the smoke was black instead of red.

"Sor'kodich?" I said to the smoke.

Sor'kodich's body disappeared. From somewhere outside the small circle of boulders, someone turned off the crazy music.

"Any idea what's happening, *pacho*?" Jocko asked.

I walked to the edge of the circle and peered around a boulder, taking in the cavern. The mulchers had stopped attacking the hunters. Instead, all of the creatures stared toward me, a collective look of awe on their toad-like faces.

"No idea," I said. Then the first mulcher fell to a knee, and the others followed. Within seconds, every mulcher that had been hanging from the ceiling or clinging to a wall was on the ground, joining the others already bowing their heads. From somewhere distant, one of them barked. Then another. Then the lot of them, until their strange grunts almost sounded like a human word.

Mah-ster. Mah-ster. Mah-ster.

Master.

18

As the mulchers chanted, Jocko clapped a hand to my shoulder.
"Hey, *pacho!*" His voice was far more cheerful than it should've been for someone who'd just been smacked around a subterranean cavern by a demon. "I found Spud and Perry for you. Good going with that nasty demon! Does that count as my kill or yours?"

I threw off his hand. Jocko had manipulated me on the last level, and we hadn't parted on good terms. Still, I wasn't able to keep the grin from my face.

"By the Dregs, *majoré,*" I said as we clasped forearms. "You got your butt kicked."

Jocko shrugged. "Good thing you had it under control, eh?" His eyes widened as he noticed Cara, who'd just stepped into the circle of boulders. "*You,*" he hissed. In an instant, his sword was at his side and he'd dropped into a fighting stance. I could tell he was a split second away from teleporting. Just as quickly, Cara raised her pistol.

"Whoa!" I said, grabbing Jocko's arm. "We're on the same side now. Jocko, I've given Cara my word that I'm going to help her, and I plan on seeing that through. So you'll stand down. And Cara, I know Jocko killed you, but he did it to protect me. You're back now, aren't you? Put away your weapons."

Jocko didn't look happy, but he sheathed his sword. "You're the boss, *pacho*," he said.

I glanced at Cara, who still hadn't lowered her pistol. "You shoot, and our deal is off," I told her. "You and Jocko can play ravens together in the Kingdom of Death."

Cara looked like she might shoot anyway, but a few seconds later, she finally let the gun drop.

"What now, then?" she asked as she shoved the weapon into her waistband. "You murdered the master of the mulchers, so you're their new leader?"

I scanned the cavern. *It certainly seems that way. Maybe this is why my Wisdom power brought us here? Wherever here is.*

I glanced around the cave, though I didn't see Skeev or the other pirates. I did see Geeta, though, which meant she'd survived.

If Cara's right and I'm the master of the mulchers, they should listen to me. Let's test that theory.

I held up my hands. "Silence!" I roared.

The mulchers stopped chanting.

"Whoa," Spud gasped. "You're like their father, Crow!"

I shook my head. There was no point arguing with Spud.

"What do I do?" I asked nervously, speaking to no one in particular. I knew how to handle a lot of things, though commanding an army of monsters wasn't one of them.

"Maybe you could talk to everyone, *pacho*?" Jocko suggested. "Try to keep them from killing each other?"

"Good idea," I said. I tried to think of what I'd say, though this was uncharted territory.

"He needs some moral support," Spud said. "Hey, Jocko, give us back to Crow." To me, he said, "We're here for you, buddy! Don't be scared."

Jocko handed Spud back to me and I set him on my shoulder. Then I added Perry to my bandolier.

"Go on, Crow," Perry said encouragingly. "They're waiting!"

I didn't normally get nervous in front of crowds, though I found myself shaking. Every eye in the cavern was on me, hunter and mulcher alike.

"Ah, gr… greetings, hunters and mulchers," I stammered. I hadn't anticipated giving a speech, but I couldn't stop now. "Only moments ago, you were at odds. Now, we have cause to align ourselves. A common goal! A common enemy."

Someone deeper in the cavern yelled something.

"What did he say?" I asked. "Anyone catch that?"

"He said they can't hear you," Xena murmured.

I cast about, hoping a megaphone might drop from the sky, but I got something better. Jocko snapped his fingers and said, "Nori! Is she still alive?" He looked out onto the cavern, then cupped both his hands around his mouth and yelled, "Nori, are you out there?"

The crowd rippled and I saw a woman making her way toward us. She was small and slender, her curves hugged by a black cocktail dress that was completely ridiculous in the dungeon. Her hands were dyed black. I couldn't place her until she got close enough for me to see the butterfly tattoo on one palm.

Then I *definitely* recognized her.

Iron Banshee (Nori Belmont)

Nori Belmont was born in Helios and rose to fame on the merits of her voice. Her lyrics were known for their sharp satire and playful jabs at the city's elite.

Inspired by the ever-escalating antics of August Morgan, Nori composed a humorous song making fun of Morgan and the Empire. As the song spread, it ignited the ire of Morgan, who saw Nori's song as an affront to his authority.

In a swift response, Morgan accused Nori Belmont of treason and she was sentenced to Toroth-Gol.

"Hey, Jocko," Nori said as she approached. "Glad to see you survived. And Nathaniel. What a surprise."

"Uh, hi, Nori," I said sheepishly. Nori looked too exhausted to be upset at seeing me, though it would've been fully within her right. Back when I'd played lightball, Nori had often sung the Empire Anthem, which meant she frequently hung around the various stadiums where we played. I'd thought she was cute, and we'd had a whirlwind relationship that had ended in large part because of my immaturity. It'd been a few years since I'd seen her. "Didn't know you were in the dungeon."

"Yup."

The tension was almost palpable as Jocko looked back and forth between the two of us. "Seems like you two know each other?" he said. Neither of us answered the question he left hanging. "Right," he said. "In that case, this might be a lot to ask, Nori, but can you help everyone hear him? They're having trouble in the back."

Nori sighed, but she nodded. She laid a hand on my bicep, her small fingers wrapping around the muscle, and for a moment I felt like I was back in Steel City.

But just for a moment.

"Sonic powers," Nori said. "Keep it short. Not sure how much I've got left."

"I just talk?" I asked. My voice came out so loudly the cavern shook. People clapped their hands to their ears and I swear stalactites threatened to crash from the ceiling. Then one actually did, the formation shaking loose from its moorings and falling to smash against the ground.

"Yes," Nori said. "Try again."

I wanted to apologize to Nori for what'd happened the last time we'd seen each other, but I had a horrible vision of opening my mouth and airing my dirty laundry to everyone in the cavern.

There'll be time later. But only if you keep everyone from killing each other first.

Cautiously, I opened my mouth. When I spoke again, my voice was loud enough for everyone to hear me, though not so loud it'd destroy the cavern.

"Hi there," I said. "My name is Nathaniel Valentine, but you can call me King Crow. If you're not a dungeon native, you might know me from my lightball games."

"*Hammer fall!*" someone shouted, giving voice to the chant that regularly swept the Stadia during Sledgehammer games.

"Right," I said. "I was a lightball player for the Steel City Sledgehammers. Like you, I was sentenced to Toroth-Gol, and it doesn't matter that I'm innocent. All of us are trapped here, and that includes the mulchers."

At the mention of their name, a cry went up from the mulchers. Many of them beat their broad chests with their fists.

"Keep it... moving," Nori said, her voice strained. "This is taking a lot out of me."

"As I was saying, we have cause to align ourselves," I continued. "A common enemy. A common goal. I'm not sure where we are, but if I guess correctly, we're still in the Valves." I pointed to the door that led back to the Decrepit Ruins. "But through that door is the third level of the dungeon, and a chance to bring our fight to the Empire!"

That wasn't exactly true, though the message would serve my purposes. If we rescued my father, I was sure we could figure out how to use the Medic's portal research to escape the dungeon.

The crowd reacted with admirable enthusiasm.

"But we need to work together!" I continued. "Before we can escape, we need to take a facility called Prey House, which is run by an organization called the Medics. They're the antagonists of the next level, and they have the technology we need to make our escape."

"You've got about thirty seconds left," Nori gasped.

"When you head through the door, you're welcome to go your own way," I said. "But if you want to get out of the dungeon and take the fight to the Empire, stay and fight the Medics with us. The choice is yours." An idea came to me, and I said, "Is there a leader of the mulchers? Someone who speaks for the group?"

I heard a loud roar, and saw a mulcher threading its way through the crowd. Because of his size, hunters scrambled to get out of his way, and the nearby mulchers showed him deference, pounding their chests and bellowing as he passed.

While he approached, I addressed the hunters: "For those who would fight, set up camp and see to your wounded while you await further instruction," I said. "This week, you escape Toroth-Gol." A murmur went up from human and mulcher alike. I held up my hands for silence. "I ask only that before we go, we defeat the organization known as the Medics."

I started to say something else, but Nori let go of my arm and started to collapse to the ground. Both Jocko and I tried to catch her, but she pushed me away, instead letting Jocko keep her standing upright. I met his questioning eyes as he peered over her shoulder and gave a slight shake of my head. I'd been young when I'd known Nori, and she'd deserved better than me.

I hoped she'd found it before Toroth-Gol.

"Thank you," I said to her. That was all I'd needed to say; anything more would've been self-serving. I glanced back to Jocko. "I'm going to talk to the head of the mulchers. Can you head through the door and start getting everyone organized?"

Jocko nodded. "You're talking to the Desert Blade, *pacho*," he said. "Organizing troops is what I do."

I wished I shared his easy confidence. "I doubt we'll have much time before we need to move," I said. "If we wait too long, the Medics will bring the fight to us. Get the troops into fighting shape. I'll find you."

"Don't you worry about it," Jocko said. "Focus on talking to that monster."

I glanced at the massive mulcher that had almost reached me. Now that he was closer, I saw he was covered from feet to shoulders in bone-white plates that clacked and clattered as he moved. He carried a staff with a skull on top; I had no idea what animal it'd come from. The skull had curved horns like a ram and multiple rows of needle-like teeth, each as long as a finger. Within the eye sockets were two fist-sized emeralds that glowed with sickly green light.

"G'or ki ha'acka?" he said as he came to a stop in front of me. I took that to mean, "You called, master?"

Mulcher Shaman (Tharok the Mauler)

In a mulcher tribe, command goes to the most powerful, with each mulcher honor-bound to serve the will of the leader.

From a young age, Tharok exhibited extraordinary physical prowess, surpassing the most seasoned warriors of his tribe. As a shaman, his powers extended beyond his formidable physical abilities; he possessed an innate connection to the primal forces of the jungle. His roars could split the very earth, and his mastery of jungle flora and fauna made him a formidable adversary in guerrilla warfare.

As Tharok grew in strength, he yearned for more than just dominance within his tribe. Instead, he sought to unite the disparate mulcher clans scattered throughout the dense jungles. However, after being bested in single combat, Tharok lost control of the mulchers to a demon named Sor'kodich. When Sor'kodich spared Tharok, the former leader became honor-bound to serve him.

Now, the mantle of leadership amongst the mulchers has passed to Nathaniel 'King Crow' Valentine, which puts Tharok at Crow's command.

As I finished reading, the mulcher turned his head to expose his muscular neck. The meaning was obvious: *my life is yours.*

"Oh, that's cool!" Spud said. "Your very own pet mulcher, Crow. Look at that! And he comes with friends!"

I didn't know anything about mulcher custom, and I certainly didn't speak their strange, grunting language. But the mulchers seemed to understand me well enough, so I nodded my thanks and said, "Well met, Tharok. My speech wasn't only for the hunters, but for you as well. If you'd do battle with us against the Medics, I will see you out of the dungeon, if that's possible, or to the best life you can make for yourselves here."

Maybe it was a mistake. Even if the mulchers *could* leave the dungeon, I couldn't exactly see them having a pint at the Empire's Guard in Steel City, or taking a leisurely stroll through the Pleasure Gardens. But there was plenty of land between Hub and the Arid Dominion, and if they preferred wetter, swampier climes, they could certainly make a life for themselves between Ironwood and the Crescent. For now, my priority was raising an army to help me save my father.

"Kulknej li'ok nak," Tharok said, which I guessed meant, "We will fight with you, my brother." Tharok beat his chest with a fist and the bone-white plates clattered. Before I could stop him, he turned to the assembly and raised his hands. "Kulknej li'ok nak!" he yelled, and his words sent the mulchers into another frenzy.

The roars were deafening.

"You can follow me out of the chamber," I said to Tharok. "Get your soldiers ready to fight. But don't harm any of the hunters! They're our allies. There will be plenty of things to hunt once we bring the fight to the Medics."

Tharok nodded, so I could only assume he understood me. "Jiak li'ok rekor goot," he said, which I took to mean, "I am honored to fight by your side." He banged his staff against the ground. "G'or nedak!"

Whatever that meant.

He turned to go, but I stopped him. "One more thing, Tharok," I said. I pointed at Jocko, who was just about to exit the cavern. "If I fall, or if the situation requires it, you'll answer to him. He's a mighty general of my people. My second-in-command. You'll follow his orders. Does that make sense?"

"Korim oot," Tharok said, which I assumed meant, "Yes, I agree."

"Uh, yeah," I said. "Korim oot." I hoped I was saying the right thing.

Tharok looked puzzled, but then he shrugged. "Korim la," he said. "Grok!"

I followed him as he stalked toward the door, bone plates clattering.

That's when I saw the Kinetoscope.

19

On the last level of the dungeon, I'd made a promise to Elvis Madden: I said I'd stop at the next Kinetoscope I saw. I could've ignored that promise, as I wasn't even sure Elvis was still alive. The last time I'd seen him, he'd faked a heart attack to let my impassioned words reach the screens of everyone in the Empire. It was a brave move for a man I typically thought of as a coward. Although I hoped the Empire hadn't punished him for it, I wouldn't have put it past them.

All the same, I was a man of my word. Instead of following my new army back to the Decrepit Ruins, I approached the Kinetoscope and pressed my face to the cool foam that cradled my forehead.

Confirming... Live on *Elvis Madden's Hunter Talk* in 3... 2... 1...

Elvis appeared on the screen. *He's alive. But maybe not unscathed?*

Something was wrong with Elvis. The usually dapper host had his shirt open, and his collar had stains the color of dried blood. The skin around his eyes was wrinkled with crow's feet. His forehead had an unhealthy sheen, as if the room in which he sat was burning hot.

"Crow!" Elvis said, and his voice was high and brittle, like someone selling snake oil at the market in Gomindor. "How nice to see you! An absolute pleasure, Crow. *King* Crow! You're royalty. You're famous. Wow! It's really *you.*"

The words and their cadence were unnatural. "Uh, nice to see you again, Elvis," I replied. "How have you been feeling?"

Elvis didn't laugh. He *tittered.* "Oh!" he said cheerfully, waving a dismissive hand. "Think nothing of *that,* Crow. Rotten hearts run in the family." He tapped the area above his heart. "In my chest, some slight distress. A woeful waltz of muscular duress!" His smile grew wider.

"Right," I said cautiously. "So, uh, do you still want to interview me? Or you could talk to Spud? I can put Spud on, if you want."

From my shoulder, I heard Spud draw in a sudden breath. "Don't put me on!" he hissed in my ear. "I can't see the guy, but I can hear him. He's fried, Crow. That's not the voice of someone sane."

Elvis kept smiling at me. I thought the feed might've been frozen until I saw his hand: he tapped his breastbone above his heart.

Tap.

"Elvis?" I said. "You okay?"

Tap. Tap. The host continued to smile at me.

"What's going on, Crow?" Perry whispered.

"I can't admit to feeling like myself lately," Elvis said. "But don't worry, Crow. It's just you and me here. No one else is watching yet. We'll get to that. For now, I need you to know something: I want to destroy the Empire just as much as you. The two of us are going to get along famously, and I'm going to help you! Do you know what you get if you rearrange the letters in my first name?"

He started to turn his head, looking over his right shoulder. His head reached the point where it should've stopped, but it *kept* turning, rotating all the way around until I found myself staring at the back of his skull. It continued turning until I could see his right ear, and went even farther, until we stared at each other once again.

His smile remained.

"Rearrange Elvis and you get 'Evils,'" the host said.

Then Elvis' head snapped back around. The smile left his face, and the hand that had been tapping his breastbone disappeared under the desk. A second later, I found myself staring at Madden as he'd been at the beginning of the call. Unwell, perhaps, though not demonic.

"And we're back, now talking to the famous King Crow!" he said as if I hadn't just seen his head turn all the way around on his shoulders. "There's some rip-roaring good stuff happening down in the dungeon. Cara Thorne has returned! I can't say we saw that coming. And Crow has reunited with Jocko! Tell us, Crow: why'd you decide to bring Cara back?"

I don't remember much of the interview after that. I know Elvis asked a few easy questions, and I gave short but informative answers. I don't think I said anything that would've gotten me in too much trouble, but I wasn't really sure, because all I could think about was Elvis' head turning all the way around on his shoulders. And the way he'd uttered that single word—*evils*—like the spirit of something dark and malevolent had found its way into his body.

"I won't take up too much more of your time!" Elvis said cheerfully. "But before we go, there's one final thing to discuss." Madden's eyes twinkled with mischief as he leaned toward the camera, a conspiratorial smile playing on his lips. "We've had another Empire Vote, Crow. Do you want to see what you've won this time?"

Casually, Elvis reached under his desk, pulling out a nondescript wooden box similar to the one he'd used to send me Perry. His voice was warm as he continued, saying, "After the Empire Vote, you're now the proud owner of..." He trailed off as the panel in his desk slid to one side, revealing a chute. He pushed the box into the chute and the panel slid closed. "I think I'll let this one be a surprise. You'll have to tell us what you think. Good luck!"

The feed winked out and I stumbled backward, glad to be away from the Kinetoscope.

"By the Dregs," I gasped. "What was *that?*"

"We could only hear him, Crow," Xena said, worry in her voice. "He sounded messed up. What was going on? Was he sick?"

I wasn't sure. But at that moment, the door on the Kinetoscope popped open to reveal Elvis' box.

"I don't think this is good," Spud said, shaking himself so vigorously he almost fell off my shoulder. "Crow, remember when we got a box from Elvis and it contained Perry? Don't touch that thing. Just burn it. We'll all be better off!"

"Actually, the last time we got a box from Elvis, it contained a pair of levitating boots that allowed us to escape a hotel-turned-armory where we were backed into a corner and getting attacked by mulchers," Perry said. "That gift saved our lives."

Nearby, I watched hunters and mulchers continue filing through the doorway to the Decrepit Ruins. *I could join them right now. Walk over there and leave the box behind.*

But Perry was right: the last time I'd taken a gift from Elvis, it'd saved my life.

Even so, I couldn't keep my hands from trembling as I reached for the box.

"I'm telling you, Crow, this is a bad idea," Spud said. "I've never steered you wrong. You gotta trust me!"

The box was surprisingly heavy. On one side was a little golden clasp, which I flipped to one side before lifting the lid. There, nestled on a bed of green fabric, were five pieces of produce. The biggest was a coconut, which sat in the middle of the others. There was also a strawberry, a green bell pepper, a jalapeño, and a sweet potato. Taped to the inside of the lid was a piece of paper, folded in half.

"*No,*" Spud whispered as all of us stared into the box. "What have you done? Crow, this is why you should've listened to me!"

I waited for the produce in the box to offer their opinions, but none were forthcoming. Carefully, I reached inside and turned the coconut around, looking for a face, prepared to pull my hand back at the slightest sign of gnashing teeth. However, there was no face. I turned it over and realized it was just a coconut.

"Is this a joke?" I asked. "If it's a joke, I don't get it."

I lifted the sweet potato next, but that didn't have a face, either. In fact, none of the produce had faces. They were just regular pieces of produce.

I snagged the note and unfolded it to reveal a crudely drawn picture of a pitchfork. That was it. There was no text.

"I'm not sure I get it, either," Spud said. "Unless we're supposed to use the pitchfork to destroy what's in the box? Oh, that's probably it. Don't delay, Crow! Get to destroying already!"

I understood what the note was actually saying. I already knew the pitchfork could steal souls. With my Bulletsmithing power, I could get them back out.

Perry also caught on. "Remember that poem from Gray Moor, Crow?" he asked. "The one that Justice Maron showed us from his *Book of Prophecy*? It was called 'The Gardener,' and it foretold that someone with eight pieces of produce would reach the end of the dungeon." He closed his eyes and then recited, "'Tuber, nightshades, berry, drupe. Eight in total mean the end—a cut upon the loop.'" His eyes flashed open. "I'm a nightshade, and so are Xena and Spud."

"I'm nothing like you, Twinkletoes," Spud spat. "I'm a *tuber*."

"You're not, though," Perry said. "Like it or not, you're a member of the Solanaceae family. That means you're a *nightshade*, just like the jalapeño. Sweet potatoes are tubers, but they don't belong to Solanaceae. So in that box, you have the sweet potato as the tuber, the coconut as the drupe, the strawberry as the berry, and the jalapeño as the nightshade. That fits the poem, and when you include us, it makes eight pieces of produce. See?"

"The spell I learned in Bulletsmithing would let me put souls into these," I said. "That would give me eight pieces of talking produce."

"That's just it," Perry said. "A prophecy about a man and his eight pieces of talking produce who will reach the end of the dungeon and save the world from certain destruction? I don't know. Until now, I didn't really put any faith in that poem. We should try to learn more about it, Crow. I really think there's something here."

Xena grunted. "But how would this Elvis character know about any prophecy?" she asked. "Correct me if I'm wrong, but he doesn't seem like he's your friend, Crow. Why would he want to help us reach the end of the dungeon?"

I shook my head. I didn't have any more answers than my friends, and I thought the prophecy was ludicrous.

Unless, of course, it wasn't.

20

Prophecy or not, I now had the means to rescue my old friend Devora. Her soul was trapped in the Soulskewer, and I could use Old Thuin to pull it back out.

I don't have her original body, though if she's amenable, I could put her into one of the pieces of produce Elvis just sent me.

I set the box on the ground in front of me and pulled the Soulskewer out of my Inventory. The twin streams of glowing smoke, red and black, still danced inside the haft.

"Check me on this, Xena," I said, raising the Soulskewer. "We know this weapon is capable of stealing souls. And not just stealing them, but storing them inside the haft, which the description told us was made of the same material as a soul core."

On my shoulder, I felt Xena bob back and forth in a nod. "I'm with you," she said. "What about it?"

"If the Soulskewer is basically a giant soul core, don't I have an Old Thuin spell that can move items from a soul core into another body?" I replied.

"You want to move Devora from the soul core to one of the pieces of produce in that box?" she asked.

"Exactly," I said. "I won't force her, though. If this really works, saying the spell will let me appear in her soul space, and I'll be able to have a conversation with her. We don't have her original body, but if she wants to come back, I can make her like you. If she'd rather go beyond the veil, I'll release her soul to the Kingdom of Death. Either option has to be better than being trapped inside a magic pitchfork."

"You never gave me that choice," Spud grumbled.

"Do you want me to release your soul?" I asked.

"No way. But it would've been nice if you'd asked."

I turned my attention to the box Madden had sent me. I hesitated to put a former ally into something as silly as a coconut, but of my options, I thought it was the best choice for her.

And it's not like I'll force her to come back. If she wants me to release her soul to the Kingdom of Death, I'll do it.

The coconut was big, though so were my hands. It was one of the reasons I made a good lightball center. I took the fruit into one palm, the fiber coarse against my skin.

"Okay," I said. "I'm going to try it."

Before I lost my nerve, I spoke the proper words in Old Thuin, and found myself in Devora's soul space.

The soul space looked like a pub, which made sense given what I knew about Devora. I remembered the words of the description I'd received the first time I'd seen her: "She yearned for a quieter life, one where she could put down roots and leave the battlefield behind… she bought a small plot of land in the city of Ironwood and began construction on a bar…"

The bar had cobblestone floors and wooden tables and chairs, and each table had a small vase filled with live wildflowers. On one side of the room, a cauldron bubbled over a crackling fire. The whole place smelled of roast chicken. Above the hearth, sausages hung from the wall, framing a gleaming, two-handed broadsword.

I found Devora on the other side of the room, sleeping atop a fifteen-seat bar counter. As expected, she was in the form of a coconut. Her body was perfectly round and covered in furry brown fibers, and she had big eyes and a cheerful mouth. The description I'd seen the first time I'd laid eyes on her reappeared in my vision, though this time it contained a caveat: "By combining esoteric magic and the prophecies of an ancient cult, you've placed Devora's soul into a coconut."

Strangely, Devora wasn't alone. There was another woman at the bar, her skin so pale it was almost translucent.

No, that's not right, I thought as the woman turned to face me. *This is Devora's soul space. There shouldn't be anyone else here.*

And yet, there was.

The stranger wore a robe of black lace, delicate as spider silk, with a high collar that framed a diamond amulet around her neck. Her hair was the color of dark chocolate and her lips were the bright red of fresh blood. When she smiled, I wasn't at all surprised to see fangs.

Lilith

WARNING: DO NOT ENGAGE.

"Hello, Crow," Lilith purred, her voice soft. "So glad we could *finally* meet."

In one hand, Lilith clutched an ornately wrought silver chalice that was as translucent as the rest of her. It looked to be filled with blood. With the other, she extended a single finger and stroked Devora's side, almost intimately. At least, she tried. Her translucent finger went straight through the coconut. Poor Devora shivered and mumbled something.

"I don't know who this is, but I'd be very, *very* cautious right now," Perry murmured from his spot on my bandolier. I'd forgotten my friends could enter the soul space with me. I rested a hand on the tomato's fuzzy head, which was surprisingly comforting.

"Who are you?" I asked the woman. I was suspicious, but not impolite. "And what have you done to Devora?"

Lilith swirled her chalice. "Your friend is resting," she said. "As for who I am, let's just say I'm someone with your best interests at heart. Someone *powerful.*"

Her answer did nothing to put me at ease. Even without her

description, I would've known Lilith was dangerous. She exuded the type of "don't-mess-with-me" vibes that I got from lightball enforcers, the athletes who spent the game trying to hurt other players.

"How can we help you?" I asked.

Lilith took a sip from her chalice, which left her lips a brighter shade of red. "I heard you met one of my brothers lately," she said.

I racked my brain, trying to think of who that might be. *Sor'kodich?* This woman appeared demonic enough, though something about that didn't ring true for me.

"And who might that have been?" I asked.

Lilith laughed, the diamond amulet around her pale neck catching the light as she threw back her head. "You met my brother Ramses, though you wouldn't have recognized him. He's currently inhabiting the body of a man you once knew as Elvis Madden."

I froze. Elvis *had* acted strangely when I'd last spoken to him, but did that mean he was possessed?

"Let's stop playing games," I said. "What do you want?"

From my shoulder, Xena grunted. "Careful," she said softly.

Lilith set her chalice down on the bar. "Right down to business," she said. "Good. I don't have much time, either. My real body is trapped beneath one of the Empire's twelve great cities, but I possess the unique ability of astral projection, which lets me move about. It does leave me weak, however." She pinched her arm, the ghostly fingers moving through her own body. "You can help me. And I can help you."

I glanced toward Devora. Lilith saw where my eyes went and smiled.

Might as well hear her out.

"How's that?" I asked.

"The fifth level of the dungeon is a museum called the Library of the Lost," she said. "Inside, you'll find something called the Votive Compass. It's something that once existed outside the dungeon, but was sent *in* by accident, and I need to get it *out* again. Find it, and get it to Geth. As long as it's in the city, my people will find it."

I understood now why Lilith wanted to help me. For whatever reason, she needed this device.

And she needed me to retrieve it.

"And if I refuse?"

Lilith laughed again. "I'm very old and very powerful. Those who have lived as long as me understand the carrot works better than the stick. But don't cross me, Crow."

Lilith held a hand over Devora's new form. *She's going to hurt her!* I thought, my eyes growing wide with panic. However, nothing appeared to happen, and Devora seemed fine. She gave a single loud snort and mumbled something.

"What did you do?" I asked.

"I'm showing you how I can be a good friend," Lilith purred. "Before this, your friend was weak. She was a slave to the drink that was rotting her from the inside out. Fittingly, the power she chose in the entry to the dungeon reflected her disease. It was nothing useful, especially if you're to face what's coming. I cured her of an illness and also gave her a sliver of my power. You can see it now, if you like."

She waved a hand toward me.

Concussive Blast (Devora)

This power allows Devora to generate a blast of concussive force from her body. The force can be projected in a 360-degree wave around Devora, or focused in a tighter range for a more powerful effect.

When focused in a tight angle, Concussive Blast can break the hardest substances in the world, including glassinine.

My father's cell is made of glassinine. While I hated to admit it, the power certainly made her more helpful than a sentient coconut who could get very drunk and pass on her inebriation, which had been Devora's primary power as a Brewmaster.

I narrowed my eyes at Lilith. "What happens now?"

The woman lifted her chalice. "I leave you to your business. Don't cross me, Crow, and don't fail me, or you'll start to see my wrath."

Her hand pulsed with light, and for a half second, I saw a shadow appear around her in the shape of a hulking, winged beast. It was fifteen feet tall, with a face like a bat: pointed ears, a flat nose with slits for nostrils, and red, glowing eyes. It dwarfed the ethereal woman. The diamond amulet around its neck, which was identical to Lilith's, told me I wasn't looking at a second entity. This *was* Lilith, her true form, the one that was trapped.

"So long, Crow," Lilith said, and the winged beast spoke the words along with her, a low baritone that underscored her melodious purr.

Between blinks, she was gone.

I ran to Devora, who blinked rapidly and came awake. "Where am I?" she mumbled. "Crow? Is that you?"

It's never easy to tell a friend they've been killed, their soul trapped in a magical pitchfork, and that they've been stopped from passing through the veil to the Kingdom of Death. It's even tougher to share how, if they want, you'll be able to bring them back to life, but only as a coconut.

I explained as best I could.

Devora took everything in stride. "I *thought* something strange was happening," she said. "So we can go back to the dungeon? But I'll be a coconut?"

"The new form takes some getting used to, but you'll be fine," Xena said from my shoulder. "I dealt with it! Admittedly, not having hands is a little weird. But honestly, the worst of it is listening to Spud's jokes."

Spud scoffed. "My jokes are *crispy*," he said. "Don't get it twisted, lady."

"The bandolier has a massaging feature, which I really like," Perry added. "Puts me right to sleep every time."

"If you don't like this body, I can try to find you a new one," I said. "Or I can release your soul and let you die, I guess. Go beyond the veil. It's your choice."

Devora considered. "Well, I don't want to die yet, so that option is off the table," she said. "And honestly, I've always liked coconuts."

I smiled. "There's a lot to catch you up on," I said. "I'll let the crew fill you in."

"We're going to have so much fun together, Devora," Perry said from my bandolier, a note of childish excitement in his voice. "I'm so glad you're back!"

A moment later, we reappeared in the Valves.

21

I walked back through the doorway to the Decrepit Ruins with Cara on my heels. Since the fight with the mulchers, she'd been quiet, though now she spoke up.

"Can we find my brothers, now? If you can bring Devora back from the dead like that, you might be able to do something similar for me."

That's not a bad idea. For whatever reason, I wasn't able to move Cara's soul from her body to Skeev's master soul core, though the Soulskewer might have different mechanics.

"I'm open to the thought," I said tentatively. "But I'm not going to take the blame if the process kills you."

"Let's talk about it with my brothers. I'm sure we could come to some arrangement."

When I got back to the Decrepit Ruins, I was surprised to see how quickly Jocko had gotten things organized. Already, the hunters and mulchers were arranged into little camps between the ruined piles of stone, and there was a field hospital set up nearby, with hunters walking rows of injured and administering whatever aid was necessary.

I found the pirates almost immediately; they'd set up camp near the entrance to the ruins, their chosen spot indicated by a flag they'd draped over one crumbling wall. The flag was black and featured a grinning human skull.

I wonder where they got that, I thought as I approached.

The pirates sat around a fire, talking amongst themselves, though they fell silent when they saw me. Skeev reached for the gun at his waist, though stopped when Cara held up a hand.

"Love what you've done with the place," I said, stopping a few feet away from them and nodding to the flag.

Skeev's eyes narrowed. "Cara, we should kill him and be done with it."

"Hush," she said. "He wants to help."

When none of the pirates spoke up, I took that as my cue to continue. "I haven't forgotten about the deal I made," I said. "And Cara had a good idea." I pointed toward the coconut hanging from my bandolier. "This here is Devora. Devora, these are the pirates we told you about. That's Skeev, Marland, Roderick, and Craven."

"Ahoy!" Devora said cheerfully. "Do you guys actually say that? I've always wondered."

"Sometimes," Skeev said. "So you've got a new friend, Crow. How does that help Cara?"

"Well," I replied as I took the pitchfork from my Inventory and held it toward her, "this weapon is capable of stealing souls." I tapped the haft. "The black smoke is the soul of the demon I fought earlier. Until a little while ago, this pitchfork also contained Devora's soul."

Skeev raised an eyebrow. "And?"

"Now, she's in a new body," I continued. "For some reason, the backward spell I tried didn't move Cara's soul to your soul core, but this weapon is two for two on getting souls out of a body and into its haft. Cara and I are thinking that from there, the spell *might* be able to move her soul back into her body. That's what I did for Devora, only we didn't have her human body, so we used this coconut."

"It's not as bad as it sounds," Devora said. "This form suits me."

Skeev looked incredulous. "You want to *stab her?*" he said. "No way. I'm not letting you do that."

"We're not asking for your permission, Skeev," Cara interrupted. "It's my decision to make and I say we're doing it."

"Wait just a minute," Skeev said, jumping to his feet. "I won't let you do this."

"Stand down, first mate!" Cara said. Although she was a foot shorter than Skeev, she clearly held the upper hand. "I'm the captain of this crew. If I say I'm doing this, and I don't want a blood debt, that's the call getting made. Unless you're leading a mutiny?" She jabbed a finger into his chest. "Is that it, Skeev? You want to lead this crew?"

Skeev looked like he'd fight back, and I lifted one hand to wrap around Perry.

If the situation comes to blows, I'll have to take out Craven first, as he's the closest to me. Then I'll toss Spud at Marland. Roderick is beside Craven, though in close quarters like this, his massive weapon will be more dangerous to his crew than to me, so I'm not as worried about him.

Skeev shook his head. "No, captain," he said. He sat back down. Cara remained standing.

"Crow and I didn't have to come find you," she said. I wanted to hug her. "He has an army at his back. Heck, he could've had us all arrested and put down like dogs. But he gave us his word and he's here to follow through. He and his friends have tried to do right by us. So no blood debt. Promise me. All of you. Even if this doesn't work and something bad happens."

"Promise," Roderick and Craven murmured at the same time. Marland signed something, which I assumed meant that he promised, and Cara turned her full attention to Skeev.

The pirate's expression suggested he'd rather go on a date with Spud. Finally, he sighed.

"Aye." He sounded utterly spent. "I promise."

Cara faced me. "How do we do this?"

I had no idea, but of course I didn't say that. Instead, I said, "I'm going to set my friends down, because anyone close to me when I say the words will also enter the soul space. The rest of you should back up as well." I took Spud and Xena from my shoulders, then removed

Perry and Devora from my bandolier. They rolled away, joining the pirates in a wide circle around me and Cara. Once they were in position, I said, "Skeev, can I have my equipment back? And when you see Geeta and Brynn, you should give them their weapons back as well."

Skeev hesitated, but one glance from Cara and he pulled my gloves and battery pack out of his Inventory and handed them to me.

"Thanks." I slipped the familiar gloves over my hands. It felt good to have them back. I clipped on my battery pack. "Lie on the ground, Cara," I said. "It'll be easier for both of us."

Cara lay on the wet stone and pulled up her shirt to reveal the smooth, tan skin of her stomach.

"Do you think it'll hurt?" she asked.

I wasn't going to sugarcoat it. "Do I think getting stabbed with a pitchfork will hurt?"

"You know what I mean!"

"I'll try to do it gently."

Cara looked at the sky. "Gently," she said. "I'm ready."

I lifted the pitchfork. *Here goes nothing.* "Close your eyes," I said. Cara did as instructed, and I looked at the group around us. "Turn away if you don't want to watch."

When none of them did, I stabbed Cara Thorne.

Cara had closed her eyes, but they flew open the moment the tines slid into her stomach. Her mechanical eye showed no emotion, though the violet pool of her other eye was turbulent with fear. She gasped like she'd just jumped into an icy pond. Her back arched and she wrapped both hands around the pitchfork's haft.

"*Agh,*" she hissed. "It really hurts."

I didn't know what to do next. It was one thing to stab an enemy in the heat of battle and another entirely to intentionally hurt someone you wanted to call a friend. I felt sick. But I couldn't give up now. I doubled down, swallowing bile, and put all of my weight behind the thrust.

The tines pierced deeper, moving all the way through her until I felt them hit the ground.

"It's so cold," Cara rasped.

She fell back against the stone. Her eyes fell closed and her grip loosened on the haft. I pulled the pitchfork out of her body and it came away trailing golden smoke. From behind me, I heard Roderick gasp as the smoke moved from Cara's body, through the tines, and up into the weapon's translucent haft. After another few seconds, there was no smoke left inside her; her entire soul was trapped inside my weapon.

"Do you still feel her?" I said to Xena.

The eggplant shook back and forth. "No," she said. "She's gone."

Skeev and the pirates had promised not to hurt me, though I didn't want to test my luck by sticking around. Additionally, when I'd stabbed Sor'kodich, his body had disappeared. If that happened to Cara, I didn't know how to explain why I couldn't put her back in her original body, but instead needed to use a sweet potato, or a jalapeño.

I said Justice Maron's magic words, the ones that would allow me to move Cara's soul to her body. The group around me was completely silent. At tense times like this, Spud usually had a distracting word or two, but even he remained quiet.

I wasn't surprised when, between eye blinks, I reappeared on the beach I'd seen when I'd tried to move Cara's soul into Skeev's soul core. Only this time, Cara stood next to me.

"Beautiful, isn't it?" she said as she stared out over the ocean. "This is a little what death looked like, only there wasn't a pirate ship, and there was a film that separated the beach from the water. It stretched as far into the sky as I could see." She looked down and ran a hand across her unblemished stomach. "Not a scratch," she said. "But that really did hurt."

The purple storm I'd seen earlier still raged on the horizon. But where we stood, the beach was warm and pleasant. The surf reached the tips of my boots before running back to the sea with a calming *hiss*.

"Sorry," I said. "For what it's worth, I do think this will work."

Cara nodded. "It will. I can feel it. I'd never say this in front of anyone else, but we're alone now, so here goes: I'm sorry. I'm sorry about a lot. You've done a lot to earn my trust. When we spoke in the

Valves… well, it was nice. I haven't been vulnerable like that in a long time."

That was nice of her. She'd known I'd needed to hear those words, though I also knew what she needed, which was to be relieved of the responsibility of making a sappy speech.

"You don't need to say any more," I said. "I understand."

"I want to say more," she replied. "For years, my life has been so confusing. I don't remember parts of my childhood, and then I got older, and even parts of my teenage years are missing. I was angry. I *am* angry. I have flashes of this other life. I have these *feelings* toward you, but…"

My heart raced as she trailed off. *Cara also has parts of her life she doesn't remember. And she has visions of me, too?*

But that hadn't been exactly what she'd said. Rather, she'd said she had "flashes of another life" and "feelings" toward me.

Are those the same thing?

"Cara." She turned to face me. Because I was so much taller than her, she needed to look up. I didn't hesitate. I bent, my face moving toward hers, and she moved to meet me. In spite of what I knew about her, and about who she'd been and what she'd done, our kiss felt like the most natural thing in the world.

"That was nice," Cara said after a while.

"That was nice," I agreed. "Do you think we ever knew each other? In the parts of our lives neither of us can remember?"

"I've had that thought. Like we've met before. In another time. Another place. Back when I was a better person, I think." She surprised me again by pointing to the storm. "Do you know what that is?" she asked.

"If you think it's a physical manifestation of the holes in your memory, then I'd say yes, I think that's what it is, too. I don't know too much about these spaces, but that feels right."

Cara stared into the distance. "I'm glad you brought me back. It would've been so disappointing to die without more answers. Why can't we remember our pasts? Who did this to us? And why?"

I didn't have an answer, though I knew someone who might. "My father might know more."

"The father that's currently trapped in Prey House."

I nodded. "When this works, and I put you back in your body, I could use your help rescuing him. You and your crew. If you're up for it."

"I think something could be arranged. If it means answers. And if it means we get to destroy the Empire."

She grinned at me. I pulled her into my arms and she came willingly, rising to meet me for another kiss. She wasn't heavy, but I found myself falling to the sand, Cara tumbling after me. She landed on top of me, her face no more than an inch from mine.

"I'd like nothing more," I said.

22

An eye blink later, we reappeared in the Decrepit Ruins exactly as we left: me standing over Cara, pitchfork in hand. I stumbled away from her prone body as she sat up, and her hands flew to her stomach.

"Gah!" she yelled. She patted her body, though there were no wounds where the tines had slid into the skin. "That was cold! Never again!"

"My goodness," Xena said. "I can't feel her, and her eye isn't purple anymore. By all the monsters in the Kingdom of Death, I think it worked!"

From nearby, I heard a strange sound. I looked up and saw that Skeev was *laughing*. Not a cruel laugh, either, but a genuine expression of mirth.

"You're alive!" he said to his sister, stepping forward to help her to her feet. Then he stepped back and looked her over, one hand resting on her shoulder. "And not a scratch on you! By the gods of the sea, you're back!"

It was true: Cara Thorne was alive and back in her own body.

Like I'd promised.

"You did it, Crow!" Perry shouted. "Nice work!"

Before I could reply, Skeev turned toward me and offered his hand. "Aye, mate," he said. "You've done right by the crew."

He burst into tears.

It was so incongruous with his earlier behavior that I didn't know how to react. I stood there awkwardly until Cara stepped forward and wrapped her brother in a hug. "There, there," she said comfortingly. "*Shhh.* It's okay. I'm back."

"I thought we'd lost you!" Skeev wailed. "I was so worried!"

Cara met my gaze over Skeev's shoulder and rolled her eyes. *Sensitive,* she mouthed. I nodded. I could see that, though it still came as quite a surprise.

"We can go," I said. "Maybe we'll check in later?"

"Good idea," Cara said. "And Crow? Thank you."

I collected my friends, who rolled to meet me. It was nice to finally believe the pirates weren't coming after me, though they needed to process what had happened. In the meantime, I planned to check in with Jocko.

"That was weird," Spud said after we were out of earshot. "Honestly, I wouldn't have pegged Skeev as the crying type."

"Did anything, uh, *interesting* happen while you were in that soul space, Crow?" Xena asked. "Anything you want to tell us about?"

I felt a blush creep up my neck. "Nothing," I said. "Why do you ask?"

"No reason," Xena said knowingly. "Just curious."

"Oh my gosh," Devora said. "Crow and the pirate? Really?"

"What's she talking about, Crow?" Spud asked. "Were you and Cara kissing?" He gasped. "You *did* kiss her, didn't you? You sly dog! When were you going to tell us?"

I was saved from having to answer by Geeta, who dropped from the sky and landed on the path before us.

"What's up?" I said. "Everything okay?"

From the look on her face, I knew it wasn't. "After we came through the door, Jocko sent scouts to Old Town to gather intel," she said. "I was one of the first ones back, and he asked me to find you. It is not good. Remember that explosion we heard before we went back to the Valves? It was a bomb. The Medics have destroyed Old Town."

"*Destroyed?*" Perry replied. "Like, all of it?"

Geeta nodded. "Most of it," she said. "You should see."

I followed Geeta toward the path that wound back to the cemetery, and from there to Old Town. As we walked, I found myself thinking of Mega.

Whatever happened, I hope he survived, I thought, dread curling around my stomach.

Before we exited the ruins, we heard a shout and turned to see Brynn and the mulcher leader hurrying to catch up with our group.

Tharok. That was the strange mulcher's name. They were an odd pair: Brynn was short and manic, while Tharok was hulking and measured. However, they looked right together. Not in a romantic way, but as complementary fighters.

Brynn was breathless as she spoke. "Glad we caught you. Saw the pirates and they said you were heading this way. Got my stuff back, too. Thanks for that. Oh, and this is for you, Geeta." She handed Geeta her stiletto, which had appeared in her hand. Geeta nodded in appreciation and made the blade disappear. "If you're going to Old Town, we're coming with you. Jocko's orders. Got to keep our golden child safe. And I wouldn't want to miss the chance to see Spud at the height of his powers."

Spud gave a squeal of delight. "I've always liked you, Brynn," he said. "And not just because you complimented me. I like your weapons and I like your style. And I definitely liked that time you flicked Crow's eyeball."

"What?" Devora said.

"I'll tell you later," Spud said. "But it was awesome and gross and it caused Crow pain. So pretty much everything I enjoy."

Brynn flashed Spud a smile before jerking a thumb at Tharok. "Boss didn't tell this one to come, but he heard I was looking for you and started shadowing me," she said. "I don't think I could stop him if I tried."

Tharok banged his staff on the ground. "Jiak nak tor lat," he said, which I thought might mean, "I'm definitely coming with you, so don't try to tell me I'm not."

Our small group started picking our way through the woods. Despite Tharok's size, he was surprisingly adept at moving without making any noise. Numerous times, I tried to ask Geeta what we might see, but each time she only shook her head and said, "You need to see it for yourself."

As we got closer to Old Town, I smelled smoke. The trees became warped, twisted by some dark magic that had recently been used. Although the flora had looked old before, it hadn't looked like *this*. Scant few trees had leaves, and all were withered and lifeless.

"Gor'lan ika be'douk," Tharok said from my side, his nostrils flaring, which I assumed meant, "I don't like the scent of this at all."

"Reminds me of the time we raided the Helios suburb of Kinosia," Brynn muttered. "The one and only time we used alchemical fire. That is not a happy memory."

More than one of the burned trees had been used as a gallows, and I tried to ignore the bodies that swung from their branches. I felt a pit in my stomach that only intensified as we broke the tree line and saw the source of the smoke, and the explosion we'd heard before jumping through the door to the Valves.

What had once been a street was now little more than a crater. Whatever explosive the Medics had used had flattened the buildings for two blocks and ripped a smoldering furrow ten feet into the ground.

"Okay, this is *worse* than Kinosia," Brynn said. "Why would the Medics do this?"

I wasn't sure, but I hated to think it had something to do with Mega's plan to overthrow them. My thoughts turned to my spandex-wearing friend, and I wondered how he'd fared.

Is there any chance he survived? I needed to know.

"I need to check on a friend," I said. "Be on your guard. The Medics could still be out here." I flipped on my battery pack and brought Spud to hover above my hand. "Stay quiet," I told him. "No flames until we engage an enemy." Then I turned to Geeta. "Can you be our eyes in the sky? Let us know if we're about to run into a pack of wargs?"

"I will do that," the reptilian said. Her wings snapped out from her back. I felt the rush of displaced air as she flapped them, once, twice, three times, and then she was fifty yards away and twenty high, rising into the sky.

"She's so cool," Spud whispered.

Brynn nodded in agreement. "I don't want to say I foresaw this exact situation, but it *always* pays to have a friend with wings," she said. "Even if you have to have them installed."

Carefully, we continued through the town. With each turn of a corner, we saw more devastation: ruined bodies, flesh savaged by both magic and wargs, and bombed-out buildings. The houses of Old Town had never been vibrant, but they'd been orderly. Now, broken furniture lay overturned, and personal belongings were scattered everywhere.

I kept my eyes open for any sign of survivors, yet there were none. The Medics had swept through this part of Old Town like a plague.

"This is horrible," Brynn said as we passed a group of vultures picking entrails from the split stomach of a dead hunter. The woman's eyes were open, her face a rictus of agony. Luckily for her, she was dead, her eternal, silent scream catalyzed by whatever weapon had torn her open. "I hate to say it, but not even the Empire would've done something like this. They've swept through many Thuin settlements, to be sure, but their goal was always eradication. They wanted quick, clean death. They didn't want this."

She was talking about the joy the destroyers of Old Town had taken in their killing. The evidence was there: hangings and dismemberment. Bodies didn't just lie where they'd fallen, but had been arranged in sick and twisted poses. The Medics hadn't just killed these residents of Old Town, but tortured them. They'd inflicted as much pain as possible before finishing off their victims and leaving them for the flames and vultures.

A shadow fell across the street and I glanced up to see Geeta perched on a stone arch. At one time, the arch had sported a wooden facade, though the wood had burned away.

"Anything?" I asked.

She shook her head. "Nothing alive between here and the square except carrion birds," she said. "But I came across something bad. If you plan to continue to the square, you should cut over. There are things this way you do not want to see."

"Worse than the hangings?" I asked. "The bodies savaged by wargs and left to rot? Senseless murder and the destruction of a town?"

Geeta didn't respond. At least she'd tried to warn me.

23

As we got farther down the street, I saw the bodies. They hadn't just been dismembered and left to rot like the others. Rather, the Medics had set them in rows of chairs they'd pulled from the nearby houses, five deep and eight long. The glistening entrails that spilled from their cut stomachs had been used to secure each body to its respective chair, then pulled farther to wrap around each head in a cruel mockery of a blindfold. Each mouth hung open, the tongue removed, and ears had been sliced from each head. The message was clear: *This congregation has been rendered senseless. They can't see, can't speak, can't hear.*

The message was driven home by the pillar the bodies faced, which stood in the middle of the street. I wasn't sure how the Medics had gotten it there. It was at least twenty feet high, and must've weighed thousands of pounds.

They probably used magic. Sigils had been drawn in blood on the nearby street and walls, and since there were no vultures or flames here, I guessed the swirling designs formed some type of spell that preserved the scene for any who might think of defying the Medics.

Like me.

At the base of the pillar, I saw the missing eyes, ears, and tongues of the grim congregation. Secured to the middle of the pillar by a rope of his own entrails was Mega.

"Oh no," I said. Without thinking, I moved Spud from my hand back to my shoulder. He didn't complain. With my now-free hand, I covered Devora's eyes. Although I didn't know much about her, I remembered she'd had a crush on the big man. How had I forgotten?

"It's fine," Devora murmured from beneath my hand. "I want to see."

I removed my hand. Together, all of us stared at the man hanging from the pillar. He held his own head in stiff hands. His legs had been cut off at the knees and I saw the severed appendages on the ground below him.

Deceased Human

Loot? Yes or No.

The "Yes" button was grayed out, but I hardly even noticed.

I was too disturbed by the sight before me.

He tried to help others. He tried to help me. And this is what he got for it.

Behind me, Brynn retched. "Sorry," she said. "I'm not usually bothered by violence, but this is something else."

"G'or em'la," Tharok spat, which needed no translation.

I reached for Xena, but she stopped me. "There's no coming back from this, Crow," she said quietly. "I'm sorry."

"But we can try," I said, fumbling the box I'd gotten from the Kinetoscope out of my Inventory. I still had the bell pepper, the sweet potato, and the jalapeño. "His original body might be ruined, but if we can find his soul, we can put him in a different one. Xena, we need to try!"

Xena had already told me there was nothing she could do, but perhaps because of the desperation in my voice, she said, "Okay. We'll try."

I felt a cold chill on my shoulder as she activated her ability. I knelt, set the box on the ground beside me, and picked out the sweet potato. The coconut would've made sense for Mega, though I'd already used it for Devora, so I went with the next-heartiest piece of produce.

It doesn't matter what form he takes, though, as long as we can bring him back, I thought as purple smoke drifted from Xena's body.

I waited with my stomach in my throat as a minute ticked by, then two. I tried to imagine what Xena was seeing: the beach, the veil, and whatever was beyond it. On some level, I knew she was humoring me, though I forced myself to maintain hope.

Just when I was about to call out to her, Xena yelped in surprise. "I've got him!" she yelled. "Crow, he's here! Say the words!"

I was so shocked I almost messed up the Old Thuin words. But just as practice on the lightball field had taught me muscle memory, I'd practiced the words so many times that I couldn't mess up.

A blink after I finished, I appeared outside a pavilion covered in blue and gold silk. It was nighttime, and the surrounding trees were hung with lanterns that glowed with warm pink flames. I heard crickets, and from inside the pavilion, a brass chorus, like the kind you'd hear in the streets on Empire Day.

"Anyone know where we are?" Devora asked. Everything had happened so quickly that I'd forgotten to move my friends away from me.

"We're in Mega's soul space," I said. "We should be able to find him somewhere."

I walked toward the pavilion, pushing past a flap of blue fabric and stepping inside. At that moment, it became clear Mega's soul space was a circus. There were three rings, their floors littered with sawdust, and surrounding them were high wooden bleachers. The music I'd heard from outside was coming from an old gramophone that sat on a stool in the center ring.

"A circus!" Spud said. "I wonder if they have spun sugar? Rots the teeth, though everything will kill you in the end, and most of it doesn't taste half as good."

I didn't need to remind him that we weren't in a real circus, but a manifestation of Mega's soul. The big man, now in the form of a sweet potato, sat on the stool next to the gramophone. His brown face was illuminated in a half-dozen colors by spotlights that hung from struts high overhead.

The sweet potato version of Mega had been staring up at the empty bleachers, though at the sound of Spud's voice, he turned toward us. A grin split his face.

"Crow and company!" he rumbled. "The Spud Squad! Welcome to my home." He glanced around the pavilion. "The Dewey Brothers' Three Ring Traveling Extravaganza. The greatest entertainment from the Hub to the Crescent and everything in between!"

"I can't believe we found you," Xena said, marveling at the scene around us. "Crow, do you know what this means for the study of necromancy?"

I shook my head. "I can't say I do," I said.

"We'll have to rewrite half the books ever written," Xena said excitedly. "I don't know where to begin!"

I wanted to get caught up in her excitement, though for now, I was just happy to see my late friend. Even if he was in the form of a sweet potato. Perry was thrilled as well: he strained against the magnetism of the bandolier as he whooped with joy.

"Mega!" he said. "It's so great to see you. And look at this soul space! It's so cool! Did you used to work for a circus or something?"

Mega laughed. "Work for one? I owned one!" he said. "You think I wore spandex shorts for fun? They were part of my costume!"

"I was wondering about that, actually," Spud said.

"I thought they were cute," Devora chimed in.

"My brother and I grew up here," Mega continued. "He always had the head for business, but I was better with the acts. The clown routine? The dancing bears? I was behind all of those. My brother was the one who found the funds to pay for them." He jumped up and used his body to bump a button on the gramophone. The music stopped with a warble and he landed back on the stool. "Alas, when my brother died, our show fell into arrears. I sold the carnival to pay our debts and settled in the Crescent. Got hired as a bouncer at a club with a circus theme, and they asked me to keep wearing the uniform.

Found love there, for a time. Got arrested. They didn't let me change out of the shorts before they sent me down here." He gazed wistfully around his soul space, then took a deep breath. "Ah. Sawdust and popcorn. So mundane, and yet so comforting. I'm glad I got to see it one more time before I pass."

His words reminded me why I was there. "The skill I learned in Bulletsmithing can bring you back, Mega," I said. "We can't use your original body, but I can make you like the Squad." I jerked my thumbs at Spud and Xena, who sat on my shoulders. "Later down the road, I can try to get you into a real body, if you want."

Mega looked thoughtful. "Terrible business, what happened with the Medics," he said. "They said they wanted to meet under a flag of peace. I didn't fall for such an obvious trap, but they found me anyway. It was Robyn who gave away our location. She was good to Jinx, which is why I let her stick around, but she came from a family of swindlers. It's hard to outrun your past."

He hadn't addressed what I'd said to him. "If you don't want to come back, I'll respect your decision, but we're outgunned right now and we could use all the help we can get," I said. "Can I bring you back?"

Mega shook back and forth in the gesture I'd come to recognize as a shake of the head. "I appreciate the offer, Crow, but I'd rather you didn't."

"*What?*" Spud said incredulously. "What are you talking about? You're a hero, Mega! We need you!"

Mega smiled wanly. "That's nice of you to say, Spud," he said. "But I really don't want to come back. My life hasn't been easy. Running the circus with my brother was the best time of my life, though since he died, I've felt nothing but pain. I wasn't a good husband. I was addicted to static. I still am. Esmé was making me a tincture to help with the withdrawal, but I've been living on borrowed time since I came down here."

I shivered at the mention of static. I hadn't seen the drug since I'd lived in the Dregs, and I'd made a point of trying to never think about it again. Everyone in my tenement had been addicted. Although the substance the Empire gave its working class kept them blissed out and pain-free, it was also highly addictive. If you went without static for too long, you became little more than a zombie, willing to do anything for another hit.

I'd seen static junkies kill for just a few flakes.

"When I died, I appeared on a beach, and I felt peace," Mega continued. "I heard a voice from beyond the veil, calling me through. I don't know if it was real or not, but the person sounded like my brother. It might sound silly, and a few hours ago, I would've told you I didn't believe in an afterlife, but now I'm not so sure."

"It's real," Xena said.

"I'll respect whatever decision you make," I repeated.

"And I appreciate it," Mega said. "I've made my decision, Crow. I'll put this in terms you'll understand: I've carried the ball downfield as far as I can go. Now it's time for me to get off the field and let you handle the goal."

Honestly, I didn't blame him. I thought of the journey I'd taken so far, and how nice it would be to rest. The responsibility of keeping my friends safe and leading an army was enough to make anyone tired, and I'd only been doing it for a few hours.

"I understand," I said quietly.

Spud wasn't of the same mind. "You're just going to let him go?" he yelled. "Wait a minute. I don't like this one bit. Come on, Mega! Join us! I won't make any bad jokes for two… no, *three* hours! Perry, tell him. Crow, you gotta say something. Devora, charm him with your wiles. We can't just give up on him!"

But I wasn't giving up on Mega. Rather, I was trusting him. We all knew it, and on some level, Spud must've known it, too, because at my silence he gave a pained sob.

"I really like you, Mega," Spud cried. "I don't want to lose you!"

Mega smiled comfortingly. "We've all got to go sometime," he said to Spud. "This is my time. I can feel it. When times were tough at the circus, my brother had a little poem he liked to recite. I'll pass it along to you, yes? Keep these words alive." He cleared his throat, and when he spoke again, it was as if he were talking to an invisible audience that filled every seat in the grand pavilion:

Do your all and do your best,
The things that yield a hero's death.
In living fully, strong, and true,
We'll find our peace and earn our due.

"It's so sad," Spud whispered through his tears.

Mega turned his attention to me. "You're a good man, Crow," he said. "I assume your goal remains the same? You're taking the battle to the Medics to save your father?"

I nodded. "We have a chance now," I said. "In the Decrepit Ruins, I found an experiment the Medics were running. It led back to the Valves, and I was able to create a doorway to this level for the hunters who'd been trapped there. I also beat the leader of the mulchers, so they follow me now, too."

Mega smiled delightedly. "You've been busy! While I was getting myself killed, you were building an army." His face grew somber. "What time of day was it, when you found me?"

"Dusk."

"If it was dusk on the day I was killed, the meeting I'd planned with the Ghosts is at first light tomorrow. You can still make it. You'll find the entrance to their territory to the east, beneath a mausoleum. You'll know it when you see it. Great big building with all kinds of horrible things carved into it. Looks like the entrance to Toroth-Gol, actually. I wish I could tell you more, but the group is called 'the Ghosts' for a reason. They've only managed to survive this long by flying under the radar."

I nodded. "That's fine. I'll find them. See if I can convince them to join us."

"You'll find the research your father started in my basement. Remember how to get inside?"

I thought back to when I'd woken up in the house Mega had taken over from my father. "Turn that fifth burner on the stove," I said.

"Right. If you end up heating water for tea, you've turned the wrong one." He winked. "Oh! And I left a little present for you down there. Picked it up from another hunter right after you left. Thought we'd see each other again tomorrow morning. I'm not telling you what I got you, though, so don't ask. You'll see it for yourself soon enough."

"Thank you," I said.

"One more thing," Mega added. "I don't know how many of my people survived, but if you see Robyn, watch out for her. If you find Jinx, take care of her for me. Goodness knows she can take care of herself, but she's just a kid. Help her, if you can."

I remembered the quiet girl who had been hiding behind Mega's legs when I'd first seen him. *What are the chances she's still alive? Would Leslie and the Medics have killed a child?*

The answer came to me more quickly than I would've liked, and it wasn't pleasant.

Those monsters would kill anyone, and revel in it.

Still, I didn't need to mention that to Mega. "I wish we could've gotten more time to know each other better," I said.

"It was good while it lasted," Mega said. "Give 'em hell, Spud Squad."

I blinked, and then I was back in Old Town.

24

Once I'd packed up the sweet potato, we continued to Mega's house. Unlike many of the houses closer to the cemetery, Mega's was still intact, untouched by the fires that had plagued many of the other buildings we'd seen.

However, it wasn't unscathed. The wooden door had been blown off its hinges and the glass in the windows had been shattered.

Cautiously, I entered the home, Brynn and Tharok following behind. Geeta remained outside, ready to alert us if she saw the Medics returning.

"They really didn't spare anyone," Brynn said as we stepped inside.

The house was a mess, the furniture smashed and the cracked cups I'd once used to drink tea with Mega now broken into a thousand pieces on the floor. But it was the bodies that held my attention.

Esmé hung from the rafters, held up by the chain that ran between her two daggers. The chain had been wrapped around her neck several times.

Robyn's body lay half on, half off the bed; she had a stab wound in her chest; a blossoming flower of blood stained her tunic.

"This is awful," Spud murmured. "Pure evil."

I had to agree. "Brynn, do you mind pulling that sheet over Robyn. She may have betrayed Mega, but she deserves some dignity."

As Brynn went about the business of covering Robyn, I walked over to Esmé, touched her dangling foot, and pulled her body into my Inventory. I didn't know her well enough to invite her into my party as a piece of produce, though I could at least give her a proper burial at some point. As for Robyn… well, if what Mega had said was true, she was the one who'd given away their location and gotten them all killed. Her soul could take care of itself.

That done, I turned my attention to the cupboard that covered the secret passage. It was still intact, though the glass in the doors had been broken and the shelves ripped out.

"Stay here and keep watch," I said to Tharok and Brynn. "I've got something to grab from the basement."

I approached the stove and turned the knob that unlocked the door. Now that I was listening for it, I heard a soft *click*. When I pushed on the cupboard, it slid to one side.

"Korlan g'oot," Tharok said, which I took to mean, "Cool secret passage."

I stepped toward the door, though before I hit the steps, a creature rocketed out of the darkness, all anger and fury and gnashing teeth. I might've lost an important vein in my throat if Brynn hadn't been there in a blink, snagging whatever had leaped from the passage and pulling it tight against her body. Tharok had also jumped into action, the tip of his staff an inch away from the creature's throat.

The creature was Jinx. The girl snarled and thrashed, trying to escape Brynn's grasp, but the engineer had one of the girl's arms twisted up behind her back, and Tharok stepped forward to press the tip of his staff against the girl's chest.

"Stand down!" I shouted as relief flooded my body.

She's alive. Was she the gift Mega left for me?

But I knew that wasn't right. Whatever Mega had gotten me, he said he'd picked it up from another hunter; he'd also said he didn't know whether Jinx had survived. Her presence was a bonus, so his real gift was still inside the basement.

I held up my hands, pleading for Tharok not to stab the girl and for Brynn not to break her arm. At the same time, I started talking to Jinx, trying to keep her from taking a bite out of Brynn. When I'd first seen the young girl, I'd been surprised at the ruthlessness of the Empire, and the idea that they'd sent a child into Toroth-Gol. Now, after three levels in the dungeon, nothing truly surprised me.

"Jinx, the Medics are gone," I said. "We're friends! I was down here yesterday. Remember? We wanted to help Mega. Everyone, just calm down!"

It was the word 'Mega' that did it. The word appeared to be a salve to Jinx's furious thrashing, and she immediately fell still. Tharok lowered his staff, and Brynn released her.

I stared at the young girl, my heart breaking. She couldn't have been older than twelve. Her eyes were red-rimmed but hopeful. I couldn't remember if she just *hadn't* talked or *couldn't*, though I got my answer as she pointed at me, threw her arms wide, and flashed a thumbs up, head cocked to one side in a question.

The big man. Is he okay?

I couldn't bear to string her along. "He's gone," I said delicately. "But we've got you now. We'll help you."

I hoped that was true. I knew less about children than I did about romantic relationships, and that was saying something. If there was a book about handling kids, I hadn't done the homework. If mothers and fathers were the ones who were supposed to provide a model of parental duty, I was out of luck there as well; I didn't have any memory of my life before I woke up in the Dregs. By the time I came to Sal's house, Violet Valentine was already dead, and although Sal was my *adoptive* father, he was really more of a coach than a parent.

If Jinx wanted to learn how to play lightball, or defend herself against political enemies, I'd be all right. As for the normal things a kid needed to learn, I didn't know any of them.

Unlike me, Brynn knew exactly what to do, and she wrapped Jinx in a hug. "You poor little lady. You'll let Brynn take care of you, won't you?"

"I want to help too!" Spud shouted from my shoulder. "I *love* kids.

That's why I was counselor of the year at camp. Camp Green Lake! That's what it was called, I think. I don't really remember. But kids and I are a perfect mash!"

As usual, it was a terrible joke. To my shock, Jinx looked over at him and *smiled*. Shyly, it was true, but that was her nature. Considering the destruction around us, that smile was worth a lot.

"Can you watch her for a minute while I get what I need from the basement?" I said to Brynn, though it was Spud who answered.

"I'd only be too happy to help," he said. "Kids keep me feeling young. Go on down, Crow. We'll see you tater!"

I rolled my eyes and set him on the table. I set Perry beside him.

"Watch Spud," I said quietly. "Don't let him teach her any dirty words or anything like that."

"The guy is a liability, Crow," Perry said. "There's nothing I can do!"

I sighed and set Xena beside Perry. "Keep the boys from fighting. Devora, you want to come down or stay up here?"

"I'm always up for adventure," the coconut said. "Let's see what's in the basement."

"We'll be right back," I said, then stepped through the doorway of the secret passage.

The smell of old wood hit me as I made my way down the rickety stairs to the table where my father had once sat. It was strange to be headed back into that basement and to know that *both* of the great men who'd used it before me had been bested by the Medics.

Although I hadn't flipped any lights, they came on automatically. On the far wall, I could still see all of the research on the Medics, which would be invaluable in the coming battle. I touched each sheet and sent it to my Inventory. When that was done, I turned my attention to the table, where I saw the gift Mega had left for me.

It was a gun, though that was like saying Spud was a potato. The resemblance was there, but the reality was something totally different. The whole thing was made from some type of futuristic-looking, matte-gray metal, the details accented by jet-black lines that almost looked like wet ink. In the middle of the weapon was a rotating cylinder.

Titan Armament

When the dwarven weaponsmiths who lived in the dungeon discovered that proximity to the Heart of the World disrupted their technology, they turned to artificing, a skill that blended machinery with supernatural forces to create weapons that worked even in the lowest levels of Toroth-Gol. The Titan Armament is an example of one such weapon.

Primarily mechanical in operation, the Titan Armament uses magic to hold itself together. Magic also instills each cartridge with additional velocity and is responsible for the weapon's "SmartLoad" feature, which lets the Titan Armament shoot any object that fits inside one of its eight chambers.

The Titan Armament is worn on an arm and fired via mental connection established when a new user wields the weapon for the first time. The weapon only responds to one user at a time, and a new one can only be added upon the previous user's death.

"Not a bad gift," Devora murmured. "You know what it's meant to fire, right?"

It took me a moment to realize what she was talking about, and then I wanted to kick myself for not catching on sooner.

This is a replacement for my gloves. The weapon's massive cylinder looked like it was made to hold cannonballs. Or sentient produce, which was probably why Mega had chosen this particular weapon for me. I read the description again: apparently, the Titan Armament could fire *any object that fit inside one of its chambers.*

Was it a coincidence that the weapon could fire eight shots, and the prophecy that had influenced so much of my time in the dungeon predicted I'd carry eight pieces of sentient produce?

"Hmm," I grunted. I didn't know how to feel about giving up my gloves. For as long as I could remember, lightball had been a part of my life. When I lived in the Dregs, the occasional lightball games were one of the only things that kept me motivated. After I'd been adopted, I'd taken to the sport almost immediately.

Now, it was time to let the gloves go. From what I understood, I wouldn't need the battery pack, either.

I lifted the Titan Armament in both hands. For something so big, it was surprisingly light. The black accent lines glinted in the dim light. Beneath the gun, I saw a note.

For King Crow. Happy hunting! Love, Mega and Co.

With a traditional gun, one held the stock and pulled the trigger, which caused the hammer to strike the firing pin, which in turn hit the primer of a cartridge. The resulting spark would ignite the powder in the cartridge and send the bullet shooting from the barrel. With a revolver, the cylinder would then rotate, lining up a new cartridge with the hammer.

From what I could see, the Titan Armament didn't have a stock or a trigger. Rather, the whole thing was mounted atop a mesh sleeve I was supposed to slide over my arm.

"You gonna gawk or try it on?" Devora asked.

I slid the weapon onto my right arm. The mesh sleeve had been pretty sizable, but as I pushed my arm through, the sleeve automatically tightened around my skin. It was snug enough to keep the weapon from sliding, though not uncomfortable. And the gun didn't weigh me down. It had a heft to it that let me know it was there, and I had a feeling it could take a few good hits without breaking, but I could keep it lifted without exhausting myself.

Hello, Nathaniel 'King Crow' Valentine. This is the Titan Armament.

Form a mental connection with the Titan Armament? Yes or No.

I thought back to the description: "The Titan Armament is worn on an arm and fired via mental connection established when a new user wields the weapon for the first time."

If that were true, I needed to establish the connection to use the weapon.

Yes. I felt a tickle at my right temple.

Thank you, Nathaniel 'King Crow' Valentine. Connection has been established with the Titan Armament.

Load? Yes or No.

Hmm. Just to see what would happen, I thought, *Yes.* Soundlessly, the gray aperture on top of the cylinder slid open to reveal eight empty chambers, each of which looked just big enough to fit Devora.

"You're going to ask me to jump in there, aren't you?" Devora said.

"Are you opposed?"

Devora sighed. "You only live once. Or maybe twice, in my case. Either way, might as well have your soul ripped from your body and anchored to a tropical fruit so you can get shot out of a magical weapon."

"*Artificed* weapon," I corrected. "Blend of technology and magic."

"Whatever. Drop me in, captain."

I lifted her from her spot on my bandolier and placed her into one of the chambers. Immediately, the plates on top of the cylinder slid shut.

"How are you doing in there?" I said. "Can you hear me?"

Devora's reply was muffled, but audible. "Hey Crow! It's like a soul space in here! I thought it might be a tight squeeze, but I have all the room in the world. There are couches and a popcorn machine! These chairs will massage my back, I think. Yes! Oh my goodness. It's *amazing!*"

I raised my arm and sighted down the barrel at the far wall.

You have one (1) cartridge available to fire.

Cartridge A: Devora
Special Ability: Concussive Blast

Fire? Yes or No.

WARNING: You are about to fire the Titan Armament in a confined space. Damage to your eardrums is likely. Damage to the integrity of the structure above you is likely.

Are you sure you want to fire the Titan Armament?

I lowered the gun. "On second thought, maybe let's wait until we're outside to fire this."

"No complaints from in here," Devora replied. "I'm going through the movie selection!"

I turned back to the staircase and climbed the stairs. When I reached the top, I saw my group sitting around the kitchen table. Spud and Perry were on one side, and Jinx sat on the other. Xena, Brynn, Tharok, and Geeta stood around her. Between Jinx and Spud, there was a ravens board. One of my friends must've pulled it out of their Inventory.

Perry was yelling at the potato. "Do *not* move there, Spud! You have sixty-three different moves you could make, and that's *literally* the worst one."

"Worst one?" Spud cried. "If I take out her harpy, I can invoke the squiggle time contingent and bring my aerie piece to the backline."

Perry rolled his eyes. "I don't know how to say it more clearly: that's not a rule. That's not even close to a rule."

The group looked up as I cleared my throat. Spud took the opportunity to pretend like he'd been scared, give an exaggerated yelp, and knock the board with his body, upsetting all the pieces.

"Oh *nooo*," he said. "I didn't mean to…" He trailed off as his eyes fell on my new weapon. "In the name of all that's crispy! What's *that?*"

I held up the Titan Armament, which still encased my right arm.

"Got a little upgrade over my gloves. Anyone want to see how it works?"

25

As we walked from Old Town back to the Decrepit Ruins, I explored the capabilities of the Titan Armament. The weapon was *epic*. Perry had better words to describe it, and Spud's language was more colorful, though I stand by my choice.

One by one, I loaded Spud, Perry, and Xena inside.

"Anyone here seen any of the *Smoothie Boys* movies?" I heard Devora say as the top of the cylinder slid closed.

"I *love* those movies," Spud said. "Whoa! That's a *massive* telescreen!"

"We're *not* watching those," Xena said. "Look here! They have footage of every lightball game for the last ten years."

"Ooh, let's put on the Steel City versus the Crescent Necromancers in the Lightning Cup," Devora said. "That's the one where Crow got his ribs broken by Tamlin Muir!"

"We've got that?" Although I wasn't inside the weapon, I could hear the amazement in Spud's voice. "Put that on *immediately!*"

I was glad to hear that my friends were enjoying the comforts of the Titan Armament, but I was more excited by the weapon's functionality. For one, it would work in the lower levels of the dungeon, whereas my gloves might not. Also, it appeared to be a breeze to use.

All I needed to do was pick my cartridge, think *Fire,* and *bam!* The cartridge would rocket from the barrel.

Now that we weren't in a confined space, I decided to try it out. I raised the weapon.

You have four (4) cartridges available to fire.

Cartridge A: Devora
Special Ability: Concussive Blast

Cartridge B: Peristopheles Magnesis IV
Special Ability: Acidic Vomit

Cartridge C: Xenandor of Kratha
Special Ability: Nightmare Fuel

Cartridge D: Spud Spuddington
Special Ability: Hot Potato

Which cartridge would you like to fire?

Cartridge D. The gun's cylinder whirred. From inside the weapon, I heard a yelp of surprise.

"Whoa!" Spud said. "You're not gonna believe this. I was watching you get your ribs smashed when a siren went off. All the lights in here turned red, and then this robotic voice said, 'Battle stations! Battle stations!' A chute opened beneath my chair, and I fell into this little compartment. *I can see straight down the barrel!* This is wild!"

Cartridge D loaded.

Fire, I thought.

Whoomph. There wasn't much recoil, but the gun was *loud.* Spud shot from the barrel so quickly that it took another second before I heard him screaming.

"*Arghhhhh!*" He smashed into the trunk of a distant tree. Instead of becoming lodged in the wood, however, he blasted straight through it, continuing for another hundred yards before he was stopped by a boulder. I started running toward him.

You have one (1) cartridge available for recall.

Cartridge D: Spud Spuddington
Special Ability: Hot Potato

Would you like to recall Cartridge D? Yes or No.

Yes. Spud rocketed toward me, falling straight through the aperture and right back into the gun.

By the Dregs. This weapon is fantastic!

The only downside to the Titan Armament was that it almost worked too well. Given the velocity at which it fired, it was great for putting my friends in difficult-to-reach places and made me glad I could return them to me with a thought. The catch: if I wanted to shoot it *at* something, I needed to use the harder-bodied produce like Devora and Spud. If Perry or Xena had hit a tree like Spud, I was liable to end up with pulp.

Titan Armament, do you have a velocity modulator? Any way to slow down your shots?

Despite my mental connection with the gun, it didn't answer my questions.

Until I find an instruction manual, I'll have to save my shots at harder objects for Devora and Spud.

Still, I wasn't too bothered. The gun could *fire.* As we walked, I shot Devora at the wall of a nearby house, and she punched through the crumbling stone like it was wet paper. She hadn't even activated Concussive Blast.

"I'm definitely going to miss my gloves, but this thing is pretty incredible," I said as I mentally called her back.

I'm not sure what type of force the weapon used for that little trick, though it was akin to magnetism. Devora soared back toward me and the weapon did all the heavy lifting. When she was close, the top of the cylinder slid open and she dropped straight inside.

As we neared the camp, I saw that cook fires had become ubiquitous. For a group that had just finished one battle and was soon to enter another, the mood was surprisingly cheerful. Hunters shared food or clinked drinks, and a few of the hunter bands even mingled among the mulchers. I was pretty sure they couldn't understand each other, though food was a universal language. Now that the animosity between the groups had been quelled, both the hunters and mulchers were willing to try and get along.

"The Desert Blade has outdone himself again," Brynn said, marveling at the camp. "You should've seen our setup in the Wastes. Man, that ran like clockwork."

I cast my gaze over the arrangement of cook fires and tents. "Speaking of the Desert Blade, do you know where we can find him?" I asked.

"Sure," Brynn said. She pointed toward the center of the camp. "Just that way. Turn the corner and you'll see a big orange tent. You can't miss it."

"Thanks," I said. I started that way, then stopped and let my gaze wander until I found the pirates. They were seated around one of the fires and drinking some type of liquor. As I watched, Skeev pulled a lit branch from the coals and used it to breathe a jet of fire into the sky. Craven gave a whoop of appreciation, and both Roderick and Cara clapped and egged him on. A silent Marland sat on a stump, sharpening a knife.

Hmm.

I started toward them, my group following in my wake. Marland was the first of the pirates to notice us. His sharp eyes darted from me to my new weapon, then to my comrades, and finally to Jinx. He stood, and the whetstone he'd been using to sharpen his knife disappeared into his Inventory.

It was fitting that he was the first to catch sight of us, because he was the one I wanted to address. I lifted a hand in greeting. Marland gave a curt nod, and the other pirates looked up and saw us.

"Welcome back," Cara said as she got to her feet to stand beside her brother. "What's up?"

I told them about what I'd seen in Old Town, and about Jinx.

"She doesn't speak, but she knows how to sign, and she could really use a friend," I said to Marland. "It might be asking too much, but I was wondering if you could talk to her?"

My request sounded dumb. *Why'd I think this was a good idea? He's a pirate.*

Marland didn't seem opposed, which was a first. He glanced over my shoulder and his eyes fell on Jinx. Although he didn't acknowledge my question, he stepped around me and walked toward Jinx, shoving his knife into his waistband as he moved. When he reached her, he lifted a hand in silent salute.

Jinx returned the gesture.

Maybe the vicious pirate does *have a heart,* I thought as I watched them.

Marland signed something to Jinx, then opened his mouth to show that he didn't have a tongue. Jinx's eyes widened slightly. She shook her head and signed something back, and then the two were having a full conversation.

"Would you look at that," Cara murmured from behind me. I'd forgotten she was there. "Usually, Marland hates kids. He'd rather abandon them on an island than sail with 'em."

Marland *laughed.* It was strange to hear a sound coming from the pirate other than the manic whoops I'd heard while he and Skeev had chased me through the Valves. Until that moment, I hadn't known the stoic pirate had been capable of smiling. But there it was, his lips pulled back from his teeth in a grin. Jinx was smiling, too.

It was a moment of joy in an otherwise heavy evening, though I still had my work cut out for me. As fun as it would've been to let loose with the pirates, I needed to speak to Jocko.

I also needed to prepare for my meeting with the Ghosts.

"Can I leave her with you guys for a bit?" I asked. It seemed crazy to leave a child with *pirates*, though there was something different about them now. I knew Cara would keep Jinx safe.

"Don't you worry about a thing, Crow," Cara said. "We'll treat that girl like family."

I knew how much that meant to the pirates. "Thank you. See you soon." I walked back over to my group. "We're going to leave Jinx here. Anyone want to come with me to speak with Jocko?"

Brynn looked horrified. "Not at all. I'm not talking to him again until this is over. He'll make me do something, and I've done enough for one day. So no thank you, Crow. I'd rather stay here with the pirates. Tharok will keep me company, won't you, big guy?"

Tharok had been watching the movement of a large ant that was walking across the frozen ground nearby. Upon hearing his name, however, he looked over at her. "Gor'el makiak dorthala?" he said, which I suspected meant, "Will it be fun?"

"Sure," Brynn said, clapping him on the shoulder. "Gor'el makiak dorthala." She raised an eyebrow at me. "I have no idea what I just said," she whispered. More loudly, she said, "You know where to find us."

I turned to Geeta. "What about you? You want to come meet Jocko with me?"

The reptilian shook her head. "I am going to find something to eat."

I sighed. "Catch you guys later."

I turned and walked through the camp.

26

Jocko's tent was easy enough to find, as it was four times the size of the others. As Brynn had told me, it was also made from bright orange fabric. I didn't know where he'd gotten it; it certainly wasn't discreet, though that fit with Jocko's style.

"I'm excited to see Jocko again!" Spud said from inside the Titan Armament. Now that I had the gun, all my friends had taken to spending time inside instead of on my shoulders or bandolier. "I'm going to ask him how else he plans to manipulate you."

That was one part of the conversation I *wasn't* excited about. In the heat of rescuing Jocko from Sor'kodich and moving my new army out of the Valves, Jocko and I hadn't had time for a personal reconciliation.

Do I need one? At this point, I understood the Grass King: he'd do anything to keep me safe. As long as he thought he was acting in my best interests, he wasn't shy about lying.

Still, an apology would be nice.

I looked down at the weapon covering my arm. "I thought you guys were watching me get my butt kicked in old lightball matches," I said.

"We finished that," Perry replied, his voice floating from the weapon. "Spud convinced us it'd be fun to watch your reunion with Jocko instead. We've got a great view of Jocko's tent."

"I *love* drama," Spud said. "Your Lightning Cup matchup against the Goblins has nothing on this!"

"I don't plan on having it out with Jocko," I told him. "The last time we saw him, he saved my life. I'm interested in hearing what happened to him after I got shot and before we found him again, but that can wait. We need to discuss how we're going to save my father and that's about as dramatic as our conversation is going to get."

"That's very mature, Crow," Xena said.

"Very *boring*, is more like it," Spud said. "If you're not gonna fight, why would I bother watching? Devora, let's play ravens instead. I have a feeling I'm finally going to win a game. Perry, you're on my team!"

With my friends distracted, I pushed into Jocko's tent. As it turned out, I didn't need to worry about having it out with him. He stood at a large table in the center of the tent with several other hunters, including Nori, my old flame, and I wouldn't be getting into anything personal while they were around.

The hunters around the table were so distracted by their conversation that they didn't notice me enter.

"We're lost if we wait," one man said. He was dark-skinned with neat black hair. As he spoke, he slapped a fist into a meaty palm for emphasis. His hands were dyed black like mine. *Treason.* "We need to strike while we have the element of surprise!"

Stone Galvanizer (Goran Peretz)

Originally from the coastal city of Salmae, Goran dreamed of joining the Empire Guard. At sixteen, he ran away from home and traveled to Bellablanco, where he worked in the kitchen of a local restaurant until he'd saved enough money for passage to Helios. After arriving in the center of the Empire's power, he lied about his age and joined the Empire Guard, eventually rising to the rank of Sergeant Major.

When Goran was thirty-eight, his forces were sent to eradicate the griffins of Peakskill. Objecting to the genocide of an entire race, Goran allowed many of the griffins to escape.

When Goran returned to Helios, he was convicted of treason and sentenced to Toroth-Gol.

"It doesn't make sense to attack if we don't know the terrain," Nori said. "You've led squads of soldiers, Goran, so I shouldn't need to tell you this. If we head in blind, we're going to get crushed."

"You're not *listening*," Goran growled. "I'm not saying we launch a full assault on Prey House while we don't know the terrain. But we need to *act*. Get an advance force to clear the area, then send in scouts to map it out. We're sitting ducks out here!"

They argued back and forth, stopping only when I cleared my throat. All of them looked up.

"Hey, *pacho!*" Jocko said cheerfully, waving me over. "We're putting the finishing touches on a plan. Come on over!"

I approached the table. As I did, Goran looked me up and down. From the sneer on his lips, he seemed to find me lacking. "So this is the leader of our forces?" he asked. "The great King Crow?"

I didn't know what I'd done to offend him, but I decided to nip his attitude in the bud. "Jocko is your leader," I said. "I'm just the person who saved you all from the Valves."

Goran grunted, though he was willing to concede the point. I came to stand beside Jocko and studied the drawings on the table. They were all copies of the same four maps, which showed all of the ground we'd covered so far on this level of the dungeon: Prey House, Old Town, and the Decrepit Ruins. Scattered across them were clusters of multi-colored pebbles.

"What are these showing?" I asked, pointing to the small rocks.

"Good question, *pacho*," Jocko said. "You remember how there were several different room types in Gray Moor, each with its own set of advantages?" I nodded. "Well, the General's Quarters allowed those who stayed in them to link up with five scouts from Talon

Lake. The scouts could mark points of interest on their Maps, and the person who stayed in the General's Quarters would see the same thing on theirs." He jerked a thumb at Goran. "He took the General's Quarters, and we set him up with a few of the scouts, so we're getting information on the location of enemy troops in real time."

"Hence the pebbles," Nori added.

I nodded and pointed to a cluster of pebbles. "I assume the different colors mean different things?"

Jocko nodded. "The Medics are easy enough, *pacho*. We matched the colors of their stones with the colors of their robes. We used black stones for the mulchers. The gold stones indicate a hunter." He tapped the map on the table directly in front of him. "This map shows what's happening in the field right now, while the others are sandbox maps we made to model various scenarios."

"Why do your maps look like a child drew them?" Spud asked, his voice coming from the Titan Armament.

Many of the hunters around the table looked shocked to hear a voice coming from my gun, but I didn't explain. Besides, Spud was right: the drawing of Prey House was terrible.

Jocko looked sheepish. "To be honest, we're having a bit of trouble with that one. We've built the map we have from interviewing Geeta, and a few of the other hunters here who saw the inside of the facility, but their reports differ somewhat, and we can't see anything on our Maps. The Medics have blocked off the building. Maybe you could tell us what you remember?"

For the first time in a while, I checked my own Map. Sure enough, Prey House was now nothing more than a gray box.

But it didn't matter. "I can do better than that." I removed the detailed maps I'd taken from Mega's basement from my Inventory and dropped them on the table. "Here's the intel you need."

The group crowded around to get a better look. "This is incredible!" one of the gathered leaders said. Interestingly enough, she was the only reptilian in the room; her hands were dyed black like mine, which meant she'd been sentenced to Toroth-Gol for treason.

Unseen Spy (Lamuel Ros'i)

Like most reptilians, Lamuel was born in the Emerald Isles. In her youth, she made her way to the Red Hills and then Crystal Keep, where she apprenticed with a gnomish glassworker and learned the secrets of glassinine.

When the Empire took over Crystal Keep, they demanded the gnomes teach them how to work glassinine, though the gnomes refused. Many of them were put to death on the spot. As an apprentice and a reptilian, Lamuel was not suspected of possessing the coveted knowledge, though she was still captured by the Empire and sent to Steel City for judgment.

Lamuel was accused of sedition and sentenced to Toroth-Gol.

"The detail here is down to the individual room!" Lamuel continued. She looked over at Goran. "You would've had us attack an hour ago, before we knew any of this. Is this not reason to take a more cautious approach?"

Jocko clapped me on the shoulder. "Well done, *pacho*. Thought we'd go in blind and have a rock fight."

Goran narrowed his eyes at Lamuel, then turned his angry gaze toward me. "Where'd you get these maps?"

I met Goran's gaze. I didn't care if he was an ally; I didn't play well with bullies.

"I got them from a friend," I said, "who got them from my father. He mapped out this entire level. Not only that, but he wrote detailed reports on everyone inside Prey House. If you want to know about the enemy's firepower, maybe spend less time antagonizing your allies and more time doing your homework."

Goran looked ready to jump across the table at me, but Jocko raised a hand. "I won't see us arguing," he said. "We're on the same side, *pacho*. This is good news! Crow, let's see what else you've got."

I took the rest of the research out of my Inventory and set it on the table. There were pages upon pages of information. Although it was far too much for anyone to read completely in an evening, the group could divide and conquer. There were definitely details here that would lend themselves toward a more successful infiltration.

"This is a gold mine," Lamuel said. "Should we get started?"

Everyone except Goran nodded. After a moment, he deflated. "Fine." He lifted a page from the table. "I suppose more caution is warranted."

From the corner of my eye, I saw Jocko wink at me. "Let's see how we can break this out. Crow, why don't you join me and Goran in handling the maps? The rest of you can dig through the personnel profiles and pull any that look particularly dangerous. We'll reconvene in two hours for a check-in, and once we've gone through all the research, we'll work on an infiltration plan."

Part of me wanted to help, but I shook my head. Those with more practical experience in leading troops could handle this part of the plan.

"It was a pleasure to help," I murmured. "But I have another responsibility. Feel free to find me if you need anything else."

It only bruised my ego a little bit when no one insisted I stay.

27

The next morning, I woke up early and couldn't get back to sleep. Perhaps it was the magnitude of the task set before me. Whatever the reason, my dreams had been troubled, and Devora's snoring didn't help. Every inhale was like the blast of the Titan Armament.

Soon, it was time for my meeting with the Ghosts. As the sun rose above the horizon, I made my way toward Old Town. One by one, the members of my squad awoke. By the time I reached the edge of the city, all of them were awake.

"So we're looking for a mausoleum?" Spud asked from inside my weapon. "If you ask me, this whole town looks like a mausoleum."

"Mega did say we'd know it when we saw it," I replied as I eyed the charred wreckage.

"I've got my eyes *peeled*," Spud said. "Get it?" He laughed, though no one else responded.

Xena sighed. "Aren't mausoleums usually on the outskirts of towns?" she asked. "Like, in the town graveyard? That was how things worked in my day."

I shrugged. "You'd think. But this one isn't, apparently."

Ignoring the smoky stench clinging to the air, I ventured deeper into the town. As I walked, my boots crunched on debris, echoing eerily in the silence. Every so often, Spud would try to lighten the mood with a quip, but the humor fell flat against the backdrop of destruction.

I'd been wandering through the remnants of the once-thriving town for over an hour when I turned the corner and saw our destination. It stood untouched amidst the devastation, its austere stone walls and iron gates a stark contrast against the wreckage.

"Uh, this has to be it, right?" I said. The mausoleum was a dark monolith, an imposing structure that consumed the light around it. There were intricate carvings on its stone walls: faces contorted in agony and despair, their mouths open in silent screams.

I remembered what Mega had said: "Great big building with all kinds of horrible things carved into it."

A chill ran down my spine.

"I'm going to say yes," Spud replied. "Does anyone else feel like they just walked into a horror story?"

"Only every day since we met," Xena responded.

I ignored them, my thoughts focused on the task ahead. If what Mega had said was true, this was just the beginning. We were about to delve deep into the underworld, looking to recruit those who lurked in the shadows.

I reached the gate of the mausoleum and felt a tingling sense of apprehension. *What if the Ghosts don't want to help us?*

With a deep breath, I pushed the heavy gate. It groaned in protest, its ancient hinges crying out.

Cautiously, I stepped inside. The entry was little more than a small room, with dust motes that floated in the beams of light that shot through high windows. In the center of the floor was a staircase that led down into darkness.

"Dark, creepy, probably infested with rats!" Spud exclaimed. "How exciting. Crow, you need a light?"

Before I could respond, Spud moaned and the barrel of the Titan Armament started *glowing*.

"Huh," I said, looking at the gun. "That's actually really helpful."

I started down the stairs. The air was dank. I walked carefully, my path illuminated by Spud's soft glow. To either side of the staircase, the walls were lined with empty, dusty alcoves.

As we descended deeper, the air around us grew colder. Eventually, the staircase leveled off and we found ourselves in catacombs. The air was heavy, filled with the musty scent of decay and the faint smell of... something else.

Mulchers? No, that's not it. But definitely something damp.

"What are we looking for down here, exactly?" Perry asked. "Or let me guess: we'll know it when we see it."

"I think you nailed it," I said.

My footfalls echoed off the damp stone walls. Shattered statues and remnants of ancient tapestries lay strewn about, all veiled under a thick layer of dust. I couldn't shake the feeling that we were being watched.

One wall drew my attention; it was cleaner than the rest. It contained a stunning piece of art, a myriad of tiny, colorful tiles intricately arranged to create an elaborate scene of gods and monsters.

"It's—*arghhh*—a mosaic!" Spud shouted. "Such detailed artistry. And look at the detail on that—*ugh*—centaur's buttocks. Divine! *Yearghhh!* Simply divine!"

"Seriously?" Xena said. "We're in a creepy mausoleum, potentially surrounded by an invisible gang, and you're commenting on a centaur's buttocks?"

"These are—*ooh*—difficult times, Xena," Spud said seriously. "One must—*ah!*—appreciate beauty wherever it is found."

While the two bickered, I studied the mosaic. There, among the chaos of gods and monsters, was something resembling a small, unassuming potato. It floated above the hand of someone who looked like...

Me.

What's going on? Curiosity piqued, I reached forward. As my fingers brushed the potato, the whole mosaic slid aside, disappearing into a recess in the rock.

Behind it, I saw a bustling tavern.

"Oh," I said. "I think we've found the Ghosts."

The tavern was filled with a motley crew. On one side of the room, musicians had been playing a jaunty tune, but the music and merry-making came to an abrupt halt and every eye in the room turned to stare at us in surprise.

"Uh, hi," I said. "You must be the Ghosts. Anyway, I have a meeting with your boss, if that's okay. So I'll just be going to find, uh, your boss?"

As I moved to take another step, one of the Ghosts stood and hurled a weapon at my legs. It was a bola, two balls connected by a rope. Before I knew what was happening, it had wrapped around my legs and sent me sprawling.

"What was—*urgh*—that?" Spud yelled from inside the gun. "Crow, are you okay?"

The person who'd thrown the weapon sauntered toward me with a smirk on his face. He was thin with wavy white hair and a weather-beaten face. His off-hand was wrapped in a bandage that ran from his wrist to his elbow. But the hand he'd thrown with was visible, and it was dyed red.

A murderer. That's not ideal.

Boleadoras (Tavian Stormrider)

Tavian Stormrider was born into a family of fishermen in a coastal town just south of the Crescent. From a young age, he was drawn to the sea, spending his days watching the horizon and dreaming of distant lands. When he came of age, he left his home-town to join the crew of the *Storm's Bounty*, a formidable trading vessel known for its daring voyages and fearless captain.

Under the mentorship of Captain Silas Ironbeard, Tavian honed his maritime skills and learned the art of navigation, ship manage-ment, and swordplay. His adventures took him to far-flung ports, from the bustling marketplaces of Helios to the hidden coves of the Lobster Isles. When Silas Ironbeard was accused of sedition for

**running goods to the Thuins, Tavian lashed out against the guards
sent to bring Ironbeard to Helios.**

Tavian was convicted of murder and sentenced to Toroth-Gol.

"Caught you now, didn't I?" Tavian purred.

"I'll take care of him, Tavian," another criminal growled from a
nearby table. This man stood, one hand going to the wooden spoon at
his waist, and I saw the hand was dyed purple.

Sentenced for magic.

As I struggled to extricate myself from Tavian's weapon, I scanned
his description.

Grim Chef (Gideon Whitaker)

**A native of Wick, Gideon was a hunter during the Cursed Winter,
which saw the area's normally abundant hunting stock struck
with a terrible wasting disease. At least thirty percent of Wick's
population died of starvation before town elders sent scouts to the
Crescent for help.**

**Unwilling to put his trust in the Empire, Gideon went northwest
to seek help from the Thuins. While the scouts who went to the
Crescent brought back a wagon filled with meager supplies,
Gideon returned with a spell that could greatly expand the yields
from harvestable crops. The scouts from the Crescent also
returned with several members of the Empire Guard, who came to
see the situation in Wick for themselves.**

**Gideon was convicted of practicing magic and sentenced to
Toroth-Gol.**

"He said he wants a meeting with the boss," Tavian said. "So let's
get him to the boss. She'll decide what to do with him."

"The boss!" shouted a man at the bar. He was clearly drunk. He laughed, giddy with excitement, which caused ale to spill into his lap. It didn't seem to bother him. "The boss! The boss!"

I didn't like the way the man was repeating the word, but what could I do? I was still ensnared, though I fought against the rope as Gideon approached.

"A wooden spoon?" Spud asked, his voice coming from the Titan Armament. "What are you going to do, bake us a cake? Stir us to death?"

"Maybe now isn't the time to antagonize anyone," I hissed at him.

Gideon's smirk faltered. "And here I was going to help you," he said. "I'll teach you to make fun of me!"

"No, wait!" I yelled as he swung the spoon at my head. The second it touched me, there was a loud *crack*, and then everything went black.

28

I awoke to a throbbing ache pounding at the forefront of my skull. My vision was smeared with indistinct shapes and shades. In the depths of my ears, I heard the ghostly remnants of a *crack:* the sound of a magical wooden spoon meeting my skull. My tongue detected the flavor of iron, like someone had put a penny under it while I was knocked out.

"Awake at last," Spud said. His voice was unmistakable. I attempted to combat my blurry vision by blinking rapidly, and my reward was the sight of Spud, Perry, Xena, and Devora trapped beneath bell jars.

"What happened?" I asked my friends. They looked like trophies for some deranged collector.

"Maybe you don't remember this, Crow, but you got knocked out *with a spoon!*" Spud said.

"Ugh," I managed to utter, my voice creaking like an old hinge. Quickly, it became clear I was bound to a stiff, unyielding chair, with my limbs effectively immobilized with strips of leather. I strained against my restraints, but to no avail. "I remember. You just had to antagonize that guy, didn't you, Spud?"

"Sorry," Spud said.

I blinked again, willing the fog in my vision to dissipate. "Any idea where we are?" The room in which we sat bore a striking resemblance to Justice Maron's Machine Shop from Gray Moor: gears, cogs, and brass pipes crisscrossed the ceiling in a maze of metallic veins. Glass tubes filled with liquids of varying hues lined the walls, their contents bubbling and churning. A brass telescope stood nearby, an anomaly in our subterranean confines.

"The guys who put us here said we'd stay until the boss was ready for us," Perry said, his voice muffled by the glass of his jar. His usually rosy cheeks were flushed a darker shade of red. "We tried breaking out, but the jars are impenetrable. They're harder than glassinine! I used my vomit, though all I managed was to get myself covered in my own sick. And Devora's Concussive Blast didn't do a thing."

Spud's laughter rang out in the chamber, a coarse, grating sound that echoed off the cold, stone walls. "Trust me, Crow, Perry throwing up on himself was pure comedy."

The corner of Perry's mouth twitched. "At least I didn't end up screaming like a baby when I tried to burn my way out."

Spud looked indignant. "I didn't sound like a baby. I sounded like a man! A strong, powerful man!"

"Oh come on," Devora said. "Not *another* argument."

"Get used to it, honey," Xena said. "It's pretty much an hourly occurrence. The weird thing is, they're super protective of one another."

The ensuing squabble was abruptly interrupted by the ominous creak of a door. A figure stepped into the room, and I squinted through the semi-darkness, attempting to discern the face that hid beneath the cloak.

This must be the boss, I thought, dread worming its way through my stomach. The cloaked figure walked toward me, each step precise. As they approached, their head turned toward the bell jars. When they noticed my friends, they changed direction, making a beeline toward them.

"Hey!" I called to them as I strained against my bonds. "Over here! I want to talk to you. Mega sent me! I'm with Mega!"

The figure didn't respond, instead reaching for the jar that held Spud. I saw the potato's eyes grow wide with fear.

"Take me, but spare Perry," he said, his voice muffled by the glass. His body exploded in flame. "Promise you won't—*argggh!*—harm a leaf on his adorable head!"

Xena rolled her eyes. "See?" she said to Devora.

The figure lifted the bell jar away from Spud. When they spoke, they didn't sound evil. Instead, their voice was warm.

"You're safe," the person said. I wracked my brain, but I didn't recognize the voice. "I'm not going to hurt you. Your friends are safe, too."

"We're… safe?" Spud said as he let his flames gutter out. It was more of a question than a statement. "Who are you, lady?"

The mysterious figure pulled the cowl away from her face.

Surprisingly, I recognized her.

"Rayne?" It was the Thuin witch I'd first seen on the train to Toroth-Gol. The one who'd spat in Lucca Bert's face. Later in my journey, Rayne had been the one to build the bone battery that had gotten us out of the Castle of 1,000 Doors.

But the Rayne I knew hadn't been able to speak—or so I'd thought.

After setting Spud's bell jar back on the table, Rayne released Perry, Devora, and Xena. "Apologies for your treatment," she said. "The Ghosts are used to a rougher form of governance. I was indisposed when you came in, and I'd been expecting Mega, so it took a while for news of your arrival to reach me."

Rayne walked toward me, the light of the laboratory now illuminating her fully. With her braided hair pulled back from her face, I saw that she had sharp features, with eyebrows manicured to match. Two metal studs ran through her left eyebrow.

"You're the leader of the Ghosts?" I asked.

Rayne bowed. "In the flesh. Did Mega come with you? Or send you in his place? I guess I'm a little confused."

Might as well rip off the bandage.

"Mega is dead."

Rayne looked sympathetic. "I'm sorry to hear that. From what I understood, he was a good man."

From beneath the folds of her cloak, she drew a dagger. I tensed as she approached, but she only used the knife to slice through the ropes holding me to the chair. Then she used the blade to gesture at a nearby box.

"Your equipment is in there," she said. "Let me know if anything's missing, and I'll talk with the men."

From the way she'd said the word "talk," there was no doubt what she'd meant.

"Okay, you need to catch me up, here," I said as I massaged blood back into my numb hands. "Who are you actually? And how did you come to lead the Ghosts?"

Rayne put her knife back into her cloak. "That's an interesting story. It starts when my brother and I lived in the Wastes. When we were planning this venture, Jocko and I agreed that—"

"Uh, I'm sorry," Spud interrupted. "Did you just say *brother?*"

Rayne winced. "I did, didn't I? I didn't mean that. I meant…" She trailed off, then massaged her temples. "*Ugh.* Yes, Jocko is my brother. It's supposed to be a secret, but I'm the shield to his sword. Second-born of our father. Do you know what that means?"

I shook my head. Now that she mentioned it, I saw the resemblance: the same hair color, tan skin, and hawkish nose.

"In our culture, the firstborn of any royal line is known as the sword," Rayne continued. "The second is the shield. In Thuin, we say, 'Kala bay'im, sala yab'im.' Or, 'The sword goes and the shield follows.' In other words, it's my sworn duty to protect Jocko, and it's a role I've held proudly for many years. He decided that when we reached this level, I'd do what I could to establish myself in a position of power. I saw the Ghosts were weak, and it was simple enough for me to take over."

"You run the Ghosts," I said incredulously. "Just like that? Have you spoken to Jocko since we went into our separate towers?"

The charms in Rayne's hair jangled as she shook her head. "No.

But I've known the game for a while now. Years. I knew what had to be done."

"You can help us," I said. "You and the Ghosts. Jocko and I have a hundred mulchers and another fifty hunters waiting just outside of Old Town. We're going to take Prey House and free my father."

Rayne smiled. "Of course I can help you. When do we start?"

29

It was nice to see Rayne reunite with Jocko and Brynn. Additionally, many of the Ghosts recognized the hunters I'd rescued from the Valves, and the tension that suffused our camp over the upcoming battle was tempered with joyous shouts.

I didn't allow myself to celebrate, as I knew how much blood was about to be spilled.

According to the plan our leadership had devised, the main body of our forces would remain in Old Town. We knew the Medics were watching us, and this would keep them from growing suspicious. Meanwhile, a smaller contingent of mulchers and ranged fighters would hide along the path leading to Prey House. My father's notes had suggested that the Orange Medics, the most dangerous of the enemy's forces, used that path every morning when they returned from their patrol; when they did, we'd ambush them, surrounding Prey House and eliminating a potent threat in one move.

That's how I found myself in the shivering dawn, peeking through tree branches at an empty path some twenty yards away. Other than Tharok, who stood just behind me, I couldn't see any more of our troops, though I knew there were at least fifty of them hidden amongst the trees.

Cold dread turned my guts to water. Although I'd played lightball for years, this was different.

Lightball was a game. This was life and death.

"They're coming," Xena said, her voice muffled by the Titan Armament.

I passed the message to Tharok. He nodded and hit his staff against the ground. The air around us filled with magical bird calls, the sound echoing among the trees.

The world held its breath.

For a while, I didn't hear anything. Then came the snuffling and growling of wargs. Heart hammering, I peeked out through the brush and saw the wolf-like creatures in a column, their orange-robed riders sitting atop their backs.

They don't know what's about to hit them. I counted their forces as they moved past us. *Ten. Twenty. Twenty-five. Just as we suspected.*

When the last warg moved past our hiding spot, Tharok tapped his staff against the ground once more. The cry of a hawk split the air, as shrill and clear as a clarion call.

That was the cue for us to start attacking.

I stood, shooting Spud, then Perry, then Devora. I kept Xena in reserve, as she wouldn't be able to help until our enemies started dying.

All around me, other hunters with ranged weapons emerged from the brush, firing arrows and bullets that hissed through the air like a plague of deadly locusts.

The rear guard of the Orange Medics melted as wargs toppled and bucked their riders. Steam rose from pools of black blood and gaping wounds. The sound of the monsters in pain was a new signal, as was the reverberating bass line.

A second later, the mulchers spilled from the trees.

We'd hit the Orange Medics so quickly, many of them hadn't realized anything was wrong. Now, however, it was obvious.

The Medics turned and saw their comrades fallen on the cobblestones. "We're under attack!" one of them shouted. As I looked at him, I saw that it was Skor Dratvir, the Medic I'd seen in the courtyard when I'd first left Prey House. He hefted a two-handed greatsword into the air. It must've come from his Inventory, because there was no way the sword had fit under his robes. "Draw your weapons, Medics!" he called. "Rally the defense on me!"

The jet-black warg upon which Skor sat let out a snarl. From the description in my vision, I saw that it was Zannius.

Spud's voice cut the cold air: "There was a golden one—*urgh*—who vilified the golden sun and lived a life in furs!" he sang from inside the Titan Armament. "Fire me, Crow! *Yearghhh!*"

I shot him toward an Orange Medic who'd recovered enough to pull a mace from beneath his robes and was in the middle of swinging at a mulcher. My shot was dead accurate, but the warg the Medic rode must've sensed something, because the animal's great gray head swiveled toward me and it leaped away. The quick-moving warg saved its rider, but the off-balance Medic missed his swipe, and the warg's leap was interrupted by an arrow that pierced its heart. Instead of landing clear, the warg crashed into the bodies of two other wargs. A rider on one of these fell to the ground as its mount reared, and then the mount came down and its rider was crushed.

"My turn!" I heard Xena cry from inside my weapon. Purple smoke wreathed my arm and a dead warg rose from the ground to attack its comrades.

I chambered Perry, who'd dropped back into my weapon after my initial shot, and fired him toward a Medic. Of course, I aimed slightly to one side to keep Perry from smashing against the man's face. As Perry soared past the fighter, his acid took the man in the eyes. The liquid also ate through his mount's fur, causing the creature to yelp in pain and leap toward another grouping of wargs.

"Nice aim—*argggh!*—Perry!" Spud yelled from the thick of the battle as he lit a warg on fire. "Look at me, baby! I'm *toasty!*"

It was chaos. Despite our best efforts, the Medics weren't immediately routed. Although we'd prepared for resistance, that didn't make it any easier to stomach losses. As a ranged fighter, I'd stayed amongst the relative safety of the trees, but those who'd closed with the Orange Medics faced fierce opposition. The same mulcher I'd seen gut one of the Medics had its throat torn out by a warg; the giant wolf snarled in victory, its snout covered in black blood and viscera. Farther down the line, a Medic lobbed a grenade at two approaching hunters and I heard screams of agony as it exploded.

Don't focus on that, I thought, coming back to myself. *Just keep shooting. Fire, repeat. Fire, repeat.*

The line of fighters parted. The movement gave me a view into the center of the column, where Zannius and Skor Dratvir faced off against a howling Tharok.

"Tharok?" I said. I glanced behind me, where the leader of the mulchers was supposed to be. Of course, he wasn't there. I didn't know when he'd left the safety of the trees, though that certainly hadn't been part of the plan.

"It occurs to me that if Skor Dratvir kills Tharok, the mulchers might choose to follow *him* as their new leader," Perry said as he dropped back into my gun. "You know, similar to how they chose to follow you after you bested Sor'kodich?"

"By the Dregs," I hissed. He was right. Right now, we had more troops than the Medics. We'd emerge victorious, but I didn't like our chances if the mulchers switched sides.

With a snarl, Zannius charged Tharok, black lips pulled back from bloody teeth. Skor swung his sword in a blurring arc, its movement followed by a *crack* that echoed across the battlefield. But Tharok was *fast*. He launched himself directly at Skor. Although his ankle caught on the body of a fallen Medic that lay across the cobblestones, the leap was enough to carry him past Zannius' snapping jaws—and over Skor's swing. Tharok missed his own swipe at Skor, though he recovered and slammed an elbow into the leader of the Orange Medics, knocking him from his mount. They tumbled to the ground, falling away from each other and scrambling to their feet.

Tharok raised his staff for a spell, but Skor lashed out with his sword, catching the mulcher on the side of the head with the flat of his blade. There was another *crack* and Tharok was thrown sideways as if launched by a cannon; that glancing blow would've been fatal if Tharok hadn't been shielded. To my relief, he *had* gotten off a spell, summoning three golden, ethereal eagles that circled his head, and it was one of the birds that had taken the brunt of Skor's blade to protect its master.

Tharok staggered, though the eye on the side of his head where he'd taken the blow from Skor was now swollen and closed. The other two eagles screeched and dove at Zannius, who'd circled Tharok and was trying to attack him from behind. They flashed their talons at the wolf, which snarled in return, its predatory eyes filled with bloodlust. Neither had an edge on the other, but the eagles took Zannius out of the fight, letting Tharok focus solely on Skor.

With my mulcher army on the line, I didn't have any silly notions of honor. The fight didn't need to be decided by single combat.

I shot Spud directly at Skor.

The leader of the Orange Medics didn't look up as he angled his sword. There was a *crack,* and then Spud was flying back toward me as if shot from my own weapon, repelled by whatever magic Skor had used. Instinct saved me, and I ducked before the flaming potato took off my head. Spud slammed into the tree behind me, embedded several inches into the trunk.

"*Ugh,*" he moaned. "Ouch."

At some point, Tharok had gotten himself covered in blood, the off-white plates of his armor stained red. Zannius looked much the same. Skor Dratvir had managed to keep his robe clean, though he looked no less dangerous for it.

The mulcher shaman banged a fist against his chest and I heard the sound I'd come to recognize as a sign of mulcher enjoyment.

Tharok is crazy. He's loving this!

Once again, Tharok charged Skor, making the leader of the Orange Medics adopt a defensive stance. He raised his sword and I feared the worst.

At that moment, a mulcher shaman I'd sworn was dead got to its feet behind Skor, obsidian knife glittering in its hand. As Skor raised his sword to take another swipe at Tharok, the undead mulcher plunged the knife to the hilt in his back.

"Got him," Xena said gleefully. I glanced down and saw the Titan

Armament wreathed in purple smoke. "The body was *just* together enough for me to use."

Then the smoke dissipated and the mulcher that had stabbed Skor dropped bonelessly to the ground. So did Skor. I didn't know if he was dead or not, but Tharok closed the issue by punching the tip of his staff straight through Skor's throat.

From there, the Orange Medics fell like dominoes. I watched with grim satisfaction as a hunter put an arrow into Zannius' side.

Win at all costs, I thought, watching as our soldiers mopped up the rest of the Medics. *No mercy.*

But as we collected loot and tended to our wounded, I knew the real battle was about to begin.

30

With the Orange Medics routed, the full might of our troops joined the assault force around Prey House. The gates stood open and I took it as a good omen that a single crow sat atop one of the iron spikes.

Beyond the gate, wide marble stairs led to two wooden doors.

Unlike the gates, the doors were closed and locked. But Jocko had prepared for this. With a wave, he ordered forward two of the mulcher shamans, who ran at the door with sledgehammers. At the side and back doors of the facility, I knew, the scene looked similar.

Jocko and I stood with a small group of leaders on a rise far outside the gate. Through the field binoculars one of the Talon Lake hunters I'd rescued from the Valves had given me, I could see everything that was happening, though we weren't in any danger of getting attacked. I looked through them now, my gaze moving up the side of the facility. In Prey House's upper windows, I spotted the worried faces of several Medics. I continued higher and saw snipers on the roof. Although several of our ranged fighters kept them pinned, our winged hunters wouldn't be able to fly into the facility until they were gone.

I took the binoculars away from my face. From where we stood, I could still see the action, though it was distant. As the mulchers banged away at the doors, one of our ranged fighters shot an arrow toward one of the high windows, shattering the glass and scattering the Yellow Medics who peered out from behind it.

"Nori, help me out," Jocko said, and my old flame ran over and put a hand on his arm. When he next spoke, his voice was amplified.

"Focus on the snipers!" he yelled. "You're going to create enemies out of scared citizens. We wait for the mulchers to break through and we accept any surrenders."

I didn't blame the lone hunter for firing; my nerves were just as frayed. At the doors, the mulchers continued to try and break into the facility. *Clang! Clang!* They worked in rhythm, bashing at the thick doors.

The whole time, I expected Red Medics to pour out of Prey House to stop us, though none came. That was almost more nerve-wracking than if we'd seen them.

Where are they? I thought, bringing the binoculars back to my face. *They've got to be up to something.*

It didn't take more than a minute before a mighty blow from one of the shamans smashed Prey House's front door off its hinges. Per our plan, those who could detect traps moved in first, while the melee fighters waited behind. I didn't hear the hunter who gave the all-clear, though it must've happened, because our troops surged forward.

That's when everything went wrong.

Boom. I felt the explosion's shockwave from where I stood. The ground bucked, and a wall of fire ripped through the courtyard, evaporating our front line as well as half of Prey House's façade. It was so bright I was forced to pull the binoculars away from my eyes.

From inside the Titan Armament, I heard Spud yell, "In the name of all that's crispy! What was *that?*"

I peered back through the binoculars. The ground in front of Prey House was alternately heaped into haphazard piles or pocked with deep pits. There were bodies everywhere. The front of the building had been torn off, and now Red Medics streamed from the exposed rooms and hallways.

Jocko uttered a Thuin curse. "I *knew* they were up to something," he growled. "I didn't expect them to blow up half their own facility."

I heard more distant *booms*, and I imagined they were detonations from other bombs. Jocko cursed again and my stomach dropped.

"What do we do?" I asked. "We've got to find a way inside."

I wasn't a battlefield expert by any means, though with the number of Red Medics still pouring from Prey House, it looked like even the best-case scenario would end in a stalemate. That would lead to a siege, which would eat up time.

If we were going to rescue my father, time was the one thing we didn't have.

"You could always try a more subtle approach," Brynn said from behind me.

I turned to see her, Geeta, and Tharok coming up the rise; they were covered in dirt and leaves. I didn't know where they'd been, and I didn't ask. As Brynn raised a hand, I saw she held a disc that looked like an Empire mark. It was slightly convex on one side and glimmered with a silvery sheen.

Brynn's Top Secret Invisibility Modulator IV (BTS-IM IV)

Capable of distorting light around an object, the BTS-IM provides functional invisibility. This is the fourth iteration of the device, which holds up to fifteen minutes of charge and can be activated by tapping its convex side. To function properly, the BTS-IM IV needs to maintain a constant physical connection with the object one intends to make invisible.

WARNING: Full functionality of the BTS-IM IV can be disrupted by magical interference.

From beside me, I felt Jocko stiffen. "Why didn't you mention this earlier, *pacho?*" he asked. "If we'd been able to sneak into Prey House, we wouldn't have needed to launch an assault like this."

Brynn shook her head. "It wasn't working earlier," she replied. "I tried to use it in the cemetery to save Crow from the pirates and it almost got all of us killed. The magic from the Heart of the World interferes with its circuits."

I nodded, remembering how she'd appeared in fits and starts.

"This is a *slightly* updated version," Brynn continued. "I just finished whipping it up. It's still not perfect, though it might work in a pinch." She tossed the disc to me and I caught it out of the air. "Your friends are made of magic. If you want to use it, you'll have to leave them behind. Sorry, Spud Squad."

There was a chorus of protests from the Titan Armament, though I silenced it. "If it gives us a chance to save my father, I'll try it. Geeta, will you watch the squad?"

The reptilian nodded. I ordered the Titan Armament to disengage from my arm, then handed it to Geeta. As she took the weapon, the top popped open. It wasn't Spud who jumped out, but Devora.

"If you're going inside, you need to bring me," the coconut said. "Your father's cell is made of glassinine and you'll need my Concussive Blast to break through."

I shook my head. "It won't work. You heard what Brynn said."

I glanced over at the engineer, who looked thoughtful. "You could *probably* get away with a single magical item, but no more than that. Of course, Devora will need to maintain contact with you at all times or she'll become visible. And you'll definitely need to leave behind the other magical items in your Inventory."

That was good enough for me. I didn't know how to get the cells open, and in a worst-case scenario, she'd provide a turnkey solution.

Had Lilith foreseen this when she switched Devora's power? But it wasn't the right time to think about the implications.

"All right, Devora, load up," I said. The coconut jumped from the top of the weapon to my shoulder.

I lifted the BTS-IM IV and was about to press the convex side when Jocko said, "I'm coming with you too, *pacho*."

I turned to face him. "How? You could teleport, but that's magic. If you use your power, you might disrupt Brynn's device. That's not a risk I'm willing to take."

I thought he might suggest I give *him* the BTS-IM IV, but he said, "Brynn said the device will cover Devora as long as she stays in contact with you. Why wouldn't it cover me as well?"

I shook my head. "So I'm giving you a piggyback, or...?" I trailed off as I saw Jocko nod.

That's his master plan? I'm giving the Grass King a piggyback ride?

I pictured myself invisibly sneaking through Prey House, Jocko on my back and Devora sitting on his shoulder. The image was ridiculous.

"Would it work?" I asked Brynn. Having a fighter like Jocko to back me up would be a significant advantage.

Once again, Brynn looked thoughtful. "Probably? You might not get all fifteen minutes of battery life, though, conceptually, it *should* work. This is all very experimental! To confirm everything, I'd need to run some tests."

"We don't have time for tests," I said.

"But I know we don't have time for tests," Brynn continued, throwing me an annoyed look. "I'm reasonably confident you'll be fine."

Jocko smiled. "Ready when you are, *pacho*."

31

The top of the Titan Armament opened, and this time all my friends hopped out, each finding a perch on a different part of Geeta. Spud took one shoulder and Xena took the other. Perry jumped to her open palm. The reptilian looked uncomfortable as my friends settled, and though she didn't say anything, I knew she'd protect them.

"Good luck on your wild mission!" Spud shouted. "Usually, I like to be intimately involved in any scheme that involves daring and danger, but I trust the three of you to win the day and bring glory to my squad."

"Uh, thanks," I said. "Stick with Geeta and listen to her orders. If there's an opportunity to come after us, feel free to take it, but I don't want you putting yourselves in any unreasonable danger."

"Don't worry about us, Crow," Xena said. "We've got your back if we can swing it. Otherwise, I know we all look forward to meeting your father after you break him free."

"If he's as nice as you, I'm sure he's a great guy!" Perry added.

Jocko clambered onto my back, and I tapped the BTS-IM IV. There was a collective gasp from everyone except Brynn, who grinned. I didn't notice anything different until I looked down and realized I couldn't see my body.

The device worked. I'm invisible.

"You can thank me later," Brynn said. "The clock on the battery life is ticking. Go, Crow!"

I started toward the entrance to Prey House, still not totally believing I was invisible.

If this works... I didn't let myself finish the thought. *Celebrate later. You have enough to think about now.*

Once I was through the gate, I made a wide arc to skirt the worst of the fighting that continued in the courtyard and entered the building through an unguarded hole in one wall. I found myself in a bathroom, the tile floor slick with water from a broken pipe.

"Make sure you dry your shoes before the next room, *pacho*," Jocko whispered. "I don't want wet footprints giving us away."

It was an obvious point but a good one. I opened my Map. When I'd tried to look at Prey House's layout from the Decrepit Ruins, it had appeared as a gray box. Now, the Map was functional again, and I saw details and names of each room.

Whatever technology the Medics are using to shield the facility's layout, it doesn't work once I'm inside. Interesting.

Using the Map, I charted a path toward the cells. When I found the route, I cautiously stepped from the bathroom into a long hall.

The facility was silent. There were no traps, and no resistance came to greet us. At one point, we passed a trio of Yellow Medics, but they scurried past without seeing us, books clutched protectively to their chests.

That changed when we reached the doors to the cells, which were guarded by three Red Medics. The first held a machine gun so big it was supported by a turret, and the other two carried rifles. When their names popped up in my augmented vision, I racked my brain, trying to recall details about each of them from my father's research, but the only ones I remembered were about the third Medic, a man named Alden Rorschach, who possessed some sort of ability to control rock.

We should make a plan before we try to get past them.

I returned the way I'd come, walking until I was sure we were out of earshot. Only then did I whisper to Jocko.

"What do you want to do?" I asked.

"It's only three guards, *pacho*," the Desert Blade replied. "Put me down and give me seven seconds."

I didn't doubt Jocko's prowess, though I thought three against one was poor odds, even for him. "You don't want help?" I asked. "Devora and I can take one, at least."

Jocko climbed down from my back, keeping a hand on me to remain invisible in case someone came around the corner. "You're a good fighter, Crow, and getting better, but you're not ready for this," he said. "Seven seconds. Then you come around the corner and rescue me if something goes wrong."

I nodded, then realized he couldn't see me. "Fine," I whispered. "Do it."

"I move on the count of three," he said. I heard a *snick* as he drew the blade that was always at his side. He tapped my shoulder.

One.

He tapped it again.

Two.

A third time.

Three.

Leaves fell to the ground around my feet.

Since I was invisible, I could peer around the corner without the risk of being seen, though I almost wished I hadn't. There was a spray of arterial blood as Jocko drew his sword across the neck of the first Medic, and he'd done the same to the second before the first had even lifted his hands to his neck. The third had just enough time to turn before Jocko's sword exploded from his chest. The three enemies fell to the ground with successive *thuds*, dry leaves drifting around them.

He'd asked for seven seconds, though he'd only needed three.

I rounded the corner and approached Jocko. "I'm here," I whispered so he'd know where to find me. "Nice work."

Jocko wiped his sword on the robe of a downed Medic, sheathed it, and held out a hand. I grabbed it and he once again turned invisible.

"Shall we continue, *pacho?*"

"I'll guide you. The cells are just beyond."

As we pushed through the doors, I felt a sudden dread. *Could the Medics have killed all their prisoners in advance of the battle?* I wouldn't have put it past them, though I was relieved to find my suspicion unfounded. The prisoners were alive; they sat with their knees up and their heads down, or else they lay on their backs with gazes turned toward the ceiling. Their clothes were threadbare and dirty.

We'll rescue them all, eventually. For now, Sal is our priority.

There were no Medics in the chamber, which was good. As we walked toward the cell where I'd last seen my father, I saw my hand flicker in front of me. I didn't know if the BTS-IM IV was failing because of magical interference or because the battery was running out, though either way, we'd arrived at the perfect time.

Since there wasn't a need to remain invisible, I turned off Brynn's device and released my grip on Jocko's hand. Then I pointed to the cell that contained my father.

"There he is!" I said. Even at the sight of his emaciated form, I couldn't help but feel a surge of triumph.

We made it. Thank goodness for small victories.

As if he could hear us, my father glanced up. When he saw Jocko and me, his eyes widened.

"Back away!" I shouted to him. I knew he couldn't hear, though my hand motions must've been clear enough to him, because he stood and backed away.

"Poor Sal," Jocko murmured from beside me. I glanced over to see a look of pained sympathy on his face. I knew what he was feeling. My father had always been spry, slowed down by his career-ending light-ball injury but still a force. Yet, the man in the cell before us didn't just look old.

He looked broken. Defeated.

"He's not looking so good, is he?" Devora said. She jumped into my hand. "Let's get him out of there, Crow. We're so close!"

From beside me, the Grass King rested a reassuring hand on my shoulder. "He might not look great, though Sal's mind was always his strongest asset, *pacho*. We'll get him out of there and he'll be right as rain."

I hoped that was the case. When my father was as far away from the front of the cell as possible, I lifted Devora. "Ready?"

"Do it," Devora replied.

I threw her at the glass and she *smashed* into its surface. The shock-wave generated by her impact almost blew me off my feet, and a crack rippled through the glassinine of Sal's cell.

Did it work? Can Concussive Blast actually break glassinine?

As if in answer, the cell *shattered*.

Glass rained to the ground in a thousand tiny pieces. Devora fell to the ground amidst the shards, whooping with joy, and Jocko cheered, too. Even I couldn't help but smile.

We did it! With the odds against us, we'd successfully pressed into Prey House, brought the fight to the Medics, and freed my father. *Now, we just need to get him out.*

I wanted to be the first to reach my father, but it was Jocko who took that honor, disappearing in a whirlwind of fallen leaves and reappearing before Sal with his arms wrapped around the man's emaciated frame.

"We're here, *pacho*," Jocko said as he clutched my father. Sobs of joy wracked Jocko's wiry body. "We're doing it. Almost three levels down, and everything is exactly as we planned."

A pang of jealousy ran through me, but I could hardly fault the Grass King; Sal Valentine had been like a father to him, too. For over a decade, Sal and Jocko's father had planned this incursion into Toroth-Gol, and when the old head of the Thuins had died, Jocko had stepped into his role. I knew many of the "business trips" my father had taken over the years had actually been spent with Jocko, training and refining their plan as they prepared for the most ambitious venture of their lives.

I suppose Jocko deserves this. I'll have my own moment.

My father was several inches taller than Jocko, and he made eye contact with me over the smaller man's shoulder. Then he grinned. It wasn't a joyous grin, like the one a father might give to a son during a happy reunion, but a grin like the one Elvis Madden had given me: an expression of sly trickery and self-satisfaction. As soon as I realized the incongruity, I tried to warn Jocko, but my shout came too late.

The Grass King stumbled away from my father, the hilt of a dagger protruding from his back.

"What?" Jocko asked. He stared at my father in disbelief, then tried and failed to grasp the dagger's smooth handle. From the slow, sloppy way he moved, I suspected it wouldn't have mattered if he'd reached it.

The blade must be poisoned. But why?

"What have you done?" I asked my father. It was a testament to the stress of the assault on Prey House that I still thought it was him.

The Grass King teleported away, but it didn't remove the dagger from his back. Like his clothing, which stayed on his body whenever he used his skill, the blade was treated like a part of him; he reappeared halfway between me and my father, still trying to reach the knife, and fell to his knees.

"Don't try to speak," I said as I ran to him. "Jocko, I'm sorry. Stay with me, *majoré*. We can get you help!"

Even as I spoke, I knew it wasn't true. Jocko looked at me, and I was horrified to realize he seemed peaceful.

"I think… that's it… for me… *pacho*," he gasped. "I never expected to… make it out. You should… agh… I'm glad… I'm glad we…"

He didn't finish. With a final gurgle, he fell forward, his sword crushed awkwardly beneath him.

The leaves that drifted to the ground around us were the color of blood.

32

When is a father not a father? It sounds like the start of a bad riddle.

Inside the Cell Viewing Chamber of Prey House, I looked at the man pretending to be Sal Valentine.

The man stared back at me, grinning.

"You're not him," I said. My father didn't grin like that, and he wouldn't murder Jocko.

As I continued staring, the man's face shifted. His rakish appearance turned doughy and dumb, the shadow of stubble disappearing from his cheeks. His jowls sagged and his chin lost definition. His sharp eyes became piggish, and his salt-and-pepper hair pulled into his skull to reveal a smooth, shiny pate.

Then his fleshy lips parted, and from a tongueless mouth, I heard the sound of guttural laughter: *urk, urk, urk.*

I found myself staring at Gerald, the Red Medic who'd been guarding my room when I'd first awoken in Prey House. I remembered the notes from Mega's basement: "In the entrance to the dungeon, Gerald took a mimic ability that allowed him to copy the likeness of any hunter he saw."

Now everything became clear: the Medics *knew* we'd come for my father. They'd laid a trap for us, and we'd fallen right into it.

"You," I hissed at Gerald. Before I could say anything else, the glass of every cell in the chamber drew up into the ceiling. The prisoners rushed out, all pulling weapons from beneath their dirty clothes.

Not prisoners, I realized as they surrounded me. *Medics disguised as prisoners. This whole thing was a ruse from the start.*

A voice rang out from the other side of the chamber: "Crow!" I glanced over to see Leslie. My father stood before her, his hands tied behind his back. The leader of the Medics stood far enough behind him that Sal couldn't deliver any of the half-dozen disarms of which I knew he was capable.

She also had a pistol pointed at the back of his head.

Is this my actual father or another dupe?

"Pink quilts and navy beans," Sal said. Taken at face value, the words didn't mean anything. But they were a code of sorts, words only we knew and a way for us to prove our identities to each other if it ever became necessary.

My father prepared for every contingency. But how could he possibly have prepared for this?

Now that Leslie had my attention, she stepped forward and delivered a savage kick to the back of my father's shin. It was his bad leg, and I saw pain lance across his features as he fell to his knees.

"Don't touch him!" I shouted, stepping toward them. As I did, the Medics closed the gap between us. They formed an orderly wall, those with blades filling the spaces between those who clutched blunt weapons like clubs and mauls.

I also knew that Leslie pulled their strings. *Pathifery. She's control-ling their emotions. Is there a way to break them free?*

"Wake up!" I yelled at them. "We have an army in Prey House. You're outnumbered, but you can still do the right thing!"

The gazes of the Medics who surrounded me were implacable. I wasn't surprised. *She has the power to convince some of them to cut out their own tongues. What chance do you have of making them help you?*

"That's enough of that," Leslie said. The wall of Medics parted so I could see her again; as I did, she beckoned to me. "Come closer, Nathaniel," she continued. "I don't like to yell when I speak."

I didn't want to be anywhere *near* Leslie, though I clearly didn't have a choice. Cautiously, I started toward her, trying not to look at Jocko's body as I passed. When I glanced toward Devora, Leslie clucked her tongue.

"None of that. I won't have you killing me while I'm trying to have a civil conversation. You're at my mercy, Nathaniel, and let's not mince words about it. I won't hesitate to kill your father, no matter how much you rant and rave. And yes, I knew it was your father from the start. Did you really think we wouldn't recognize one of the most famous men in the Empire?" She shook her head. "I only showed him to you when you first arrived because I wanted to see the look on your face. What's a victory if you can't gloat? Now come."

Devora and I locked eyes, and then she nodded.

"Listen to her, Crow," she said bravely. "I'll be fine."

I didn't know if that was true or not, but I didn't have another option. We both knew it. All of my weapons were outside the facility; I could've tried to use the BTS-IM IV, though it'd been glitching. Even if I could've used it, it wouldn't have helped my father.

I continued toward Leslie, stopping just a few feet before her.

"What do you—?" I started to say, but the leader of the Medics raised a hand and I felt something smash into my back. Something else hit me from the front. I knew it was her power, the one that allowed her to wield invisible walls.

"That's better," Leslie said, her face a mask of smug satisfaction. "The one with the sword was the dangerous one, but I still don't trust you, Crow." She glanced past me to her soldiers. "Go! Take the coconut and secure her. Then help your brothers and sisters fight the upstarts."

"Devora!" I shouted. At least, that's what I tried to shout. With my lips pressed against Leslie's invisible plane, it came out garbled.

"Don't worry about me, Crow!" Devora shouted from behind me. "I'm already—*oof!*"

Her voice cut off, and though I struggled, it was no use. I couldn't see what had happened to her, though I hoped she was safe.

"If you hurt her, I'll kill you!" I managed.

"Oh hush, Crow," Leslie said. "You're not in a position to be making threats. At least, I assume that's what you're doing. I can't understand what you're saying."

I almost spat more brave, defiant words, but what was the point? Leslie had me at her mercy, plain and simple. Jocko was dead, my father was on his knees, and Devora had been captured. With a thought, the leader of the Medics could squash me like a bug.

"May I make a threat on my son's behalf?" my father said calmly. "If anything happens to him, I'll pull out your fingernails one by one and dip your hands in salt."

I thought Leslie might kick him again, but she simply cast him a pitying look. "Threats from the cowed don't have much bite," she said.

"Fair enough," my father replied, "though the threat still stands."

Leslie rolled her eyes as she turned back to me. "Do you know how to eliminate a colony of ants that have invaded your home? Don't answer. The question was rhetorical. You *trap* them. You put out poison in the form of something too tasty to resist, and then you let a single ant find it. They'll bring their friends from hiding to gobble it up. Do you see what I'm saying here? Again, no need for an answer." She smiled cruelly. "I thank you, Nathaniel, for being my little ant. Thanks to you, the Ghosts and all the other hunters who wouldn't join us can all be eliminated in one fell swoop."

Leslie sighed. "In general, I don't believe in second chances. In my experience, people never change. But you're special, Nathaniel. The fact that you've gotten this far is a testament to your abilities, and they could be put to good use in the Medics. You can help us escape this prison. Destroy the Empire. Everything you've wanted. Here, let me lower the barrier so you can talk."

The invisible barrier that pressed against my face disappeared, though the ones that held my body in place remained.

"What would you like me to say?" I asked.

"My true power doesn't lie in these barriers, or my ability to wield emotions, but my ability to find leverage on those who threaten me," Leslie said, continuing as if I hadn't spoken. "Not all the Medics need persuasion, of course, but so many of them have willingly allowed me into their minds. Always, it was because I had something they wanted. It's so delicious when they finally let me in. Like eating lemon sorbet on a hot summer day." She smacked her lips, which did nothing to dissuade me of the idea that I was talking to evil personified. "I have something you want, Nathaniel. But you can't have it unless I get what I want, too. So here's my second chance: agree to submit yourself to me, and your father goes free. I'll take him with me when we escape the dungeon, and drop him off in the city of your choosing. Unharmed, on my word. You serve me and the Medics for ten years, and then you're free as well."

She paused to let me consider her offer, but my mind was chewing on something else: the words Sister Anne had spoken before she'd given me the gold coin when I'd first awoken in Prey House.

"Whatever you do, don't join our ranks."

Was this what she was actually talking about? Had she seen this coming the whole time?

I could've looked to my father for an answer. The great Sal Valentine would've come up with an answer to this puzzle within seconds, blitzing through each angle to decide on the behavior that would yield the optimal outcome. All it would take was a glance in his direction, and I'd know the correct course: a blink of the left eye for *no* and the right for *yes*. We'd had that system in place for years.

But I was a tactician, too. Or, I was in the process of becoming one. Three levels into Toroth-Gol, I was no longer a spoiled celebrity stumbling between obstacles and hoping someone would save me. I'd fought and killed. Made friends and lost them. Started to trust others.

Started to trust myself.

This is a dangerous woman. And not just for her magic. Her mind is a fine thing, all perfectly clicking cogs and gears, running without friction and polished to a high sheen.

Which gave me information about the stakes at play. I might not have known why Leslie wanted me, but I knew she *did*, and that was enough to make sure she never got me.

"No," I said.

My father cheered. "Yes!" he whooped. "Got it in one!"

Leslie barked a laugh. "No? That can't be your answer."

"It is. Do what you want with us, Leslie. We're not playing your game."

My father smiled at me. I could see pride in his eyes. "May I suggest, madame, with the utmost disrespect, that you walk off a cliff?"

Leslie's face clouded as her disbelief turned to anger. "Fine. You're fools. Both of you. Come, then! See what your obstinance yields."

33

Using her pistol, Leslie forced my father to walk before her. Since I was still trapped between two planes of her magic, I had no choice but to float along behind.

We exited the doors at the far end of the room, and I once again found myself on the platform that surrounded the Pit. I had no doubt about what was coming. I wasn't looking forward to it, though as long as we still had breath in our lungs, we had the ability to escape.

Leslie stopped a few feet away from the Pit and faced me.

"Your father lied to you," she said, pointing at Sal with her pistol. "Did you know that? He is the one who gave you the Purple. There's something about your past he wants to keep hidden. Something he made you forget. Would you like to ask him about it, before it's too late?"

I considered. In truth, I *did* wonder why there were holes in my memory, and why someone might've gone to great lengths to make me forget something. I had no doubt my father was *still* keeping secrets from me.

But I trusted him. Maybe I shouldn't have, but I did. That was more than I could say for Leslie, and I wouldn't go to my grave letting her create divisions between me and the man who'd raised me.

"I'm all right on that," I said. "You can do your worst, Leslie."

Leslie scoffed. "I hope the beasts of the afterlife choke on your bones." She turned toward my father, and I knew she was about to force him into the Pit. "You're up first. Jump."

At that moment, I heard a strange noise. *That sounds like a violin.* Leslie heard it, too; she looked around curiously.

"What is that?" she asked. The music swelled. "Where is that coming from?"

The notes rose to a crescendo before stopping. As they did, Marland Thorne appeared beside Leslie. Spud sat on his shoulder, and the magical violin that let him hide himself hung from his waist.

In his hands, he held a blunderbuss.

Boom! Marland pulled the trigger. The shot should've blasted Leslie into the Pit, but she pulled the invisible barriers from around me and threw them up in front of her like a shield. The action saved her life, though it also let me free, and made her release her hold on her pistol, which clattered across the deck before falling into the Pit.

"Wha-BAM!" Spud yelled from Marland's shoulder. "And now I burn your hair!"

He jumped toward Leslie, activating his flames.

"*Yearrgh!*" he screamed.

Leslie screamed, too. She held up her hands to ward him off, but the flaming potato juked midair and landed atop her head. When she tried to grab him, Spud jumped away, deactivated his flames, and rolled back to Marland, who snatched him up and set the potato on his shoulder.

"I'll kill you for that!" Leslie hissed as she beat out the flames in her hair. An entire patch had been burned down to the skin. Marland raised his gun for another blast, though this time Leslie beat him to the punch; she threw a barrier toward him that knocked the gun clean out of his hands. The blunderbuss lifted into the air, and went spinning over the side of Prey House. But Marland wasn't done. He snatched Spud from his shoulder and tossed him back at the Gray Medic.

Leslie wasn't done either; she used one of her shields to block the flaming potato.

"*Agh!*" the potato moaned as he bounced off the invisible barrier. "Foiled again!"

Because Leslie was facing Spud and Marland, she didn't see my father free his hands. I didn't know how he'd done it; he must've had a blade hidden somewhere on his body.

She also didn't see Geeta come up over the side of Prey House. The flying reptilian carried Brynn and Perry, who sat on Brynn's shoulder.

"My turn!" the tomato shouted as Brynn threw him at Leslie. It wasn't the best throw I'd ever seen, but they were close enough to their enemy for it not to matter. Midair, Perry's mouth opened, and he released a spray of acidic vomit. Most of it was repelled by one of Leslie's barriers, which she deployed even without looking, but some of it splashed over the top, landing on the Medic's forearms and robe. I saw the acid eat through flesh and fabric; although Leslie screamed, she didn't seem distracted by the pain.

Now, Leslie faced off against multiple hunters. Even a small distraction would mean her death, and she was smart enough to know that.

Geeta set Brynn on the deck before diving over the side of Prey House, her wings spread out behind her. Then she was gone.

To get reinforcements, I hope. Me, my father, Marland, Spud, Brynn, and Perry make it six against one, though it's always good to stack the deck in your favor.

In spite of the odds, Leslie didn't look worried. She looked around the platform, taking in the new variables; if not for her smoldering hair and acid-pocked arms, she might have been going for a stroll in the Pleasure Gardens.

"I've already killed the most dangerous of you," she said calmly. "Let's see how the rest of you fight."

Leslie moved like Jocko, seemingly everywhere at once. Despite my hatred of her, I couldn't help but admire her skill. Over the next few seconds, she held her own against *six* of us.

"I hate to say it, but she's good," Spud said as he rolled up to me. "We need to flank her, I think."

He was right. "Brynn, wheel to your left!" I shouted as she bent to scoop up Perry. The tomato, who'd been deflected by one of Leslie's barriers, had rolled back toward the engineer for another throw.

With Perry safely on her shoulder, Brynn followed my instructions. Leslie threw a barrier at her, trying to use the invisible plane like a wall to knock the woman backward. Thankfully, it didn't work. The barrier stopped five feet in front of the engineer, and the air between them rippled with blue energy. I noticed an object on the ground before Brynn, a plate about the size of my palm.

She must have a device to keep Leslie's magic from reaching her.

Leslie, who must've come to the same realization, growled and shot her barrier at *me*. As I dove to one side, I saw Brynn use the reprieve to grab the barrier-blocking plate from the ground and run to get a better angle. I almost cheered before I realized this was what Leslie had wanted. She wheeled back toward Brynn, tracking her as she readied a barrier to use like an invisible fist.

Without her plate to block Leslie's magic, Brynn was vulnerable.

To keep Leslie busy, I tossed Spud toward her. The potato screamed as he flew. At the same time, Marland drew his violin and held it before him like a club.

With both Marland and Spud approaching her, the head of the Medics was forced to abandon Brynn as a target. She brought one barrier between her and Spud and the other between her and the mute pirate.

"Your fight… is… pointless!" Leslie called, gasping with exertion. I could see the sweat on her soot-stained forehead.

"It won't be pointless if we end your sorry existence," Brynn replied. "The world will be better off without you!"

"And without the Medics!" Perry shouted. "Cut off the head of a snake and the body will die!"

"The body… will continue thrashing… and take you to the grave!" Leslie replied dramatically. She paused then, a curious move in a battle for her life. I was confused, and then I saw that she stared past

Marland, toward the door we'd used to reach the platform. Out of the corner of my eye, I saw a figure standing there.

My heart dropped.

Six on one, and we couldn't stop her. Now it'll be six on two.

Sister Anne, the pretty Blue Medic trainee who'd greeted me back to consciousness when I'd arrived at Prey House, stood in the doorway. For some reason, she held my father's duck-headed cane.

"Sister Anne!" Leslie roared. "Come to my aid!"

I turned toward this new threat, ready to throw Spud in her direction, when my father held up a hand.

"Hold!" he shouted. Sister Anne tossed him the cane, which he deftly snatched out of the air.

"What are you doing?" Leslie asked, a look of horror on her face. "I order you to fight these saboteurs!"

Sister Anne only flashed Leslie a grin.

Mega had said my father was getting his information from someone inside Prey House. It must've been Sister Anne!

My father confirmed my suspicions. "It seems you had a traitor in your midst." He turned the head of his cane ninety degrees. A split second later, black mesh spilled out of the duck's mouth, running over his arms and covering them in flexible armor. The same mesh extended over his torso, moving down his legs as well as up his neck and over the back of his head. Finally, the mesh knit itself together over his face to form a protective helmet.

Leslie growled, a feral noise that sounded more animal than human. She shot one of her barriers toward the Blue Medic, catching Sister Anne with a blow that sent her flying. The Blue Medic landed in a heap and didn't get back up. My stomach sank, but then I saw her chest rise and fall, and realized she'd only been knocked unconscious.

"You'll regret that," my father said.

Wrapped in dark mesh armor, my father looked like a living shadow. Any signs of the weakness he'd displayed before were gone as he charged toward Leslie, his movements as smooth as they'd been when he'd held the distinction of being the greatest lightball player of his day.

"Die, Valentine!" Leslie screamed as she threw up a barrier to meet him.

When my father connected with Leslie's invisible wall, he didn't falter. Instead, he pushed Leslie backward, like he was a magnet that had come into contact with its opposite pole. Her feet slid across the deck, coming to a rest only half a foot from the edge of the Pit.

"If only the Pit was a foot closer to us," Spud said from my hand.

We're so close, I thought, throwing the potato at Leslie. As if on cue, a barrier rose to meet him.

Even as Leslie fought my father and tried to keep from falling into the Pit, she'd *still* managed to keep an eye on me.

"Marland, Brynn, now!" I roared. "Hit her with everything you've got!"

With a scream of rage, Leslie flung both arms toward my father. To my horror, he was knocked backward at least two dozen feet.

"You'll never stop me!" Leslie shouted. "Your best fighters can't do anything against me!"

There was a *crack,* and a blast of eldritch energy ripped across the deck. It connected with Leslie's forehead, exploding her skull like it was a watermelon. Blood, brains, and bits of bone sprayed everywhere.

I turned to see Geeta hovering nearby with Tharok held in her arms. The mulcher shaman had his staff held out like a rifle; it was this weapon that had ended Leslie's life.

"Ork'ha bakah!" Tharok called, raising his staff in triumph.

"I knew those wings would come in handy," Brynn said.

The headless Leslie took one stumbling step backward and her foot met empty air.

She tumbled into the Pit.

I stared at the place where she'd gone over. I half expected her to rise from its depths, head restored, eyes glowing, and fingers sparking with demonic energy, but nothing happened.

This isn't a movie, I reminded myself. *This is my life.*

Behind me, my father groaned. "Ouch," he said. I turned in time to see him push himself to a seated position. Then, I was next to him, one hand on his back.

"Father," I said. "Are you okay?"

The mesh pulled away from Sal's face. I'd never seen anything like the dark armor. It was flexible enough to move with him, seemingly giving him the speed and agility of a man half his age, and it almost seemed alive, somehow, capable of responding to his commands.

"I'm fine," he said. "Let's go see about our friends."

34

After we'd killed Leslie, those under the power of her pathifery had regained control of their bodies. As it turned out, most of them were terrified. One man had been trapped for *fifteen years*, watching through his own eyes as Leslie controlled his movements.

It was a group like this that had taken Devora, who'd been shaken up but was otherwise fine. They'd returned her to me with regret and apologies.

Gerald, the Red Medic who'd killed Jocko, was also in this group. When we found him, he was curled up over his own knees and sobbing. Since he didn't have a tongue, it was difficult to communicate with him, but one of our hunters found a pad of paper that he scribbled on with loose, childlike handwriting: *I'm so sorry.*

Jocko was well and truly dead. Although Xena did everything in her power to bring him back, she couldn't find him on the beach at the entrance to the Kingdom of Death, nor could she find him beyond the veil.

Sister Anne had regained consciousness shortly after Leslie's death, and immediately insisted on giving my father a full medical evaluation. As she checked his pulse, I learned from my father that the pretty trainee was actually Nineteen, an AI he'd built in Steel City, placed in a humanoid body, and sent into the dungeon.

Although she looked human enough, Sister Anne was an android.

I'd wanted time to speak with my father, but tying up loose ends after the Battle of Prey House took precedence. The next time I saw him was at the funeral we held for our dead.

It took place that evening in the bombed-out courtyard of Prey House, and every survivor of the battle turned out. The bodies of the deceased, including Jocko and Feng, lay atop a line of pyres that stretched the length of the space.

I stood on a makeshift platform before the assembled mass with Brynn on one side of me and Geeta on the other. The Titan Armament was back on my arm and all my friends were inside.

Rayne—Jocko's sister and the leader of the Ghosts—gave the funeral rites.

"All of us have faced loss," she said, her voice amplified thanks to Nori. "Whether it happened here in the dungeon or before, as a result of some wicked machination in Toroth-Gol or under the yoke of the Empire, I doubt a person here is free from that pain. I'm no different. Today, I lost my brother."

My gaze found my father, who stood a few people away from me. Sister Anne was at his side. Sal held himself stiffly, his eyes downcast. I knew Jocko had been like a son to him, and I couldn't imagine what it was like to have to accept the finality of his death.

"But all of you are my family now," Rayne continued. "And I promise you this, brothers and sisters: we will have our revenge!"

A cheer went up as Rayne took a lit torch from a nearby fire and touched it to the first pyre. Atop it lay the body of the man I'd met on the train ride to Toroth-Gol: the Desert Blade, the Grass King, the King of the Thuins.

Jocko.

With a *whoosh*, his pyre went up in flames, and I lost sight of his corpse. Then the flames spread, moving down the line of pyres until a wall of flame lit the night.

"To our freedom!" Rayne shouted, her voice still amplified as she hoisted the torch. "Down with the Empire!"

Instinctively, I knew to shout the words back, as did the others gathered for the funeral: "Down with the Empire!"

There was another collective bellow and this time the mulchers joined in, adding their guttural shouts to the tumult.

It was enough to shake the ground.

Eventually, the crowd dissipated and my father approached with Sister Anne just behind him. Without the strange black mesh covering Sal's skin, he was back to looking his age. He leaned heavily on his duck-headed cane.

"Hello, Father," I said.

My father smiled. "Nathaniel," he said. "I suppose you and I have much to discuss."

"I'd say that's true," I replied. I glanced at Sister Anne—Nineteen. "Do you mind if we speak alone?"

When I said "alone," I didn't count my friends, who were loaded into the cannon on my arm. For better or worse, our fates were intertwined. If I was going to get answers about my past, I wanted them to hear. Maybe they'd pick up on something I missed.

Although Nineteen was an ally, I didn't trust her in the same way.

My father weighed my request.

That's audacity. The guy lies to me my entire life, gets me sent to Toroth-Gol, and then acts like he's doing me *a favor.*

Finally, Sal nodded. "I suppose I owe you that much," he said. He turned to the woman—*android*, I reminded myself—behind him. "Nineteen, go ensure Brynn has everything she needs for the transfer. I'll be with you shortly."

"Your wish is my command," Nineteen said. She walked into the crowd.

"There you go," my father said. "Now we can talk."

"Not here," I said. "Somewhere more private. Follow me."

I led my father to a boulder I'd seen earlier that week, then used my Rings of Teleportation to get to the top. I pivoted to toss the trigger down to him, though he wasn't there. Instead, he appeared beside me, his face expressionless while I tried to calm the roiling nausea in my guts.

"Why does it seem like *everyone* has a movement power except me?" I said.

"Don't sweat it," my father said. "If it makes you feel any better, I don't have an arm cannon or sentient ammunition."

My friends remained silent. They knew this was my moment, and they wouldn't take that away.

My father sighed contentedly as he sat, his legs dangling over the edge of the rock. "There are few physical pleasures left to the aged," he said. "Sitting down is one of them."

I sat next to him and decided not to mince words. "Tell me everything," I said.

" 'Everything' is a lot," he replied. "I've always taught you to be precise with your words, Nathaniel. I can only assume you mean, 'Why are you putting me through this?' Is that what you're asking?"

My cheeks flushed. "You know exactly what I'm asking," I said.

My father smiled grimly. "You're my son," he said. "My real son. Not an orphan I adopted. I did the same with your friend Cara. She's not related to us, which I suspect is a relief to you, but we needed her for our plan."

I couldn't speak. Finally, I found my words: "Why? What for? What plan?"

Sal looked pained. "Some things are bigger than all of us. We did it to save the world."

"I still don't understand," I said. "You used the Purple on me. Sent me to the Dregs. Why? So you could pretend to adopt me? You got me sentenced to Toroth-Gol!"

Sal shrugged. "I won't apologize for the past, Nathaniel. I made my decisions and don't regret them. Perhaps it's no consolation, but you agreed to this. You were a precocious child, big for your age and so incredibly smart. At seven, you were beating me at ravens, even when I was trying my best. Your mother and I knew that if we wanted any chance of success with our ultimate goal, we needed to temper you, like coal becoming a diamond. Hence the Dregs." He scratched his chin. "We did the same thing with Cara; Whitemane owed me a favor. I have a friend, you see, who runs a special school, and... well, that's not important. But she's his granddaughter. The most brilliant student he'd had in a generation. And you... the two of you..." His breath caught in his throat and he swallowed before continuing. "*The Book of Prophecy* told us what to do. It told us what needed to happen."

I suppose that explains why Cara and I both feel like we knew each other in a past neither of us can remember.

I had so many questions. Sal seemed to sense this, so he continued.

"It was your mother who found the book. It told of humanity's fight against Alkastone, and how we could finally overcome him. At first, neither of us put much stock in it, but so much of what it predicted came to pass. After that, we *had* to believe."

"But I can't read it?"

My father shook his head. "No. That much is clear. You play a central role in the book, but I can't let you see more than what you have already."

I could've pushed the issue, but what was the point? From experience, I knew that my father was one of the smartest men in the world. He was also one of the most stubborn. If he said I couldn't read the *Book of Prophecy*, it was off-limits to me. End of story.

I remained silent. Eventually, my father spoke again. "When your mother and I talked to you about the plan, you were young, though you said you understood. We believed you. Honestly, I was jealous. Can you believe that? Jealous of a child. I was accomplished, but I knew you'd achieve a glory I could only dream about. It's the hope of every father that his son outstrips his success. At the same time, it was my greatest fear. At least, I thought it was, until we lost Violet."

"What was she like?" I asked. "My mother. I can't remember her."

My father frowned. "She was passionate. Full of life. When I was with her, all the petty grievances I had with life dropped away and I was left with the joy of simply being. She loved you, Nathaniel. There was no doubt about that."

"How did she die?" I asked. "Do you know?"

"Jaguar." My father hissed the name. "The weakest of Alkastone's generals, though possessed of the greatest intellect. It was right around the time he made his bid for control of the Empire. He identified Violet as the force behind our plans and decided to take her out. Your mother was smart enough to foresee this. You get your genius from her and not me, I'm afraid. She'd prepared for it. Her death triggered the release of the prototype that would become Nineteen."

I considered my next question. "The Heart of the World. It's really Alkastone? And my goal is to destroy him?"

My father nodded. "That's it. Tomorrow, we'll finish our augmentations to the Medics' portal experiments. When they're done, everyone will leave the dungeon. Everyone except for you, Cara, Geeta, and Tharok. You'll continue to the Heart of the World."

I felt my stomach drop. I'd been *so close* to escaping. "Is there another way?"

"If there is, I don't know it," my father replied. "But take heart: you have a special destiny. You've spent your entire life preparing for it."

"What if I can't?" I asked, barely managing to choke out the words.

The empathy in Sal's eyes was everything a son could've wanted from a father. He put a hand on my shoulder, then pulled me into a tight hug.

"Every part of me believes in you," he whispered into my ear. "You've always made me proud. You won't stop now."

I started crying. I don't know if it was the hug, or the circumstances, or the realization I wasn't escaping the dungeon with everyone else.

Maybe some combination of the three.

"You're all right," my father said. "You're okay, now. It's all right."

From where I sat, I could hear the sounds of a victorious army: shouting, laughter, and the occasional whoop of joy. Why not? The hunters had beaten the third level of the dungeon and lived to tell the tale. They had the means to go home.

But not you. You're staying.

I dried my tears. I supposed it wasn't all bad. My entire life, I'd looked for meaning. Wasn't that what anyone wanted? Now, I'd found it.

I would save the world.

Alkastone, your heart is mine. I didn't know where the words came from. At the time, I hardly even knew what they meant.

I thought them just the same.

It could've been my imagination, though I heard a whisper on the breeze:

"Then come for me."

THE END OF BOOK III

AFTERWORD

WOW!

You finished *another* book! If you have a minute, please leave a review on Amazon and Goodreads. As an independent author, I rely on those reviews from readers like you.

Also! If you want to be the first to hear about new books and more, join the #SpudSquad mailing list by visiting https://kenny-gould.kit.-com/newsletter

ABOUT THE AUTHOR

Kenny Gould writes science and fantasy fiction. He holds a BA from Duke University, an MFA from Chatham University, and an MBA from NYU Stern. He lives with his wife, two cats, and a very funny dog in sunny Florida.

Connect with him on social at @thekennygould or through his website at kennygould.com.

THE ADVENTURE CONTINUES!

Get *The War of Fangs,* Book IV in the Toroth-Gol series, for FREE on Kindle Unlimited. Also available in paperback and eBook through Amazon.

www.ingramcontent.com/pod-product-compliance
Lightning Source LLC
Chambersburg PA
CBHW071459140726
47997CB00005B/1781